ADAM

By ANTHONY McDONALD

For Tony, as always.

Legal Notice

Anthony McDonald

Anthony McDonald studied history before working as a farm labourer and a musical instrument maker and then moving into the theatre. He has written the scripts of a number of Words and Music concerts based on the lives of classical composers. His travel writing has appeared in the *Independent* and his first novel, *Orange Bitter, Orange Sweet*, was published in 2001.

Acknowledgements

The author would like to thank Olivier Cuperlier, Danielle D'Hayer, Yves Le Juen and Nicole Michel.

ONE

A young sycamore, at a guess. Nearly black bark, straight, symmetrical branches, buds (opposing) precisely spaced along the twigs that reached out over his head, tight green bud-cases ready and waiting for spring to find its way to this deepest part of the wood. Its lowest branches were in reasonable reach, Adam thought, provided he made a pretty energetic leap for them. Now he sprang, caught hold of one branch, swung his body upwards and against the trunk. Grasping it as best he could with his denim-clad knees he lunged upwards at the next branch, a foot or so higher, thrusting the whole of his middle-section against the cold tree-bark as he did so. Here he paused and looked down at the narrow, weaving path he had just left.

A few yards ahead the path disappeared between evergreens but directly below him it snaked its way among the trees through a torn carpet of wood anemones. The white windflowers, almost interlocking, and ruffled by an intermittent breeze, created a pattern of trembling star shapes and made the forest floor nearly as white as it had looked when the snow still clung on up here a month ago. Adam thought for a moment about Michael, the schoolfriend he had been to bed with, and then, for rather longer, about Sean, with whom he hadn't.

As usual, once Sean was involved it all happened very quickly. The sensation was like stepping into a hot shower and feeling its effect all along the skin, all down the nerves and veins like an electric current. Only this shower was an internal one: it went the other way round, from the inside out, but the aftershock, the glow and tingle of it, suffused his limbs in the same familiar way. Letting it happen like this - on automatic rather than on manual - took him back to how things had been two years or so ago when he had had rather less control over things. Sometimes, just for a change, he rather enjoyed not being in control and letting events take their course, just as they had done all that time ago in the gym at his school in England.

Adam's body relaxed, he let his knees unclamp themselves from the tree trunk, and for a moment he hung by his arms, swinging gently, his eyes taking in the magic carpet of green and white beneath him, the rest of his attention unfocused, his mind disengaged. Then he let go, dropping, all relaxed, allowing his legs to flex just sufficiently to take the impact shock on landing. But at the very instant he unhooked his fingers

1

from the branches above him a figure materialised on the path between the evergreens and was stopped in its tracks just ahead of him by the time he reached the ground. Adam unbent his legs and rose to his full height. *"Bonjour m'sieur,"* he said.

There was a hiatus while the two strangers looked each other up and down in mutual surprise. The *'monsieur'* which Adam had come out with in his initial confusion had perhaps been an excess of courtesy, he now felt. The person in front of him was a young man of medium height and build with a dark complexion and a head of tousled black hair. He was probably in his early twenties, Adam thought. It was an age group, older than his friends but younger than his teachers, with which Adam had little regular contact. This person might have been a student, only there was an unwoken, none too intelligent look about his eyes that made this improbable. The eyes were beautiful in themselves, though: brown and lustrous, and they rode on handsome cheekbones above a full and sensual mouth.

The stranger was dressed in a black or navy sweater that was a mess of holes, and a pair of frayed and mud-spattered trousers, also approximately black. On his feet was a pair of decaying plimsolls that might themselves have once been black - or white. *"Bonjour, p'tit-loup,"* he said.

"You're new here," he went on, in a serious but unthreatening tone. Adam smiled involuntarily. The remark struck his ears as funny - as if the stranger belonged to some hitherto unsuspected woodland community: a lost tribe, perhaps, or a normally invisible population of elves.

"Not that new," said Adam. "I've lived here since September," adding - just in case the other might understand him to mean that he lived in the wood - "I mean in the village. In Courcelles."

"What were you doing in the tree?" asked the other with childlike simplicity.

"I like climbing trees," Adam answered with a more adult degree of circumspection.

"Me too. It's nice up here in the wood, *n'est-ce pas?*"

Adam thought this needed qualifying. "It's a little bleak still, though." He gestured around him. "No leaves on the trees or anything."

The stranger approached him and turned him round with a light touch on the shoulder. "This way. I show you something." He led Adam a few metres back along the path then off the track into a coppice of young hazels; here the bareness of their twiggy surroundings was alleviated by a haze of grey-green pendant catkins which formed a sort of three-dimensional yet permeable curtain. After a few more seconds' progress

2

the curtain parted to reveal a clearing and there on the ground, blazing with a shocking yellow brightness against their sombre background, wild daffodils were suddenly visible in scattered clumps, as luminous and unexpected as sparks kicked up from the dead ashes of a woodman's bonfire. "You see?" said the stranger.

Adam found himself unexpectedly moved by the sight but he was unable to find words to match the feeling - and no more so in English than in French. Instead he offered a soft whistle of appreciation. "I hadn't seen them before today," he added, as if in explanation.

"You have a funny accent," observed the other, turning to face him.

"That's because I'm not French," Adam said with some irritation. This was what young people always said to him when they first met him. Six months in France and still they said it: "You have a funny accent."

"Ah?" This was said in some surprise. "From where then?"

"Britain. England."

The stranger made to sit down on the ground, motioning to Adam to do the same, and as he bent his legs towards a crouch Adam noticed with a frisson of lightning-bolt proportions that the other's trousers gaped wide open, that he had no underwear, and that for a fleeting moment his sex was fully exposed, darkly lurking, like a bat at roost in a cave. Adam froze, halfway to a sitting position, less surprised by the sight than shocked by the dizzying effect - powerful as an adrenalin rush - that it had on him. Adam didn't know whether the man's fly was permanently undone - broken or non-existent - or whether it had been surreptitiously opened in the course of their short walk together. He certainly hadn't noticed anything amiss in that locality the first time they had stood and faced each other a minute or two ago; he would have remembered if he had.

A long-ingrained habit of politeness reminded Adam that he was halfway to sitting down and that he needed to complete the action. By which time the apparition was no longer to be seen. Involuntarily Adam checked his own fly with his fingers the way men usually do when their attention is caught by that particular oversight on the part of someone else. And clearly the stranger's attention was similarly focused because he said: "The front of your jeans is damp."

Normally Adam would have been mortified by such a comment, even from a close friend. But he found himself strangely unfazed, perhaps because of the stranger's own sartorial carelessness. *"Et alors?"* he said. "Your fly is completely open. Did you know that?"

The other gave a wheezy chuckle, but neither his hand nor his eyes strayed to his own crotch. "Why are your trousers wet?" he persisted.

"I'd just had a piss," Adam lied, flashing a disarming smile. They were now sitting on the ground, facing each other.

"In a tree!" The young man started to laugh, though not unkindly. "You climbed a tree to have a piss?" He shook his head from side to side, laughing loudly now as if he couldn't stop.

Adam started to laugh too. "Well maybe not," he admitted. Then he experienced another frisson as the other moved one of his legs slightly and gave him another view of his most private member, no longer a roosting bat but a free-standing dusky obelisk. Adam made a move as if to get to his feet. "Look, I have to go," he said.

The other ignored this but grasped the obelisk with his hand, which he then moved up and down, just once, in the most unsubtle of gestures. *"C'était ça, n'est-ce pas?"* he said.

"Yes, OK, maybe," admitted Adam. Then boldly, because he was now excited again himself: "And you?"

For answer the young man simply withdrew his hand, leaving himself fully exposed to Adam's gaze. Scarcely in control of himself, and hardly believing what he was doing, Adam leaned slowly forward and took the stranger's cock in his own hand. The size of it, perceived visually, was one thing; the feel of its size quite another. Accustomed to the modest proportions of Michael's anatomy and his own only slightly more heavyweight equipment, he was struck by yet another lightning-shock. Then suddenly, as if another part of his psyche had caught up with him and seen what he was doing, he was overcome with horror and leapt to his feet like a startled deer. "I really have to go."

"Demain," said the other, quite matter-of-factly. Tomorrow. He remained seated on the ground, making no effort to detain Adam or even to touch him.

"Demain," said Adam hoarsely, looking down. He felt more than ever that he was two people struggling for control. Suddenly he reached down between the other's legs and gave the standing penis a farewell squeeze, as if shaking a friend's hand through a car window. Then he bolted.

His flight through the hazel saplings was necessarily less of a sprint than an urgent stumble, though his pace quickened when he regained the path. Here, in his haste, he turned left instead of right, which meant he was running the wrong way - or at least the long way - home. After a minute or two his pace slowed to a walk. He now had to plough on for another quarter of an hour, round two right-hand bends and up a steepish track before he emerged from the stands of ash and hornbeam on the crest of the hill where the woods gave way abruptly to wide open country.

4

Just two meadows away the village lay below him, its bright new orange roofs (courtesy of an E.U. grant) standing out in sharp contrast to its ageless walls of grey stone. As he looked, the huddle of barns and houses really did - however hard he tried to banish the twee image - cluster around the spire-capped church like chicks around a mother hen. Beyond, and some ten kilometres away, the top of the cathedral of Langres rode the horizon, showing its west front like a capital letter 'H' in a rather small point size. It actually stood on quite a spectacular shelf of rock, though that could not be seen from here: the scarp face was on the other side. Something else that could not be guessed from this vantage-point was the nature of the terrain. The plateau looked approximately flat. But Adam knew that you only had to cycle or walk a mile in any direction before you found yourself descending into deep, wooded ravines from which you then had to wind laboriously up. There were three such between here and Langres. But these apart, the land was high: one and a half thousand feet, a height that Adam, who had been to Paris, imagined most easily as one and a half Eiffel Towers.

He now turned right along the edge of the wood: a route which would bring him out into the lane that led downhill to the village and home. In his eye-line now a water tower crowned the horizon just a mile or two away. It stood on a little rise not much higher than the one he walked on but of vastly greater symbolic significance. It was part of the watershed of France and Western Europe - the meandering line that decided the fate of every drop that fell from the sky. On this side of the water tower the rainfall and all the streams it fed were destined for the English Channel or North Sea; beyond the tower the waters slid inexorably towards the Med. Just thinking about that destination caused Adam to see it in his mind: an eye of shining blue, glimpsed between hot hills, and a far cry from this upland hillside, still in winter colours on a blustery March afternoon.

Adam busied his mind with these thoughts. He wanted not to think just yet about what had happened in the wood. He would think plenty about it in due course but he wanted to put a little space between the event and the self-scrutiny that must inevitably follow. He walked up to the log-splitter that stood at the edge of the field like a yellow-painted iron gibbet. It worked like a hybrid of guillotine and pneumatic pile driver, its blade a metre-long wedge of solid steel. At rest in its weedy corner this afternoon it wore the forlorn look that out of use farm machinery tends to favour. But for Adam it was not entirely without purpose. Propped against it, almost merging with its hydraulic pipes and levers, was his own battered bike, where he had left it, less conspicuous, fastened here, than if he had simply chained it to the field gate. He undid

5

it, bumped it across the few remaining metres of pasture, lifted it over the gate, then scrambled after it in his turn. Here in the lane strange orchids flowered in the deep verge, their yellow blooms a high-rise of thrusting, sinister forked tongues. Nearby, giant forest ants were throwing up mounds of soil and tiny sticks, each hillock a whole metre across and half as high. Because of the incessant activity of the ants as well as their countless numbers, every twiggy building block of these miniature cities seemed in a state of perpetual motion. Adam watched them for a minute or so, then he climbed onto his two-wheeled steed and let it freewheel him down the hill.

Adam thought of himself in his moments of introspection as a lonely boy. He had no brothers or sisters to share his experiences with - not that he would have told them about this one, in all probability, if he had. As for his friends, most of those he called his 'real friends' were on the other side of the Channel. Integrating at his new French school had not been easy; most of his new schoolmates had treated him with a reserve and a coolness that still persisted after six months. Though there had been honourable exceptions: Thierry, Christophe, Céline... He drew in his breath involuntarily. He could not, would not, think about Céline.

He would have liked to talk to Michael just now. He did not have a mobile, and a call from parental home to parental home on such a subject was out of the question. A fax was similarly ruled out and there was no computer at home. It would have to be a letter. Adam could not fathom why air-mails between France and Britain should take roughly the same time to travel as if they were conveyed by horse and cart, but a letter it had to be. He would write it that evening.

Back at home, as he had learnt to call the big stone house his parents had taken for the year, Adam got down to his usual Sunday evening tasks: preparing his back-pack for the morning, making sure the right school books were in it, checking that other ones were not - he hated to find himself carrying dead weight - then getting ready his clean Monday clothes. After that he would practise the cello before supper and then, later, he might watch a film on TV with his parents (good for his French) before going to bed - or retiring to his room at any rate.

But today, as the evening wore on, he found concentrating on any of these tasks increasingly difficult. The adventure of the afternoon began to swamp his consciousness, seeping into every other thought from the most mundane - shouldn't that old pair of red socks be chucked? - to the most beautiful and rarefied: how best to draw out the poetry from this or that particular phrase in the Debussy sonata he was studying. And mixed with all this, separate from flashbacks to the afternoon and yet somehow all too much a part of them, came the thought of Céline.

6

The idea of Céline colliding against the thought of what he had done that afternoon - or not done; it depended on how he looked at it, and that was changing moment by moment - that collision was a painful, jarring one. To imagine himself telling Céline about the afternoon was to imagine the unimaginable; his mind simply shied at it as a racehorse might refuse a ten-metre fence. What would Céline think of him if she knew - if she even suspected...?

On the other hand, he had no problem with juxtaposing thoughts of her and thoughts of Michael. Michael was his own age so their affair could conveniently be labelled a 'boy thing'. And then Michael was part of his past whereas Céline, he tried to tell himself, was part of the present. But then another voice, a small, cold, unwelcome voice, reminded him that even now it was thoughts of Michael that turned him on, that his physical contacts with him had been hot and exciting while his faltering approaches towards Céline had been just that and no more and had left him cold ... Adam tried to ignore the reminder. Céline was beautiful, was she not? Adam could see that, could appreciate the fact fully. So nobody could say he was unattracted by girls. Could they?

At the beginning of the school year, on his arrival in France, when everything had seemed so new and different, Adam had quickly latched on to Céline. Not just onto Céline but onto the idea of Céline. She might be, maybe would be, the person to change him. With Céline he would put away childish things, he would leave Michael behind him, and move out onto the sunlit uplands of heterosexual romance.

Only nothing of the sort had happened. Back in October he had kissed Céline for the first time, and done it rather well he thought, quite expertly and confidently and at the same time with something that could have passed itself off as passion. It was at a party with other schoolmates and later in the evening his hand had stolen its way into her shirt and cupped itself over one of her warm breasts. It was like holding a fledgling bird in your hand, he discovered. But Céline responded strangely, as if something had surprised her, as if he had unwittingly done something that betrayed him. *He didn't kiss like the other boys. He wasn't heterosexual.* She had somehow read between the lines in the language of his kissing. *Céline knew.*

Even that could be glossed over when Adam willed it. He could ignore the episode if he chose or even interpret it differently if he tried hard enough. Céline and he had remained good friends after that evening. However, nothing had happened since then that allowed him to think that they might ever be anything else.

But now there was this. That crazy creature in the woods had emerged like the incarnation of something buried in his subconscious. It had come to tell him, not with words but with gaping trousers and an eloquent erection: "Don't try to fool yourself; this is what you're really after."

It was time to write that letter. He excused himself from his parents' company half-way through the evening film, went upstairs, sat down at the little table, exchanged glances with his mascot, a small velvety penguin which wore a blue bow-tie, and began:

Dear Michael,

What is this? The shattering of all earthly constants? A letter from Adam Wheeler! Well, alright. I can hear your slow handclap already, even at this distance. But here is some news. Something happened today that maybe won't surprise you. But it certainly did me...

Adam wasn't quite sure what he had hoped to achieve by writing to Michael. Perhaps by sending his account of the event in the woods overseas he had been trying not just to distance himself from it quite literally but even attempting to make it unhappen - the way confession was supposed to cancel out a sin. Or maybe it was more simple than that. He had shared everything in his life with Michael in the three years that they had been friends and neither distance nor the awkward nature of this particular piece of news was going to put a stop to that. Whatever the case, Adam now decided he would try to erase the episode from his mind as soon as it was safely entrusted to paper and the post. Having sex with Michael was one thing - though even that they concealed from all their other friends, especially Sean - but a squalid encounter with a loutish loony in a forest was quite another. If he forgot about it hard enough, Adam thought, maybe it would go away.

When Adam at last got into bed and closed his eyes an unexpected thing happened. Against the sudden darkness he saw like tiny brilliant yellow lights the daffodils that he had been shown in the clearing in the wood. *They flash upon that inward eye*, he remembered. And then he realised for the first time that Wordsworth had not simply been inventing a line that would fit his scheme of rhyme and metre; he had been telling an exact truth. He realised in the same moment that the creature in the forest had not been just a loutish loony; he had shown Adam the daffodils, somehow aware of their power to affect him and of Adam's capacity to be so affected. There was a truth in that too, somewhere. Adam fell asleep.

Adam did not, of course, return to the woods as he had promised the strange man in his moment of rashness. Not the next day or the next. But the morning after that, as he was getting up to go to school, something else occurred.

His bedroom window overlooked the road, or what passed for one; no thoroughfare in or near the village amounted to more than a lane and few people passed along this one. He had no qualms about dressing and undressing in front of the uncurtained window, with or without the lights on. No-one ever saw him. Only today someone did. At the precise and very brief moment when he stood naked before slipping on his briefs, a bicycle happened to pass. Its rider, a boyish figure in faded jeans, grubby jacket, and wearing a furry cap of the kind that has ear-muffs, turned and saw him. And was the stranger from the woods. Trying to master both his surprise and his still moving machine, he rode round in a complete circle in the road to come to a stop under Adam's window, steadying himself with one foot on the ground when once he did. For several seconds the two of them stared at each other in disbelief. Then the stranger's eyes strayed downwards, taking in Adam's nakedness, and when they rose again to meet Adam's, the face they looked out from was grinning. The young man said something that Adam could not catch, then pushed down on his pedal and went on his way. Adam looked down at himself and dispassionately observed an extremely full erection.

Once he was dressed and had reduced the bulge in his trousers to a more manageable size, he went downstairs and entered the stone-flagged kitchen. His parents were already at the breakfast table. His mother poured out coffee as he sat to join them.

"What was that man saying to you just now?" she asked him.

"What man?" Pretending ignorance seemed the best policy.

"Chap on a bike," said his father. "Stopped outside. Looked as if he was speaking up to your bedroom. 'Course he wasn't. He talks to himself. Always cycling about the place, lost in his own little world."

"Why," said Adam's mother. "Do you know him?"

"Not exactly," said his father. "Never formally introduced. We see him down by the dam quite often though, idling around on his bike. Some of the workmen know him. He doesn't work himself. I don't think he can. He's one of the funny family." He broke off a piece of baguette and dunked it in his coffee French fashion, butter and all.

"The funny family?" queried his mother. "I don't know who you mean." Adam was quite relieved to find himself melting into the shadows, away from the focus of his parents' conversation.

"It's in-breeding. Apparently the whole family's ever so slightly nuts. They live on a smallholding down a lane along the Perrogney road. Lots of hens, pigs and children."

Conversation turned to other topics. But for Adam this had been another moment of truth. The strange man had not disappeared, along with his letter, into the post-box. He had substance and, although still nameless, an address of sorts, together with a family of some reputation.

TWO

There was no reason why Adam had to go to school in France. His father, Hugh, had explained this at a sort of family conference back in the spring, the three of them sitting round in the familiar suburban living-room after tea. He had been offered the chance to spend a year in France working on the dam repair project but he was under no obligation to accept it. There would be no negative impact on his career if he turned it down. Similarly, Hugh pointed out, if he did accept the offer with his family's support, there were a number of choices open to Adam as regards his schooling. One was a year at a French lycée, another would have been to move to a boarding school in England and the third was to remain at his present school, living with his mother's sister Helen during term time and spending the holidays with his parents in France.

Adam gave some thought to these options. He was delighted for his father that he had this opportunity to go and work abroad at this relatively late stage in his life and would not have vetoed the project for the world. With a teenager's insight he thought that the experience might prove a tonic for his parents' relationship. He imagined this as a ship in mid-cruise, long out of sight of the home port and yet nowhere near its final destination of death-occasioned separation. A year in another country might provide a welcome landmark on what Adam supposed was becoming a fairly featureless journey. As for himself, if it was a question of boarding school or a year in France, then France won hands down. But choosing between France and his present school required more careful consideration. It was hard to leave Michael and Sean and the others behind for a year - a whole year - and grow apart from them and different. Yet, although he had never seen himself as an adventurer, something in him observed an opportunity that was unusual, special in a way, and reflected that, as in his parents' case, it might never come again. On the academic front there were fewer problems than might have been imagined at first. GCSEs were just behind him and his choice of 'A'-level subjects - French, Music and English (soft options, his father called them) fitted not too ill with a year abroad. Studying French would take care of itself, the question of music was answered by the fact that his own mother was a music teacher and as for English, he felt that anyone could read a dozen books in a year prior to splicing himself back into the second-year sixth. He was a bright boy and he knew it.

Now here he was, halfway through the year in France with no real regrets about his choice. And yet...

His French was terrific now. They might still find his accent funny in this remote corner of *La France Profonde* but back home they would say his French was accentless. To say nothing of the repertoire of swearwords he had learnt.

He had gone skiing after Christmas with others from the school. A first for him, and though no-one saw in him a future champion he learnt quickly enough and found the experience exhilarating. In the summer he hoped to learn to play tennis. They played cricket at his England school and he wasn't sorry to be missing that. The game bored him and he was not very good at it, though which of those was cause and which effect he was not sure. He would miss the sight of Sean in cricket whites though: Sean not only played rather well but he looked the part to perfection.

Adam loved so many things about his new country: the food, the wine – in which he was just beginning to take an adult interest ...

And yet.

It was not so easy to replant yourself at sixteen in foreign soil. The going had been tough at first. It wasn't just his accent. Adam had an easy way with him that meant he got on well, and quickly, with most people. He was neither so aggressive in his dealings with others as to provoke hostility nor so wimpish as to arouse contempt. He had not anticipated any problems at his new school. It had not occurred to him in advance how unfathomably alien his new schoolmates would find him. He was not sure even now if he had realised the full extent of his difference.

His shoes were different. His hair was different. The way he spoke to teachers: different. Played football: different. Tossed a coin: different. Used his knife to cut lettuce leaves on his plate instead of folding them like blankets as the others had been taught. The list went on.

With no more than a couple of exceptions they were civil to him. And Thierry and Christophe were almost friends, Céline almost a girlfriend. But the almost was a big one. Just as Céline had seemed to find herself up against some invisible barrier when Adam kissed her, there existed a strange wall between himself and the two boys too. Perhaps it was the accent that did it after all. But Adam did not really think so. As with Céline, Adam thought, the barrier had something to do with *that*.

That, the thing that had - or might have - proved the stumbling block in his faltering courtship of Céline, was the most complicated thing that Adam knew about. More complicated than politics - the language of relations between people and peoples he had hardly heard of let alone understood. More complicated by far than harmony and counterpoint

12

which, however difficult, did seem to make sense on their own terms. *That* was as tenuous as a spider's web: strand upon strand of uncertainty that might (but only might) one day be seen (and then only thanks to the perspective that time bestowed) as a perfectly programmed whole. For the present those strands of uncertainty (strands plural because who would trust themselves upon a bridge made from only a single thread) took the form in Adam's mind of questions in an endless and interlocking series. Such as: what was it that he had had with Michael, that purveyor of puns and doyen of the double-entendre? Was it friendship? Or something more than that - because of sex? Why was it so different from what he felt for Sean - Sean the sportsman, forever in cricket whites? Was all of it just a phase, as he had read and seen that in many cases it could be? Would a sudden realisation of the desirability of womankind descend upon them all (he and Michael and their kind) like tongues of flame and burn up all that had gone before? Descend upon some of them but - uncomfortable lurking dread - not all? The dread was not just lurking these days. Since his failure with Céline it was up and stalking; since Sunday afternoon in the forest it seemed close at hand and ready to strike.

It was not easy to feel your way towards others in whom the same gossamer fragments were so invisibly being stitched together. Childhood relationships were as fleeting as encounters in a shoal of minnows. Few could develop. But little by little, as Adam hauled himself into adolescence, he had found some near-certainties. Michael, for instance. Well, Michael full stop. Then suddenly France. Here he was a navigator without a compass, an explorer without a map. If anyone at his new school was anywhere near to living on his wavelength he had no inkling of the fact and the next six months looked an unpromisingly short time in which to find out.

His father drove him to school this Wednesday morning. Normally he took the bus, the dust-coated creaking veteran that did the rounds of the *'montagne'* villages, trawling for children to land in Langres. But normally was not much more often than half the time. His father often had morning meetings in the town, or had to drive through on his way to the larger town of Chaumont. Often too, his mother had reason to go into Langres, either for shopping or else to give a piano lesson. When she was driving Adam used to play a little joke on the other road-users they occasionally passed. He would hold up an open newspaper between himself and the windscreen and pretend to be reading it. (This only worked because they had a British, right-hand drive, car.) Drivers approaching round the blind bends of the hilly lanes would be appalled to see, as they thought, the driver of an oncoming vehicle immersed in the day's news and with no view of the road ahead. His father wouldn't let him do this and his mother didn't really approve, either, but he did it anyway. Adam was very fond of his mother but thankful that she did not teach at his school. He pitied children whose parents taught in the same school that they went to. Especially if they shared the same funny accent.

In the middle of the usual pre-class hubbub Adam ran into Thierry for the first time this week. Thierry was an unusually tall and angular young man with straight blond hair and a strong-boned face from which projected an impressive Roman nose. He would be handsome when he reached forty but not before. They asked each other what they had been doing. Nothing special, they both said. Thierry's family had gone to visit cousins in Troyes on the Saturday. "Cousins", Thierry said, with a dismissive upward flick of his eyes. "I know," Adam had said to show solidarity. "Mind you", he went on, "that's further than I went last weekend." The unintended ambiguity and the lie it contained struck him forcefully the moment he heard the words on his own lips. "Oh, by the way," he said, almost by accident, "you don't know of any people called the funny family, do you?"

No, Thierry did not. "Why do you ask?"

"Living along the lane towards Perrogney?" Adam prompted a memory.

"No. No way." Thierry laughed and changed the subject. Adam thought it wise not to probe further. At least not with Thierry.

Later in the morning he asked Christophe, who lived a little nearer to the *montagne*, as Adam's little corner of the great plateau - round Courcelles and Perrogney - was called. Christophe was Thierry's physical opposite: dark-haired, shortish and stocky with something of the cherub about his face. But he adored Thierry for some reason that escaped Adam and went almost everywhere with him. He had no more idea than Thierry whom Adam meant by the funny family. But he did ask if Adam was interested in a day's fishing the following Saturday. They would be going to the Lac de la Mouche, the reservoir behind the dam that Adam's father was so busy repairing. It was just across the road from where Christophe lived. "I think Thierry'll come," Christophe said. "And I'm going to ask Céline." He grinned mischievously. *"Spécialement pour toi."* So that was fixed.

By the time Adam caught up with Céline during the afternoon Christophe's plans were clearly shaping up. Céline greeted him with: "It looks like we're spending Saturday together - along with *Cul et Chemise.*" (She meant Thierry and Christophe.)

14

"I hope that's OK for you," Adam said. "Don't let them drag you into anything…"

Céline gave him a look that stopped him in mid-sentence and which made it clearer than a thousand words that she was not someone to be dragged into anything she did not want to do.

"Oh, well, good then," Adam responded brightly. "Should be a great day. Oh, by the way," - he found himself under some extraordinary new compulsion to blurt this out - "my father was talking about some crazy people he sees by the dam. Riding around on bikes. Not working. I mean they're old enough to work. He calls them the funny family. But I can't place them. Do you know who he could be talking about?"

"I haven't heard them called that," said Céline, "but then I don't spend a lot of time cycling around by the dam myself. I think perhaps I know who you're talking about. But they don't all cycle around by the dam, as far as I know. There's one *mec* who does. Did your father say where they came from?"

"Perrogney, he thought."

"That sounds about right. There's a farm between Perrogney and your place where the people have a bit of a reputation. I think the guy on the bike may be one of them. My brother spoke to him once." She flicked back a too-forward lock of chestnut hair.

"What sort of a reputation?" Adam's curiosity was coming close to betraying him. He found to his surprise that he didn't care.

"Oh, you know. Country people. A bit … old-fashioned. A bit basic. What's all the sudden interest anyway?"

"Oh nothing." Adam saw he had gone a bit far, took fright and shied away. Céline and the strange but increasingly fascinating male creature must be kept poles apart, not only geographically but in the compartments of his mind, as if ideas might leak out and pollute one another.

"Anyway," Céline went on. "You ought to know them better than me. Some of the younger ones - the ones that can go to school that is - come in to the junior school in Langres. They probably travel on your bus." At that moment the bell sounded for class and the conversation was forced to an abrupt end.

"I'll look out for them," Adam said, by way of conclusion. He liked to keep his conversations tidy. "Something to tell my father." At school all parents were 'my father, my mother', *mon père, ma mère*. It rarely occurred to anyone to ask if they had names. Just as well. It would have pained Adam to hear his schoolmates tripping over the pronunciation of his parents': Hugh and Jennifer. Funny accents indeed.

The following morning found Adam coolly monitoring his own behaviour. He could not forget the apparition of the strange young man on his bicycle the previous day. His own impulsive rash questioning of everyone he met on the subject had put paid to that. So, rising from bed, he dressed at a discreet distance from the window while at the same time directing frequent sidelong glances at it - like a demure spinster, he thought to himself - curious as to whether the scion of the funny family would come pedalling past. This morning he did not. The word 'suitor' came into his head; he batted it back immediately into outer darkness.

But the next day, while Adam, just about dressed, was combing his hair in the mirror with his back to the window but not to its reflection, the young man did come slowly past and Adam spun round on a reflex, caught a smile of recognition on the other's face then, on another, unprecedented, impulse, dropped his trousers just enough to flash an unmistakeable message before reeling round and zipping up in a panicky nanosecond and resuming his concentrated grooming before the glass.

The next three mornings were like a coin idly flipped. On Thursday the stranger passed the window and stopped, on Friday he didn't pass at all, on Saturday he passed without stopping. On Thursday Adam responded with a smile, on Saturday with nothing, simply because he was taken slightly by surprise and had no time to change his expression. Though the young man grinned and slowed to a dawdle before accelerating away.

On Saturday there was school in the morning but the afternoon was free. This was the day of the arranged fishing trip to the Lac de la Mouche, and the afternoon found Adam and his French friends with rods and baskets, in position like a row of herons on the reed-fringed shore. They all wore their oldest jeans and tops, even Céline, though nothing she wore could ever look less than stylish. All she had to do was pull on old denims and tie a piece of chiffon at her neck to look like someone fresh from a fashion-shoot. Adam wondered with mixed awe and envy how she managed it.

All the previous day and night it had rained. Not for nothing did Parisian schoolchildren learn that the Plateau de Langres was the source of all their drinking, washing and bathing water. But by mid-afternoon the sky was clearing and the tattered clouds limping away like vanquished soldiers. Adam had only started to fish since his arrival in France; the activity had played no part in his previous existence. He had not arrived in France complete with state of the art equipment; his rod was an old one dragged up from the cellars of Thierry's family home, the kind of gift that costs nothing to give yet is somehow forever slightly resented by its recipient. Adam's bicycle came into the same category; it

16

had been a cast-off of Christophe's. Both items were in evidence this afternoon, the bicycle lying at its ease among the reeds by the water's edge, the rod standing to attention, propped up by the little tripod that had thoughtfully accompanied the gift.

The waters of the lake were agitated and turbid after the rain, but a few intrepid roach and small perch found their way onto the maggot-baited hooks. To keep themselves amused, Christophe had brought a camping-gas stove and a billy-can, which they filled with water from a bottle, not the lake, and into which Céline's adroit fingers plunged a great globe artichoke when once the water reached boiling. She had brought four, one each, but they had to be cooked one at a time. As each one was judged ready - they took about twenty minutes - it was hauled out and left to cool for a few minutes before being passed around from one to another like a joint. Each person pulled off a petal, dunked it in a small container of vinaigrette which Céline had also thoughtfully provided, then sucked the small titbit of flesh off the scaly covering. This procedure went on for ages and, as the petals got smaller and more time-consuming to detach and eat, the effort eventually greatly exceeded the reward. At last the choke was exposed, despatched with Thierry's sharp knife, and the meaty *fond*, the size of a sturdy mushroom, cut in four and eaten too. By that time the next artichoke would be cooked and the whole process began again. It was all accepted as the most natural part of the day's routine. Adam couldn't imagine English kids doing anything of the sort. It would have been bags of crisps or nothing.

In between sucking and scraping at artichoke petals, chatting intermittently and occasionally running to detach a silver, writhing, red-finned roach from one or other of their hooks, Adam scanned the top of the dam that formed their northern horizon. A road ran across it which was still in use, despite the scaffolded repair-site on its far side. From time to time a bicycle would form part of the traffic, and Adam would try to make out whether it might be the mysterious stranger. There was no way of telling, in fact. The distance was too great. You couldn't even determine the sex of a cyclist, let alone identify one.

As the afternoon went on the temperature seemed to rise. It did not have long in which to do so, though. The March sun was soon arcing towards the western woods like a shooting star in slow motion. At last it disappeared completely and the clear sky became a translucent blue duck eggshell which Venus, upon her eventual arrival, pierced like a silver pin. The water, calmer now, was a mirror of dulled silver, the surrounding forests charcoal grey. It was time to count the catch and be gone. They cycled to the lakeside café beside the dam where they proudly showed off their sparkling captives to the *patron* and his wife.

Thierry ordered four beers with a winsome smile. It did not work. "You know your father won't let you drink beer when you're out on your own," said the *patron*.

"Oh, come on."

"Ask him, not me. " The *patron* was firm. "Panaché, OK. Straight beer only when your father says so." This made them all feel small. Adam, whose own father would not have gainsaid a request to drink beer in the bar, felt obliged to have a shandy like the others, out of solidarity. This was the downside of living in a community where everyone knew everybody else's business. "Beer next year," the *patron* said brightly, as he poured the four shandies with an infuriating exactness as to the fifty-fifty proportion of lemonade to beer.

Adam went back to Christophe's for supper along with the others. Christophe's mother accepted without fuss the red-finned, palpitating catch and turned it into a golden-crusted *friture* with lemon and parsley for garnish. Adam thought it was the freshest thing he had ever eaten. It tasted out of this world. Finally, his father collected him and his bicycle and drove him up the forest lane to bed.

The Sunday that followed was by contrast a social desert. On some Sundays he went to mass with his mother, who was Catholic. But today - like his father who did not share his wife's religion - he stayed at home. What his own beliefs were he was not sure, an uncertainty he disguised from his parents under a mask of private conviction as if the question of his religious beliefs were akin to that of his political ones: the secrets that an adult could, in theory at least, share with the ballot paper and no-one else. This particular sunny Sunday morning he elected to practise the cello. After early misgivings about the instrument he was glad by now that he had chosen it. Boys carrying violin cases were liable to be teased or picked on, expected to be unsporting wimpish types, and whether they were or not was hard to prove; you simply couldn't risk getting into a scuffle if you were carrying such an expensive and delicate piece of kit. The carrier of a cello case, on the other hand, had more street-cred about him and would rarely be teased about his luggage. Perhaps because a cello case looked as if, skilfully deployed, it could do substantial damage to an aggressor without the instrument inside sustaining serious injuries.

Also the cello was a bit unusual and Adam liked that. All musicians, just all of them, played the piano. In particular his mother. At least he did not have to take his instrumental lessons from her. And even if she did tend to supervise his practice, he had the saving knowledge that she couldn't play the thing herself. He had passed Grade Seven before leaving England and hoped to take Grade Eight on his return. This morning he hesitated for a moment between the Debussy he had been

18

practising and the Beethoven A-major sonata on which he was also working. Beethoven won and he spent the morning in its womblike warmth until his mother's return from church signalled the approach of lunchtime.

In the afternoon he announced that he was going out on his bike, something that these days surprised his parents not at all. Back in Britain Adam had not been noted for any addiction to long solitary hikes or bike-rides. But then he had lived in a town whose rural hinterland had not been very inviting. Flat fields of wheat extended to the horizon in summer while in winter they were ploughed bare earth. The few coppices that punctuated the landscape were difficult of access and held little to capture the imagination when you got there. Besides, in England he had better friends and better things to do.

Here on the other hand, when everything in his life had been turned inside out like a glove since last September, the plateau and the wooded canyons that opened almost at his feet had become his companions. They had seemed more sure and more dependable than his new schoolfriends at first, even than Thierry and Céline. He had discovered the landscape and fallen in love with it during the initial burst of excitement that followed his arrival. That had coincided with the heady Indian summer of the region, with its astonishing fruitfulness, the upland orchards purple with damsons, branches breaking beneath the weight of fruit, while the stubble fields shone gold in the September sun.

Then winter had blown in from the Alps with all the savagery of an invading Vandal horde. The snow fell like scimitars and the animals were taken from the fields and put indoors for months. The fields and forests were out of range for idle strollers. Now, in just two weeks since the beginning of March, the snow had gone, the wood anemones spangled the forest floor and yellow splashes of carnelian cherry flower daubed the blank hedge. Adam had resumed his explorations.

He hesitated, once he had pushed his bike out of the garden into the road, before mounting it. At this precise moment he bitterly regretted the provocative gesture he had made to the stranger through his bedroom window a few days ago. If he were to run into him this afternoon on the course of his travels he would feel highly compromised and at a great disadvantage when it came to managing the encounter. For this reason he decided not to take the uphill lane to the scene of their first meeting. To appear to be seeking the creature out would only disadvantage him further. He toyed with the idea of pedalling a little way down the Perrogney road. If he met him going that way it would look like a coincidence: the young man had no way of knowing that Adam knew where he lived. But pride got the better of curiosity. Whatever might happen, if they did meet again it must be by real, not pretended, chance. Adam would not lay himself open to the charge, even from within himself, of seeking the man out. So he rode off, away from the Perrogney direction, went straight on past the turning up the hill and rounded the corner by the church, where a row of quaintly crumbling stone cottages incongruously sprouted a mushroom crop of satellite dishes. After a moment's thought and a look up and down the two other possible turnings, he made straight over the bridge that concealed the motorway running in its deep cutting below, and then off the road entirely onto a precipitous stony track which led him down such a steep descent that he was forced to skid to a stop in a cloud of dust and continue on foot, his suffering bicycle bumping along beside him like a lame horse. Thickets of bramble rose above him as he went, the path's left-side grass verge reared up and became a limestone cliff, and as nature enfolded him more and more closely, purple orchids and sun-bright celandines appeared beside the way.

The weather had taken a dizzying turn for the better during the last twenty-four hours. Yesterday's clear, temperate afternoon, together with the fishing trip it had blessed, seemed as distant as a childhood memory. Now the sun shone almost fiercely while the first butterflies of spring flitted between the patches of light and shadow that fell across the path. Here they were not the one a fortnight phenomenon of English spring times, instead they were present in scores: brimstones like flying slices of pale lemon, marbled whites like miniature checkerboards, woodland species with watchful eye-patterns on their chocolate backs, even one handsome swallowtail, a star guest who was himself his own novelty yellow and black bow-tie. A little way ahead an early blackcap piped a cold translucent stream of sound.

At the bottom of its descent the path met boggy ground. Here had been laid small logs, crosswise like sleepers but butted up against each other to provide a continuous wooden walkway across the puddly surface. On the right-hand, downstream side a wooden handrail had been erected to aid the timid and to catch those who might slide on the wet wood and fall off the path altogether into the quagmire beside it. This railing was stout enough to sit on and there today, like Little John in the Robin Hood story, perched Adam's nemesis, looking him full in the face as he approached. Adam froze. For a second or two he thought about the choices open to him: to turn on his heel and push his bike back the way he had come with what little dignity he could muster; or to push on rudely, muscling his way past the stranger's jutting knees and feet, bumping his bike over the logs as he went. But the young man's sculpted face softened into an uncomplicated smile of recognition. He said,

"Regarde ça," and flicked his expressive eyes away to Adam's left where rocks climbed away from the side of the path towards the cliff. Adam looked. He knew what to expect: the spring coursing out of the fissured limestone at head height and decanting into its mossy, ferny, pool. It was the overspill from this pool that created the boggy surface that the path traversed just here, necessitating the log sleepers and the handrail and, indirectly, this present confrontation. But today the usual tranquil picture was transformed. The rain-swollen waters gushed in four or more places from the face of the rock, their torrents meeting and splashing into each other, and the energy of these multiple collisions was throwing up a fine spray that filled the air above the basin. Right now the sunbeams slanting through the bare trees were catching the droplets and causing miniature rainbows to dance like the butterflies in the dappled light.

"Pas mal," said Adam. To have said more would have been deeply uncool. At the same time he discovered that any question of choice about what to do next had vanished as abruptly as any rainbow and he found himself propping his bike against the railings, springing quickly up and parking himself next to his no longer quite so new acquaintance, thigh against thigh. *"Pas mal,"* he said again, looking straight in front of him at the spectacle as though he and his companion were in adjacent if uncomfortable seats at the theatre. His eyes did wander down to his neighbour's lap, though, to see whether the ancient black trousers were open at the *braguette*. They were not. Perhaps he had more than one pair of mouldering black legwear. Adam felt momentarily cheated and then immediately was cross with himself for: one, being disappointed, and two, having looked in the first place.

"Juste un p'tit-loup," said the young man pensively, though whether he was referring to Adam or to himself was not clear.

Adam decided to understand the former. Some survival instinct told him that if the creature was going to call him by a name it would be safer if that name were not Adam, and *P'tit-Loup*, which meant not only 'kid' but also 'Little Wolf', would do as well as anything. "Then I shall call you Fox," he said, surprising himself by his boldness. "Fox means *renard*," he explained." (He had named Fox in English.)

The other gave a little laugh of surprise. It seemed he liked the idea. *"Viens."* He jumped down from the handrail and beckoned with his head. "Leave your bike here behind the tree," he said once Adam had followed him across the log track and onto firmer ground. "Nobody'll nick it from down here even if you leave it in the open, but hiding things always seems to make people feel better. Don't know why but it does. *Non?"*

21

The path was narrow and where they could not go abreast Fox led the way. Adam already knew its twists and turns, he had explored them last autumn, but he felt suddenly excited at sharing the lonely woodland track with someone who also knew it, and knew it better. That was not the only thing that was starting to excite him, but he pretended to himself that it was.

The path wound upwards to throw in its lot with the high banks and cliffs on the left while the waters of the spring funnelled deeper and deeper into the ravine that opened below them on the right. Soon they were walking halfway between the tree-crowned limestone heights and the tumbling, forested valley from where the now invisible stream, nourished by more and yet more springs on its descent, could be heard rushing and chuckling away. They hardly spoke. At one point Fox turned to Adam over his shoulder and said: "It's good, the fresh air and the sun, *non*?" sounding about as unthreatening as an aunt at a tea-party, and Adam replied with equal banality: "Yes, that's true."

They began to be enveloped by the sounds of the deeper woods. Chiffchaffs had arrived from Africa earlier in the week and were starting to fill the valley with their two-syllable call. Thrushes were singing, but at half power because it was mid-afternoon, and then once or twice the silvery song of a wood warbler raised the musical stakes.

The valley twisted away to the right. The path now climbed steeply upwards among the trees. In front of Adam, Fox's muscular legs were working away, the contours of his strong thighs and buttocks intermittently showing in his rather baggy trousers. Then, unexpectedly if you hadn't been here before, the path reached a sudden summit. Adam and Fox stopped. They stood in a miniature clearing which had a flat floor of young spring grass, emerald green. The path, if they chose to follow it, would turn sharply, almost back on itself, and wind down to the floor of another valley. The clearing lay atop a sharp limestone spur from which the ground now fell away a hundred feet on three sides. A wooden fence, a metre or two in length, stopped you stepping out into space and falling headlong into the panorama below. Side by side, Adam and Fox peered out across the palings. Below them, almost vertically, the rushing stream was visible again where it tumbled over boulders in its drunken haste to meet its confluents in the wider valley that hustled towards the Lac de la Mouche. The view was nothing new to Adam. But this experience was: contemplating the view shoulder to shoulder with the creature he had decided to call Fox, and wondering what precisely would happen next - though he knew in outline - and who would start it. Adam had already assured himself that there was no-one in the vicinity. The limestone cliffs made their position impregnable on three sides; on

22

the fourth the path, arriving from either direction, climbed so steeply that anyone making their way up would be heard approaching minutes before achieving the summit.

Fox touched Adam's cheek with the back of his fingers. Adam was surprised at the softness of his touch. *"P'tit-Loup"*, was all he said.

Adam felt a sudden urge to pee and told Fox this as explanation for why he was so hurriedly opening his own fly. Once he had done that, he thought, the next step was up to Fox. They were still both standing pressed up against the guard-fence and Adam thought that perhaps he could project a hundred-foot waterfall onto the treetops below. He had never seen such a thing and was curious as to how it would look. But he quickly realised, once he had exposed himself, that such aquabatics were out of the question and that the pressure-capped spring that was suddenly desperate for release was not his bladder at all but something else.

Fox took all this in at a single sideways glance. With a little giggle he undid himself and his trousers dropped, without further persuasion, to his knees. He was in the same state as Adam, though unencumbered with underwear, and as he turned towards him Adam registered his muscular brown thighs as a pleasantly arousing background to what commanded the focus of his attention. Fox threw off his ragged pullover. There was nothing underneath it. His chest was not broad but well shaped nonetheless. It was a soft brown in colour, like the rest of him and almost hairless. On the other hand, a decorative thick plume of dark hair curled its way right up from his dense pubic forest to finish in a tapering point at his navel. Without further prompting Adam threw off his pullover and, with a little annoyance, the T-shirt that lay demurely underneath. Fox pushed Adam's jeans and pants further down his legs, gently but urgently, then folded him in his arms and said, in a hoarse whisper: "Lie down."

It was more like falling down, collapsing in a heap. Fox pressed his chest, belly and sturdy cock against Adam's and for a moment Adam could not tell which bits of warm softness and warm hardness belonged to Fox and which to himself. Then, before either of them could decide what to move next, Adam came in a series of wrenching spurts. He felt as if an artery were bursting inside him. Seconds later Fox's convulsive tremor and involuntary gasp told him that he had got there too and their bodies seemed to float together in a state of sudden lubrication like high-friction machine parts in their bath of oil.

There was a stillness. Fox showed no sign of moving off Adam now their spontaneous eruptions were over and for quite a time they looked each other steadily in the face. Adam already knew that when you first have sex with someone you know, a seismic change occurs in the room that that relationship inhabits: furniture flies around; pictures fall from the walls. It takes some time for things to settle down again in their new places. He remembered the shock, the initial recoil that followed when he first did it with Michael, and as he gazed thoughtfully at Fox he wondered how soon this next reaction was going to kick in. But it didn't. Perhaps Adam had already been through that phase at the time of their first encounter, when his mood had swung vertiginously between excitement and horror for the best part of a week. This moment, by contrast and to his surprise, seemed to be laying things to rest, picking up the furniture and the dropped pictures, dusting them down and replacing them in a satisfactory place. Or perhaps there was nothing to rearrange. Maybe that was what happened when you had sex with strangers: there was no dislocation, nothing to rearrange, because there was nothing in position in the first place. Adam pondered this as he looked up at Fox's shyly mischievous face.

"You look so serious," said Fox. "You could smile, you know." Adam did, but he kept on staring into Fox's face, at the snub nose, the wide, sensual mouth and the brown eyes that seemed to express bewilderment and amusement in equal measure. How could you read a twenty-year-old's eyes - if twenty was indeed Fox's age - when you yourself were only sixteen? And if the older person were soft in the head, or retarded in some way, as Adam's father had intimated, did that make it easier or more difficult? So far, Fox's words and behaviour had suggested an age of more like fourteen than twenty. Perhaps that was how Adam ought to treat him; it would be relatively easy and an attractive prospect too: a mental age of fourteen - an age Adam had experienced already and knew how to deal with - attached to a physique equipped with all the strength and adornments of a full-grown man. "How old are you?" Adam asked.

"Twenty-two," said Fox.

Adam thought about this for a moment. Then, "Can I get up now?" he heard himself say. "I really do have to pee."

"You won't run away again, like last time?" Fox queried.

Adam did not answer and a moment later Fox slid off him. Adam rolled away a quarter turn and emptied his bladder onto the grass but then he rolled back again and for a few moments they lay side by side, still naked from the knees up, contemplating the sky through the bare trees.

"You have a funny accent," said Fox.

"You said that before." Adam did not try to conceal his weariness of the remark. "I told you before, I'm English."

"Why?"

24

"Why am I English?" Adam's mental circuitry blew a fuse.

"Why are you in France?"

"If that's what you meant, you should have said it." Adam was proud of his articulacy in his new language. Sometimes he managed better in it than Fox. But all Fox replied was, *"Hein!"*

Adam began to trot out his well-rehearsed explanation. "I'm here because of my father. He's working on the dam at Lac de la Mouche. You've seen the scaffolding."

"Why do they need an English engineer?"

Adam thought he heard the question echoing from a hundred local lunch tables. "Because," he spoke with some heat, "my father works for a French company. His little engineering firm was swallowed by a bigger French one. That's why he's here. That's why I am."

"Why does a French company buy an English one?"

Adam pretended to be exasperated by the question. "Because … oh, why does it matter?" In truth he had little idea himself.

"Will the dam collapse?"

"No, of course not. It's simply a question of reinforcing it cost-effectively by the best means that modern technology affords." He had heard his father reiterate this so often that he was now able to parrot it fluently either in English or French whenever the question arose. "It was never going to collapse."

"Lots of fish in La Mouche. Ever go fishing there?"

"Yes - No." He changed his answer hastily. He suddenly visualised a scene in which he was fishing with Thierry and Christophe - or Céline - and Fox suddenly joining them, trousers agape. He saw their speechless astonishment, their dropped jaws and bewildered eyes, heard their horrified whispered question: "You *know* him?"

"No, I haven't," Adam said. "I've never fished there." And later he would accurately date the first of his many betrayals of Fox right back to this moment.

"I'll take you sometime," Fox prattled on obliviously. "We can go together."

A relationship was already being created in Fox's mind that Adam had no intention of allowing to materialise. If he judged it expedient to have any further dealings with Fox, he decided in a sudden access of cold adult wisdom, they would be sexual dealings only. Yet how careful he would have to be. Sex was like the wooden horse of Troy, he decided. How uncomplicated a gift it seemed at first, but once you had let it through the gate how many unexpected dangers might be found to have stowed themselves away inside.

THREE

Adam had never before lived in a house where there were peacocks in the garden. Neither had his parents. The peacocks were symptomatic of the fact that the house they found themselves occupying when they came over to France was what his parents called a 'find'. It was a large, old stone farmhouse, one of several in the village, but unlike most of the others it had ceased to be a working farm some years ago and had been thoroughly modernised - almost spoilt, as Hugh had put it, "but not quite" - by a professor of architecture, who still owned it. The professor was on a sabbatical year in the United States during the precise period of Hugh's French assignment, which happy coincidence allowed Adam and his parents the use of the place while the rent, which was not cheap, was - even more happily - paid by the company. The only responsibility that went with this was that of keeping the peacocks alive until their owner's return. This had given Jennifer a few sleepless nights at first, especially when all three, one cock and two hens, had disappeared for two whole days during a prolonged snowy spell in December, but now, with summer approaching, everyone breathed more easily on the birds' account.

The garden was spacious, as a garden with peacocks has to be, and almost English in its three-way division into lawns, flowerbeds and vegetable plots. Though the last were still blank spaces in mid-March. Hugh had followed the example of his neighbours and covered the bare soil with as many panes of glass as he managed to find, stacked in an outhouse, to warm the soil after its winter ordeal by frost. In a few days seeds would go in: beans and peas, radishes, Swiss chard and - improbably - lettuces. The growing season here, though short, was fast, and the present run of warm sunny days would soon turn to real heat.

A very low, crumbling, stone wall divided the garden from the pasture beyond. Scrubby blackthorn, white with blossom at this season, straggled across it and grew from its widening fissures. The combination of stone and thorn, though easy enough for Adam to scramble over - even if he sustained a few scratches in the process - was just sufficient to deter all but the most hell-bent hoofed animal from ambling into the garden.

As a result of some quite complex negotiations in which cash played a significant part, Adam found himself hand-weeding the beds just inside this boundary wall one afternoon after school. Every time he stood up to straighten his back he found himself staring across it, over the pasture and towards the dark woods beyond. And concealed in those woods lay, almost unbelievably, the ravines, the winding paths, the cliffs and streams of last Sunday's escapade with Fox. From this vantage point the whole landscape of that adventure was invisible and subterranean, an almost perfect metaphor for the event itself. Adam remembered his walk back up the valley with Fox, alternately in single file and abreast as the terrain permitted, with Fox occasionally laying an arm lightly across Adam's shoulder and he thinking doggedly how you had to keep these things in perspective and not let them faze you. He wasn't too surprised at how quickly and uncontrollably he had come once Fox had embraced him: it was seven months since he had had any sexual contact with another person (he didn't count what had happened at Christmas) and in any case he was only sixteen, an age when you were hardly expected to have an older person's self-control. But Fox's similar suddenness had given him pause; it had more of the fourteen-year-old's gaucheness about it than of the precision-timing of the experienced seducer, and he had wondered whether Fox was perhaps himself a newcomer to the experience of sex with other people. Adam turned this over in his mind for a few moments and came to the comforting conclusion that in either case, Fox being sexually experienced or not, that precipitate ejaculation reflected quite flatteringly on himself.

Arriving back at the log-path and the handrail where they had met, Adam had almost expected to find the construction swept away in a sort of Rousseau-esque sermon from nature that illustrated the saying: there is no going back. He had been perversely almost disappointed to find the crossing still intact and had bumped his safely retrieved bicycle over it with nearly deliberate roughness. Fox's bike lay hidden on the other side and they pushed on up the last steep stretch of the track, through bushes, butterflies and orchids, together but in silence. Arriving on the public road at last, Fox looked quickly, though not nervously, about him and said: "Next Sunday, same place?" in the tone of voice of someone who doesn't expect an answer. Then he mounted his bike and pedalled off in the opposite direction from the one that Adam would be going in. Adam watched him for a moment or two, expecting him to turn back and maybe wave, but he did not. Then Adam got on his own bike and rode slowly home. Half a week had passed since then and he had not seen Fox again.

Stop dwelling on it, he told himself as crouched back down to a weeding position. These things happen. Then his mother's voice called to him across the garden. A letter had arrived for him that morning. She had put it in his room before going out herself. Had he found it? This was a perfect excuse, parent-sanctioned, for interrupting his work on the flowerbed and going indoors. Kicking off the boots he was wearing he skidded upstairs in his socks and round the sun-swept gallery (that professor of architecture had known what he was doing) to his bedroom. And there, propped against his penguin mascot, was an envelope in Michael's unmistakeable scrawl.

Your new-found acquaintance sounds a total nutter and nerd. I can't imagine anything less cool than some guy ponsing around a French forêt with his pants at half-mast. Except you. What did you think you were doing???

Jiminy Cricket misses you though. I do try to keep him under control - but you know what he's like.

Terry scored with a girl (ugh!) last weekend. Or says he did. Another thing. Sam (a new guy who you don't know) says he can get some dope for us all - if we all chip in a bit. Could be interesting, n'est-ce pas? Will let you know the outcome. (Not, of course, a reference to Jiminy Cricket.)

The sheer slowness of the postal service gave a surreal quality to the communication. It had about it the aura of a message plucked from the sea in a bottle, or something from a vanished past time discovered in an attic trunk. Michael's letter took it for granted that the first incident in the forest was an isolated one, unlikely to be repeated. Would Michael be imagining today, nearly a week after the date of his letter and four hundred miles to the north, that Adam had met the woodland creature again, that he had a name for him, and that they had more or less agreed another tryst? Or would Michael be thinking about Adam at all? Perhaps out of sight was out of mind. Perhaps he was actually busy arranging trysts of his own. And who was this Sam character after all?

Adam's friendship with Michael went back to pre-teen, pre-sex days. They had come to each other's attention as potential rivals in the classroom: two boys with the same habit of challenging their teachers with a mixture of bright questions and deliberately stupid ones that were asked just to provoke them; this had been an identity badge for both of them and they were not pleased, when they found themselves in the same class for the first time, at having to share it. This meant that the first thing that they found they had in common was a simple sense of mutual irritation. They had had the occasional ineffectual fistfight. But as their first year in school together progressed they found it made more sense for them to be friends than enemies. They discovered gradually that they had a few more positive things in common. They both liked books. They both had an interest in classical music. There was

28

something else that made their relationship an easy one. Neither of them thought for a second that the other was physically attractive - still less beautiful.

Adam knew something about physical attraction. There had been people on the television - young men in every case - whom, as a very small child, he had fantasised about to the point of believing that he actually shared his life with them (though always only one at a time). It made him embarrassed now even to think of it and he had never told anyone. There was a boy at his first school with wonderful eyelashes; they had snuggled up in bed together, exploring each other's miniature nakedness, while sleeping over at each other's houses. Then, when Adam was nine, Sean had entered his life like the morning sun to burn up all that had gone before.

Sean was biggish and square-shouldered when Adam was small and skinny-ribbed. He had blue eyes like cornflowers and his blond hair was the cornfield itself: it was normally short but it turned wavy just before it was ready to be reaped. His skin was the pink and white of hedge-roses. He had a smile. He was older by a year than Adam was but, unlike most older boys, he was easy to approach and trusting, not disdainful and sarcastic. He had an easy self-confidence that was so secure that he never feared it might be punctured by association with his juniors. He never became a friend of Adam's exactly. They just talked sometimes. The fantasies that Adam began to project upon him were a secret known only to Adam himself. A year later he left.

And a year after that, when Adam moved up to his big school, there was Sean again, neither surprised to see him nor especially pleased, but welcoming him with the same uncomplicated, generous, trusting smile. It was more than enough for Adam that Sean, now beginning to show the promise of a manly physique to come, had not forgotten his name. Adam was soon in love with the older boy, with his looks, with the way he moved, the way he spoke. And several things were, perhaps mercifully, crystal clear to him at once. One was that Sean - who was actually growing to like Adam quite a lot - did not feel at all the same about Adam as he did about Sean. Secondly, to have said or done anything to show what he felt for Sean, whether to Sean himself or to anyone else, and no matter how guardedly, would have led to instant social crucifixion. This was connected to the third thing: Adam was perfectly certain by now that most of his male contemporaries felt no similar feeling for other boys. And if they did, then (*see under Secondly, above*) Adam was unlikely to find out.

Physical sex, though, was a different thing entirely. It crept up on Adam by stealth. He had learnt as a quite small child how it all worked.

It was all in books that any seven-year-old could understand provided he was an energetic enough reader to start with. So he was well aware of where he had come from, and what his father had had to do to put him there in the first place, long before anyone thought it might be time to tell him. When he went to his big school he saw pairs of live frogs in the bio lab during February that were dedicated to no other purpose than copulation for the duration of a whole fortnight, as if to instil in the minds of the pupils a blueprint of the right way to go about things. Soon he was hearing about older boys who had actually had sex with girls - he couldn't imagine in what circumstances - and later people would point, whispering, to the occasional foolish virgin whose folly had led to the most visible of indications that she was a virgin no longer.

Somehow he made no connection between any of this and the things that were happening to him. It was in the gym lesson that he noticed them most. When he was given a choice of activity, something which happened most usually during the last ten minutes of the period, his preferences were usually not the slightly threatening beam - for though his sense of balance was not bad, he had a fear of falling and the distance to the ground seemed alarmingly large to someone of his small stature - nor the mat with its earthworm's view of life, but rather the ropes or the wall-bars, both of which offered him a panorama of the rest of the gym's occupants as antlike crawlers far below - a view of society he could not aspire to in any other situation. And high on either of these exercise facilities he was strangely untouched by any thought that he could possibly fall off. Perhaps it was the fact of being able to hold on with his hands.

By the time he was thirteen Adam was conscious of new sensations in his cock and adjacent muscles which he experienced with particular intensity whenever he hoisted himself towards the top of the bars or ropes. The ropes in particular. He did not have a name for the feeling but he found that it drew him with ever more urgency, as the weeks passed, to scale the heights of twisted hemp. At the same time his muscles seemed increasingly able to cope with the demands that his more and more energetic scrambles made on them. Then one day - and this was the first time he had really made it to the top, and proved it to himself by bumping his head on the ceiling, while his hands no longer grasped rope but the cold metal of the hooks and eyes that fastened his support to the joist that was buried in the smooth plaster - he came face to face with Michael in the identical position at the top of the next-door rope. He said, with pseudo-suavity, "What brings you here?" but Michael just looked back at him with a glazed look that Adam didn't recognise and which somehow, inexplicably, he found slightly shocking. So Adam

30

stared at Michael in his turn. If anything Michael was even smaller and scrawnier than he, but he appeared strangely transformed by his present surroundings and the physical effort of having reached them. His slight muscles were actually individually visible, defined for the first time and standing out on arms and legs. The upward haul against the rope had caused his white shorts to ride so far up his legs that there seemed scarcely room to hide anything in the gathering of the material at his crotch. His thighs were longer than Adam had ever noticed and they disappeared most provocatively into the leg-holes of his shorts at just the last possible moment. Another centimetre and...

Adam had forgotten for a second or two the increasing tension in his own nether region. Suddenly his attention was forced back to it. He felt his imprisoned cock swell and thicken as it never had before. He thought for a mad, panicked moment that he was going to piss himself before he had time to scramble back down to the ground, then realised that there was no time to do anything at all. He gasped and nearly let go of his handhold in surprise, only just finding the presence of mind among the sudden sublime chaos of body and feelings to hold on even tighter. Michael had registered the gasp and was now staring at him open-mouthed. The thought fled through Adam's mind that his own face was just now registering the same glazed, slack-jawed look that he had seen on Michael's only seconds before. A pulse of unprecedented strength and painful, delightful, intensity hammered in his cock for a second or two then died out. Horrified, Adam began to register that he was wet. Fifteen feet above the ground he felt horribly exposed. Everybody would see, perhaps already had. "Got to go. ...Slash," he burbled, barely coherent, to Michael, then shinned recklessly fast down the ropes and ran pell-mell to the nearest washroom. Pulling down his shorts in a rush he was relieved to discover that he was only a little bit wet and that it hardly showed from the outside. He was startled by the unprecedented thickness of his semi-slouching organ. But when he tried to urinate he was equally surprised to find that nothing would come out.

When he was able to reflect a little more calmly on what had happened at the top of the ropes he became increasingly certain that whatever urge had propelled him higher and higher up the ropes over the previous weeks, Michael had found his way up there under the same compulsion. And whatever it was that had overtaken him when he finally got there had been experienced by Michael too. Maybe, Adam thought suddenly with a quick jealous pang, not for the first time. He knew then, in one of those bleak moments of adult certainty that he was beginning to experience more and more often, that his friendship with Michael would never be the same again.

For a couple of days that expanded to the proportions of months in his mind Adam avoided Michael's company altogether, managing to avoid eye contact as if by chance when their paths unavoidably crossed. He felt no animosity towards his friend, just a fathomless gulf of awkwardness; they had experienced something together but whether it was a happy or a shameful secret he could not be sure. He had no idea what he could say next time they spoke.

But eventually it was time for gym again and, towards the end of the session, Adam caught sight of Michael beginning to swarm up one of the ropes. He quickly noticed, with something like satisfaction, that the adjacent rope was not in use and therefore available for his own purposes, then, feigning nonchalance, sauntered across the floor to it and started on up. He felt as if he were flying, the way one flew in dreams, without effort or exertion. How was this possible, he wondered? The tough, gruelling climb of the last few months had been transformed somehow into a gravity-defying ascent. A moment later and he was crouched at the limit of the climb, his head pressed against the ceiling. He was face to face with Michael. Who shyly grinned at him. He saw Michael move his crotch infinitesimally up and into the rope that parted his legs. Then it happened. And Adam knew that it was for both of them. Simultaneous. And he knew that Michael knew too. He grinned back.

It was no more than two days later that Michael came up to Adam at the end of school and said: "Come for a walk?"

Adam was excitedly self-conscious as they walked out of the front gates together. They had never been together outside school, having different sets of friends. He hoped nobody was watching them but at the same time wished the eyes of the whole school might be on their backs. No way would he look round to check.

The walk was a short one. They exchanged one or two safe-ish confidences about themselves, then split and went their separate ways home. The following day they talked about sex, though not especially candidly, taking care to stick to the impersonal formulae of 'some people say...' and so on. But the third day, by mutual but unstated agreement, they took a different route.

It led them to the edge of town where ramshackle sheds half stood, half tumbled, beside disused railway sidings. Adam did not think, observing the other's half-hesitating demeanour, that Michael knew his way around the buildings any better than he did. They explored and stumbled, excitedly, together. They were in one of the rotting sheds. A smell of earth and weeds hung heavily, but broad shafts of sunlight came slanting through in place of many missing planks and panels.

Michael turned to face Adam. "Show me," he said. His voice was husky with nervousness and sex. Adam did not need telling what it was that Michael wanted to see. He quickly unzipped, then everything else happened even more quickly: Michael dropped to his knees in front of Adam and caught the sudden upswing of his released cock with both his hands; Adam felt himself let go, observed his rapid discharge for the first time in startled wonderment; it looked like the brief jet from a hypodermic when a nurse is testing it for air bubbles, but milky white. His arms went round Michael's neck and pulled his head against him, his nose and cheeks against his damp, deflating organ. With his hands he ruffled Michael's hair. "Oh, wow," he said, uncertain if it was pleasure or shock or panic he was expressing. "Oh, wow."

Then Michael dragged him gently to the ground, undid his own trousers and yanked rapidly on his own slim appendage, in short staccato bursts, until his ejaculate came squirting out of him and his blurring fist slowed to a stop. They stayed looking at each other's cocks for half a minute before buttoning up. It was the first time they had seen them, after all. Adam was quite pleased to see that Michael's was considerably smaller than his own. It went some way to making up for Michael's apparently greater experience in pleasuring himself, and for his capacity to hold off longer - by some thirty seconds. Then they stood up and dusted themselves down. It did not occur to either of them to employ a handkerchief to tidy up.

In the days that followed they learnt to pace the experience, to make it last and savour it. The recoil and guilty shock that would assail Adam an hour or so after each of his first few times with Michael faded to a distant, manageable rumble of disquiet and grew fainter as the days grew into weeks. They progressed from the railway sheds to visits to each other's houses, braving parents in the hallway, overcoming the challenge presented by a visitor in the inner sanctum of one's bedroom. When they felt safe from discovery (parents not about this afternoon) and as they grew braver about exposing themselves, they would strip naked before throwing themselves onto the duvet (Michael's plain, Adam's patterned) and add a preliminary tussle/cuddle to their standard repertoire, usually to a background of Brahms or Mahler. It never crossed either of their minds that they might consider the experiment of a kiss.

Adam pondered the implications of all this in moments of quiet. The word 'gay' floated on the currents of his mind quite a lot around that time. Was what he and Michael did a 'gay' thing or did all boys do it? And then 'gay' was something else? It was not easy to discover. He had heard that some bookshops had a whole section devoted to gay fiction. His local one did not. You would need to spend a fortune buying books on the basis of a promising title, or else spend an inordinate amount of time browsing, to make this a useful avenue of research. He consulted his local library instead and got one or two leads, a few whispers of hard fact. In the end it was Michael who came up trumps. "Look what I've got from the library," he said one day. They sprawled on Michael's counterpane and riffled through the pages. "Oh hey," they both said, and, "look at this." It was a book called *The Swimming-Pool Library*.

When their affair had ripened over a six-month period into a state of comfortable constancy, Adam one day worked his way round to a question he had been wanting to ask Michael. "You remember that first time, on the ropes. I mean the really first time." Michael nodded. "Was that the first time you ever...?" He tailed off, suddenly thinking that he didn't really want to know.

Michael looked surprised. "No. No way. I'd been doing it by myself for about a year."

"By hand, you mean?" For some reason the word wank, which they all used as part of the common currency of classroom exchange, was taboo when they were in private together, doing exactly that.

"Of course." Michael paused and peered at Adam. "You, not?"

"No," Adam said softly. The conversation was sending gentle shivers around his shoulders and down his arms. Not unpleasantly though.

"But you do now, don't you?"

"Of course," Adam said staunchly. Since he had started with Michael he couldn't get enough of it; it had become a nightly ritual even when - which was most days - he'd done it earlier on with Michael.

"But you did it with me first?" Michael sounded pleased.

Adam confirmed this. "You did it to me three or four times, and I did it to you too, before I ever did it to myself."

"But that's great, man! That's truly fantastic!"

"I suppose it is," said Adam, half convinced. But something in him remained absurdly jealous of Michael, who was actually a whole three months - an aeon of time - younger than himself, for having discovered the source of pleasure between his legs, learned how to use it and found it already operational when he did so, a whole year before Adam had taken any steps in the same direction. He did not tell Michael this. But Michael said cheerfully, "Anyway, you've been making up for lost time ever since," just as though he had heard Adam's silent cogitation.

But Adam never really felt he had caught up, and even now, nearly three years later, and after his recent, riskier-seeming, experience with Fox, it still rankled: Michael's year's start on him seemed like something on which, even were he to devote the rest of his life to the acquisition of sexual experience, of whatever kind, he could never catch up.

34

Adam had mixed feelings about following up Fox's easy, same time next week, proposal. Meet Fox again. Sex with Fox again. It sounded so simple. But 'again' never was simple, not now. Back in those far-off uncomplicated times with Michael, at the very beginning, perhaps it had been simple; maybe it just looked simple now, in hindsight. But the repetition of even the simplest things was not a simple thing itself. The musician in the recording studio, the actor in rehearsal, was asked: "One more time please, just the same." (Somebody moved, a shadow passed, a dog barked, we forgot to switch the machine on.) Trying to repeat a Sunday afternoon frolic in a clearing on a cliff-edge and to expect it to go exactly as before seemed to Adam a childish folly. Better to be sensible. Wait. Things would take their course. Above all, don't look ... eager.

There was a guest for lunch this Sunday. Not, for a change, one of his father's engineering colleagues with radical ideas about grouting - Adam was slightly relieved - but a music teacher friend of Jennifer's (goodbye relief) and her husband who was a local vet. Lunch was later than usual and went on longer. With every English person's dread of cooking for French guests and being found wanting, Jennifer had made superhuman efforts in the kitchen. She had not quite reached that eureka moment of discovering that French guests were really not so hard to please. Nothing they were offered by English hosts, however simple, however surprising, turned out to be anything like as ghastly as their upbringing and education had led them to expect; they usually left the table greatly relieved at the very least, and sometimes pleasantly surprised.

When it wasn't focused on food, conversation turned from time to time to music. "You told me," said Marie-France, the music teacher, "that you were at college with Gary Blake."

"That's right," said Jennifer, pleased of the chance to speak of an illustrious acquaintance. "Though I don't know exactly what he's doing now. We had a card at Christmas. He does know that we're in France, at least."

"Ah," said Marie-France, brightening at the chance to tell her colleague something she did not know. "He's taking a break from the recital circuit. Wants to settle to a little more composition." She sat back in her chair and bit off a morsel of bread and cheese in triumph.

Adam knew Gary Blake. Knew of him, at any rate. He was a pianist of some repute who had started out in Britain but made his home in Paris for the last few years. Adam remembered his occasional television appearances during his childhood, sometimes as soloist, sometimes talking about music, and remembered his mother unfailingly pointing him out and saying: "He came to your christening you know."

"He came to Adam's christening, you know," said Jennifer and Adam slid lower in his chair. "I really must get in touch again. Now that we're over here."

Marie-France turned to Adam. "I know it's Sunday," she said, with the easy charm that her English counterparts so often missed, "but will we have a chance to hear something from you after lunch?"

A year younger and he might have thrown a teenage tantrum and marched out 'to go for a walk'. But the fact that he actually had an appointment down in the valley somehow made it impossible for him to say that he wanted to go there. He remained at his post, got out his cello and dutifully played the Sarabande from one of Bach's solo suites. It went extraordinarily well and he surprised himself as well as his audience with his beauty of tone and depth of feeling. After that he found that the arranged meeting in the valley had taken on a new importance in his mind and it was with a certain solemnity that, at four o'clock, he announced his departure *faire une promenade dans le vallon.*

He had reached the spring and the sleeper 'bridge' almost before he knew it and was immediately disappointed, then cross, to find that Fox was not sitting on the railing. He glanced to where Fox had shown him rainbows dancing in the spray above the spring basin, but the light was different and the springs less boisterous and there were no rainbows. No, he thought, you could not have a complete repetition. Even on the way down he had noticed some changes since last weekend. Hedge-mustard was pushing up its bright cressy leaves, and orange-tip butterflies were delicately reconnoitring them from the surrounding air. The first innocent leaves of nettle were beginning to green the muddy edges of the watercourses. Adam hopped up onto the rail and sat there by himself for a minute. No-one came along. He got down from his perch and began to make his way purposefully along the path he had taken with Fox exactly a week ago. Wood warblers called from the greening willows and a blackcap, mapping its territory in song from the tip of a bramble spike, sprinted off into the air at his approach. "Sorry," he said to it and thought he sounded like one of Schubert's lovelorn anti-heroes communing with the wild things, then he thought of Fotherington-Thomas and was glad there had been nobody to hear him.

Up the path he trailed, along the valley-side, until the path began its final steeper climb to the cliff-edge clearing. He stopped for a second. Nature had fallen silent for a moment; there was just the rush of the hidden stream far below. Then he climbed the final slope and emerged into the dappled light of the clearing. His journey had been in vain. It had been silly to think of Fox's casual remark as constituting any kind of appointment. It was just something people said. Fox wasn't a responsible adult anyway. And Adam had not even replied. Besides, it was already later now than the time at which they had parted last week. He was cross with himself. And alone.

Until he turned slowly round and saw Fox sitting perfectly still at the edge of the clearing, taking the sun in the manner of his furry namesake and regarding him with the same amused stare. He was naked to the waist, his dark pullover lay half balled-up under the palm of his hand, and the slanting sun laid bars of alternate golden light and bronze shadow over his chest.

"Good camouflage," said Adam. *"Tu vas bien?"* Fox looked like... Adam tried to think what. It was a photograph, a famous photograph, a very old photo ... a ballet dancer stripped to the waist...

"Et toi?" Fox didn't move or even extend a hand. He waited. So did Adam. Then he walked slowly towards Fox and sat on the ground beside him. *L'après-midi d'un faune,* thought Adam. Nijinsky.

"You came," said Fox. "I wasn't sure you would. I remember how you ran away the first time."

"That was different," said Adam, feeling like Alice addressing some strange creature or other. "I didn't know you then." Then, from a wretched ingrained habit of politeness that he regretted as soon as the words came obediently trotting out: "I'm sorry I'm late."

"I'm glad you're here," said Fox simply. Then his face relaxed into a smile and he changed the subject. "It's your first year here, no? You're going to like the colours."

"How do you mean?"

"Next month the fields turn yellow, almost from night to day. It's a soft yellow like a Chablis wine. The next month everything goes blue."

"You mean the flowers? The wild flowers colour the fields? Is that what you mean?"

Fox ignored the interruption. "Then yellow again. This time a deep gold like the butter, like the sun. Finally it all goes red. The colour of blood. Fresh blood." Fox wanted to be exact.

"Why do you say finally?" asked Adam, slightly anxious. "You've only gone as far as June or July."

"No more colour after that," explained Fox matter-of-factly "The fields are cut for hay. And then the summer bleaches all the colour out of everything. Until the autumn comes again." Fox had been looking ahead of him. Now he turned towards Adam and smiled. "But that is where you came in."

"Do you go to the cinema, from time to time?" Adam heard himself absurdly ask.

Fox took the question seriously. "Not often. But I've been to films. *On n'est pas si plouc que ça.*" Not that much of a yokel.

Adam gave an embarrassed giggle and looked down. His eyes engaged with Fox's chest. He envied its spare muscularity, its wind-tanned air of confidence, the plume of hair that showed below the navel and then dived down below the waistband out of sight. He thought how childlike his own physique was by comparison. If anyone had told him that he only had a short time to wait before the maturity he admired in Fox's frame would be his too, he would scarcely have understood. But he was not abashed either. Fox had seen him nearly naked and had not been unimpressed. Adam slowly peeled off his own shirt and vest, until his state of dress mirrored that of the man beside him. His state of excitement too, he noticed, glancing quickly down to where promising indications stretched the fabric of both their trousers.

"T'es beau," said Fox, meaning it, and Adam was happy to accept the compliment even if he hardly dared to think it true. Fox had been here. Waiting for him. It had been an appointment and Fox had kept it. Adam felt a warm glow of comfort and security. He stretched out a hand and ran it over Fox's front, exploring the smooth surface, touching the rubbery protrusion of a nipple. It felt quite solid. Adam was intrigued; he was sure that his own nipples never got like that; something to do with being older, maybe. He ran a finger down to Fox's navel. Fox gave an involuntary little half-gasp then lay back on the young grass. Still crouching beside him, Adam slipped his hand down the warm slide of Fox's stomach until the fingers were quite out of sight. Then with his other hand he started to undo the metal buttons of his denims, one by one.

FOUR

Christophe's family had invited Adam and his parents to dinner. It was one of that sort of social occasion that hurled together adults and their teenage offspring and where different worlds collided - or appeared to - like solar eclipses, with unpredictable results. At school the impending event had been acknowledged by Adam and Christophe with rolling eyes and expressively raised eyebrows. And by Thierry too. He had been invited, along with his own parents. Adam had not had too much to do with Thierry in the last few days. Adam sensed a new aloofness in him. He didn't try to imagine its cause.

Christophe's family lived in a prosperous looking modern house by the shore of Lac de la Mouche. The house was set back from the lakeside road and the driveway that led up to it ran through an expanse of long feathery grass that was referred to, with the sangfroid of the well-to-do, as a garden. There was more garden of the same sort at the back, running away to finish where forest and hillside rose up abruptly together beyond the fence. Getting out of the car, Adam and his parents were greeted with the salvo of hysterical barking from family pets that traditionally constitutes a formal welcome in rural France. Fifty metres back from the front door lay the lake, stretching away out of sight in both directions. Today it was flat and glassy, a mirror reflecting the oncoming evening. Beyond, its forested opposite shores lay black against the west. Kites wheeled overhead in the still blue air above the water. Adam had never seen birds of prey in such numbers before coming here. But up on the plateau they were everywhere. Every time you looked up it was to catch sight of a harrier or a buzzard or - more exhilarating to watch - a kite.

There were two kinds of kite here, the dark one, the 'black kite', and the red one with its more deeply forked tail. Adam had looked them up in his father's bird book. Both were wonderful to watch as they sliced through the air with the daring and skill of stunt pilots, adjusting the trim of their tails and wing primaries to take a sudden sharp corner or to deal with an unexpected change in the breeze. They would skim the surface of the lake like bats or outsize swallows, and just like swallows' too were their breathtaking changes of direction, when it seemed that the wind must catch their sails wrong-side and dash them, like their string and fabric namesakes, to the water or the ground.

"Come on. What are you dreaming about?" said Hugh. "Get inside." Christophe's front door, un-knocked upon, had opened.

Thierry and his parents had already arrived, and while Hugh and Jennifer were offered seats and aperitifs in the house with the other parents, Adam was sent out to join the other young people in the garden where they were expected to entertain each other in adolescent fashion until dinner.

A game of *pétanque* was going on. Thierry and Christophe's sister Monique were quite engrossed in this and hardly looked up on Adam's arrival. Christophe was only half interested in the game and broke off to talk and play host. "Boring," he said. "Céline can't make it."

"I didn't know she was expected."

Thierry looked up from his game. "She wasn't."

Adam looked back at Christophe, puzzled by the contradiction.

"Oh, all right," said Christophe. "If you really want to know, we had a bit of a falling-out. She and me."

"Over what?" Adam wanted to know.

Christophe was silent and thoughtfully chewed his bottom lip with his top teeth. Thierry chipped in.

"He thought he could get somewhere with her. *Tu sais?* But you know what she's like." Thierry stopped and his coal-dark eyes looked a challenge at Adam.

"Come on," said Monique. "You shouldn't be talking about her like that in front of me." Monique was one of Céline's best girl friends.

"You know what she said?" Thierry had chosen not to hear Monique. "She said that *you* wouldn't like it. You!" He sounded bitter.

"I can't see what it has to do with you if she did," said Adam frostily. He was irritated by the tone Thierry had adopted; he had not heard it before.

"Pay no attention to him," Christophe said to Adam in a conciliatory tone. He put a brotherly hand on Adam's shoulder. "He gets like this."

"I didn't know you were after Céline anyway," said Adam to Christophe. He had never thought of Christophe as 'after' any girl, he now realised, and rebuked himself inwardly for his lack of...curiosity? ...Imagination?

"Well, I'm not now, so there," said Christophe.

"He still has the hots for her, though," said Thierry.

"This is boy talk," complained Monique. "I'm going inside." And she did, while the two family dogs ran out to take her place, wagging their tails uncritically.

"But you of all people," Thierry returned to attacking Adam. "Why should she have a thing about *you?*"

"I've no idea," said Adam.

"He's winding you up," warned Christophe. "It's just something she said once to Thierry that made him think you'd made a pass at her."

"And if I had?" asked Adam. "What of it?"

"Did you?" asked Thierry.

"I said *if.*" Adam stood his ground. "And *if* I had, she wasn't Christophe's girlfriend at the time. Or yours. Or, as far as I knew, anyone's." He turned back to Christophe. "What's got into him today? I've never known him like this. Time of the month?"

Christophe was surprised into a loud guffaw which he hastily suppressed.

"No," said Thierry scornfully. "You didn't do any such thing. Not you. You wouldn't."

Adam was getting tired of this childish game but was unable to extricate himself from its illogical coils and twists. "And why not? Why not, exactly?"

"English boys," said Thierry. "English boys."

"Meaning what?"

"I'm not quite sure that you like girls at all. They say that English boys do not acquire much of a taste for girls until they're older. Quite a lot older, actually. Say, around sixty."

"Laisse tomber!" said Christophe. Drop it.

Adam would have made a dive at Thierry at that point, but he was not so far out of control as to forget that Thierry was nearly a head taller than he was and broad in the shoulder too. Christophe he could have managed, but Christophe still seemed to be on his side.

"He's joking," Christophe said. He had caught the strength of Adam's feeling from the tension in his face and forearms. "Take it as a joke yourself, *mec.*"

But Adam was not in the mood for joking, though his bad humour was not all the result of Thierry's asinine antics. Something had happened a day or two previously - something connected with Fox - that had first upset him and then left him brooding and uneasy, and, though right now he was trying to forget about that, Thierry's mad behaviour came like a stern reminder to settle a bill that has already been paid. And was about as well received.

"You're telling me I'm *pédé*. Is that it?

"You might be," returned Thierry evenly. "You might well be."

"And you would know, I suppose." Adam's anger boiled over. "*You might well be* - both of you." He drew in Christophe with a flick of his head. "You're probably the biggest pair of *petits frères* on the plateau. No wonder Céline calls you *Cul et Chemise.*"

There was a stunned silence during which Adam realised with a horrible sick feeling that he had gone much too far, and that it was beyond him to unsay something which Céline had actually said. Unable to retreat, Adam hacked his way forward desperately like someone in alarmingly thickening undergrowth. "How would I know?" he blustered. "How would I know anything? You two don't show any signs of life in you at all. I mean sex life. At least I *have* a sex life. At least I've *had* sex. A lot of it."

There was another silence. Then Christophe said: "I don't believe you." His lower lip was trembling as if he were going to cry.

"Girls or boys?" asked Thierry coldly.

"Both," Adam lied. "What about you?"

"La vie privée," parried Thierry. "You don't ask that."

"You did."

"You were bragging. I wasn't. You deserve to be questioned." He took a step towards Adam. "So who with, then? Names!" The two dogs caught the general mood and began to bark, while turning accusing stares on Adam.

"People at school," said Adam, trying not to take a pace backwards. "In England. Nobody you'd know. Or," he risked, "that would want to know you." He had no intention of boasting about anything that might have happened on the plateau. Especially not now.

Perhaps it was fortunate that at that moment Monique called from the house to tell them on behalf of her and Christophe's mother that dinner was ready. The parents had already had a flute of champagne each and the diversion occasioned by the arrival of the young people in from the garden gave Christophe's father cover while he poured a second glass for himself and the two other fathers without the women noticing, just before everybody stood up to move to the table.

Communication among the three boys was now suspended due to force majeure, and Adam switched his attention to observing the behaviour of the older members of the party. Apart from taking his mind off the unpleasantness of the last few minutes it stopped him from dwelling on what had happened with Fox.

Christophe's mother had prepared a *salade tiède* as a starter: curly endive and chopped walnuts with hot fried bacon strips and golden croutons poured on top with a vinaigrette. It was both simple and appealing. Christophe's mother served it while expressing the hope that nobody had a problem with walnuts. (One read of such alarming stories about allergies in the press.) Nobody had.

Adam's mother had served an identical *salade tiède* to guests two weeks before. Now he watched her face as she sampled this one, seeing

42

her attention to its presentation and the balance of its constituent parts. He observed her silent satisfaction at the discovery that this was definitely no better than hers and then he read a slight uncertainty in her eyes which could only be caused by the fact that she had garnished her dish with a sprinkling of finely chopped chives, whereas Christophe's mother had seen fit to leave hers plain. Adam understood only too well his mother's groping uncertainty. Were chives a *faux pas* on the Plateau de Langres? Or a brilliant innovation? Were people even now exchanging the news, goggle-eyed, of Jennifer's culinary gaffe or - even less probably - applauding her garnish as a masterstroke of originality?

Conversation meanwhile fluttered around items of local news: the inconvenience caused by road-works in the winding streets of Langres, the replacement by an estate agent's office of one of the old butcher's shops in the old town, the increasing power of the hypermarkets (but how convenient...). Jennifer told the story of how, when she first arrived, she did not even know of the existence of the two big *hypermarchés* on the town's outskirts and had attempted to buy a chicken in the town centre on a Monday. Not today, she had been firmly told. And tomorrow? she had ventured timidly. *Non.* Even more firmly. *Poulet mercredi.*

The main course was a healthy-looking leg of lamb which had been roasted on a bed of garlic. The whole cloves were served, still in their skins, alongside the chunks of meat which Christophe's father carved without undue ceremony or finesse. Green beans were the only other accompaniment. You were free to view the garlic as an inedible residue of the cooking process and leave it on the side of your plate or, more robustly, to see it as a vegetable in its own right - which Adam nowadays did, squeezing the soft milky flesh out from its husky covering with the side of his fork. When everyone smelt of garlic, he reasoned, nobody did.

It became clearer to the adults as the meal progressed that none of the boys were speaking to each other but only to the parents and to Monique. It was also clear that Monique was the only person who would be able to tell them what the matter was and, equally, that she could not possibly be asked.

The conversation of the adults grew more nervous. "We're having a swimming-pool built," volunteered Christophe's mother at one point out of nowhere, and Adam could see mortification on the faces of her husband and children. "Of course we can't afford it," she added, and there was a general shared uncertainty around the table as to whether that made the matter worse or better.

"We had ours filled in," said Thierry preposterously. "The leaks, the cleaning, the scrubbing with cyanide... More trouble than they're worth."

"Cyanide?" echoed his father incredulously while his horrified mother said: "Don't be absurd," before turning to Christophe's mother to reassure her. "He's becoming such a tease these days. We've never had a swimming-pool."

"And we haven't got peacocks either," Thierry added, looking hard at Adam.

"Did I tell you," Jennifer intervened, struggling valiantly to get the right tone in French, and looking brightly at everyone in turn except, pointedly, Thierry, "did I tell you we've got a composer coming to stay with us next month?"

This did at least shut everybody up and Jennifer was forced to elaborate. "Well, he's better known as a pianist, actually. His name is Gary Blake."

Although, apart from Adam, all the young people looked blank and so did Thierry's parents, mercifully both of Christophe's parents nodded vigorously, partly because they did indeed know of Gary Blake and partly because they were greatly relieved to be rescued from the unanticipated depths of the swimming-pool.

"He gives concerts at the Salle Pleyel," said Christophe's father in a respectful tone. "And you know him?"

"We studied together in London."

He came to Adam's christening you know, thought Adam, but for once she didn't say it. Instead she went on: "Anyway, we got back in touch recently and it appears he's taking a bit of time away from teaching and concert-giving to do some composing. He's been commissioned by the Avignon Festival. Well, it seems he wanted a break from Paris too, so he's coming to stay with us for a month..."

"Mum!" interrupted Adam in English. "A month!" He looked at Hugh who gave one of his elder statesman nods of the head that were visible only to his son.

"Nobody tells me anything," Adam grumbled childishly, but mainly to himself. His mother went on to talk about the Avignon Festival, answering the genuinely interested questions of the others, and seemed to enjoy holding court for once in a foreign tongue. Even Thierry seemed to become human again. He had heard of Gary Blake after all; he now recalled that he owned a CD of him playing the Beethoven Fourth Piano Concerto with the French Radio Orchestra and, to Adam's surprise, asked Jennifer if she didn't think it was a finer work than the better known fifth concerto, the Emperor. And Jennifer agreed and offered an

44

anecdote about a pianist of an older generation, Edwin Fischer. An even more senior musician - it was the composer Richard Strauss - heard Fischer play the fourth concerto and said to him: "Why do you make such a fanfare of the opening? You have only to leave your visiting card."

Gradually Adam found himself giving a cautious welcome to the idea of a top-rank professional musician joining the family for a bit, as if he thought that perhaps some of that glittering talent might rub off on him.

Cheese was served, including the prized local one that went under the name simply of Langres, and then Thierry said, out of the blue - it was becoming an evening of bolts from the blue - "Do you think, Adam, that people have a choice in the matter of who they fall in love with?"

"Were we talking about that?" Adam returned, icily. "I don't think we were." But his dismissive tone was a mere disguise. The remark had surprised him and touched him on a point which, since a couple of days ago, had become most sensitive. Though there was no possible way that Thierry could have known that.

"No," persisted Thierry, "but what do you think? Do you think people have a choice? With regard to the person? With regard to their sex?"

"I don't think that's a suitable subject for the dinner table," said Thierry's father, gently but firmly.

"It depends what you mean by fall in love," Adam said quickly before anyone could try to shut him up too. "If you just mean when people *think* they're in love, they're infatuated, or they will themselves to..."

"Adam," said Jennifer, "Thierry's father's right."

"...But if it's about really falling in love," Adam ran on but then his confidence in his words could be seen to falter, "then ... then maybe ... they don't have a choice. Maybe," he finished, almost under his breath.

Hugh, who had been preparing a frowning *Adam, that's enough* in support of his wife and Thierry's father now found that it would not be needed and cleared his throat instead.

After that the timbre of the conversation grew more tinkly and brittle. It was as if the young people's introduction of love and sex into the conversation had left it strewn with broken glass that had to be stepped over for the rest of the evening.

Coffee was served. Cognac was offered but declined by the men because they were going to be driving and by their wives out of an obscure but deep-rooted feeling, peculiar to wives, for what was and was not appropriate.

In the car, going home, Adam was aware of a feeling of perplexity emanating from the front seats as his parents separately tried to make sense of the undercurrents in the teenagers' dinner conversation that they vaguely recognised, the way you recognise and try to make sense of the underlying tensions when voices are raised in a foreign language.

Adam, occupying that spacious private fiefdom of only children, the Back Seat of the Car, was no less perplexed though for reasons that only slightly overlapped his parents' areas of puzzlement. Thierry's last challenge really had caught him off guard. He was full of uncertainty about the meaning of love and its implications, and never more so than now. Could he choose between what Céline represented and what Michael did? (He pushed Fox to the back of his mind for one minute longer.) He didn't *know* if he was gay or straight, he didn't *know* if the answer lay in his hands or out of them: was it a matter of will or wasn't it? One thing he was certain about, more certain after this evening's dinner party than ever. He would not be in a rush to tell the world, at sixteen, that he was gay. Especially his parents. However well they might take it (and he had no reason to doubt that they would take it well) it would be vastly more complicated to have to turn round in a few years' time and try to explain that he wasn't gay - *if* that turned out to be the case - and that his previous self-identification had been mistaken.

It was far better, he thought, just to get on with life yourself, to have your own adventures and make your own mistakes, without raising a banner over them that proclaimed: I'm this, or I'm that; of this party or of the other one. After all, as Michael had once said, if you couldn't experiment with life when you were a teenager, when could you? And that thought brought him suddenly, by an unforeseen short cut, back to Fox, finally.

He had met Fox two or three times more in the forests over the last couple of weeks, not always in the same spot, but with time and place more carefully planned and punctually observed. The weather had continued to warm gently and it was becoming increasingly pleasant to lie nearly naked in your lover's arms on the forest floor. Nearly naked because they had not yet crossed the threshold of stripping all their clothes off together. But they pulled their upper garments so tight up against their armpits, when they didn't take them off entirely, and pulled their lower ones so far down on their ankles, that quite a satisfactory degree of intimacy could be arrived at. They achieved their ejaculations by pressing and rubbing hard against each other's tummies, sometimes with the aid of a helping hand, sometimes not. It was still all over very quickly and it was still always Adam who shot first. He wasn't at all embarrassed about this. It was only to be expected when he was so much

46

the younger partner, he told himself. Instead of Mahler for background, as Adam was used to with Michael, they had the sounds of streams and birds: the chaffinch, the willow warbler, the wren... Fox imitated their songs in a sotto voce whistle in Adam's ear, which tickled appealingly, and told him their names in French. When Adam could - though this was much less often - he gave Fox their names in English too.

Then, on the last occasion, when they had both come and were lying still together, Fox for the moment on top, Adam became aware that he was wetter than he usually found himself in that particular situation, and then realised that Fox was quietly piddling on his stomach, gently but copiously.

Adam froze for a second, rigid with shock and disgust, and for a moment thought that he would spring up and throw Fox off him. But then almost at once he found himself checking that the warm rivers would fall nowhere near his clothes, and Michael's words came back to him: if you can't experiment with life when you're a teenager, when can you? So he put up with the unusual baptism, finding, much against his will, that the warm tickling sensation over his belly and around his genitals was rather soothing, and he had to blow away a tiny cloud of regret when Fox's waterworks died to a trickle and stopped. All the same, he had no wish to repeat the experience and would have to tell Fox so. Experiments were one thing; to go in for more of the same might count as kinky.

"I'd rather you didn't do that again," he said a moment or two later. "Pissing on me, I mean. It might get on my clothes. As it is ..." He was sitting up on his naked bottom, not yet willing to pull his trousers up or his T-shirt down, and casting around for handfuls of grass or windflower stalks and leaves to wipe himself with.

"I'm sorry if you don't like it," said Fox. "I knew someone ..." but he changed tack very quickly then and said: "It just happens sometimes after I've come. I can't help it. But if it happens again I'll try to aim it away from you."

"But what happens when you ... you know, in bed?" Adam felt a hot flush of prurience at the thought - the first time it had occurred to him - of Fox in bed at home, doing what all boys, he knew, did. And grown men too?

"I never do it in bed," said Fox. "For that reason mainly. I do it around the farm, or in the fields, or in the woods." He paused mischievously. "Like you do. As I caught you doing when I first met you."

Having avidly wanted to go into all this a moment ago, Adam suddenly found that he just as urgently did not want to know. In a

47

different tone of voice - the change was so sudden that Adam saw the shock of it register on Fox's face - he said coldly:

"Well, you'll have to learn to stop that pissing trick if you ever get married - or go with a woman." He was being Adam the adult, the man of the world, the superior being, talking down to the mentally fourteen-year-old Fox.

Fox looked at him solemnly for a minute. Adam became acutely conscious that Fox was now dressed but that he, Adam, was still in his unprotected state of post-sex near-undress, and also that the recent access of lust that had prompted him to ask about Fox's bedtime habits had left him with a renewed erection that seemed almost childlike in its innocence and vulnerability.

Fox's stare softened into a dreamy smile of wide eyes and half opened lips that seemed equally childlike and innocent. "I'll never get married," he said in an even tone. "And I don't want to try it with a woman. All I ever want, and everything I've ever wanted, is you."

Adam's blood ran cold in his veins. His erection wilted, something that Fox observed with a look of disappointment on his face that he only managed to conceal after a moment's struggle.

Adam hadn't come along for this. Sex, danger, experiment, yes. Fun, companionship, otherness. All those things. But not protestations of eternal commitment from a twenty-two-year-old with a mental age of fourteen. He got to his feet, yanked up his pants and jeans roughly and did himself up. Fox jumped up too. He put his hands on Adam's forearms. "Don't run away from me again, *P'tit-Loup*." There was the sound in his voice of inward tears.

Adam jerked him away, trying not to do it too roughly. He was hurt himself, he didn't want Fox to be hurt too. But he could see, and hear, that he was. He swore silently. Why did life have to be like this? So ... complicated.

"I have to go," he said. "Things to do at home." He was trying to soften it. "My cello practice."

"You play the cello?" Fox said this in a tone of great reverence as if it were the most wonderful thing about Adam that he could possibly learn.

"Yes, and I need to practise," said Adam in a businesslike voice, then turned on his heel and ran off through the wood, conscious that Fox stood rooted to the spot and desolate behind him.

The memory of this parting made Adam go hot and cold as he relived it now in the privacy of his space in the back seat of the darkened car. Oh dear, oh dear. Those moments that you wished unhappened. (Don't minute that, Recording Angel.) Or that the floor could just open and swallow you rather than go through such a goodbye again. Because it

48

was goodbye. Adam had not seen Fox since, nor would he in the future. He would avoid him as far as possible and, if they did happen to meet, which was a realistic probability, Adam would be polite but distant. Fox would be from now on simply a part of his past.

"Just look at that!" said Hugh suddenly. They had rounded the U-shaped bend at the head of Lac de la Mouche and crossed the bridge over the stream that fed it. The car's headlights showed up something on the road ahead that in a different season might have been a carpet of autumn leaves blowing steadily across in the wind. But it wasn't leaves, it was frogs. A seething horde of frogs, hopping from left to right, on their seasonal pilgrimage to mate and spawn in the cold shallows of the lake. Their eyes caught the car's lights and each one gave back a little pale green glow, so that the whole moving carpet seemed to twinkle with sequins. Adam and his parents watched with astonishment for the few seconds that it took the car to cross the frogs' path. Some no doubt were soundlessly squashed beneath the car's wheels. Adam turned round to look through the back window and there, sure enough, the little lamps continued to stream across the road, glowing a dim red now in the car's tail lights. Hugh accelerated away and up the zigzag hill.

FIVE

Arriving at school the next day Adam wondered heavy-heartedly whether Thierry would circulate the information that Adam had admitted to having sex with boys. (His lie, that he had had girls too, would not be sufficiently newsworthy to justify the bother of broadcasting it.) He found himself straining his ears every time he turned his back on a group of classmates to catch the horrified whisper: *"Il couche avec les hommes. Tu sais?"* But he never did hear it. There was no change in anyone's attitude to him. Evidently Thierry had kept Adam's revelation to himself with an oyster-like discretion that Adam could not help admiring and being grateful for. But Thierry himself had turned cool to the point of iciness, cutting him dead when their paths crossed and behaving quite ostentatiously as if he did not exist, making it quite clear in the most childish way that he had in fact seen him while at the same time acting as if he were not there. Adam felt it beneath him to challenge Thierry over such an infantile tactic and decided simply to ignore him in his turn.

Christophe was a different proposition. Adam was acutely conscious that he had treated him shabbily and would have liked to make it up with him. Unfortunately Christophe did not seem ready to make this easy for him. Several times Adam went up to him during the next two days, wanting to say sorry, but each time Christophe turned away with a wounded animal look on his face and was no more prepared to listen or speak to him than Thierry was. Clearly Adam's uncalled-for jibe had hurt him deeply.

In the end Adam had to give up. Those two days were the last two of the Easter term and what could not be settled in the course of them would have to be held over into the next accounting period. Adam was disappointed by this but not too desperately upset. He knew from experience that school holidays, on whichever side of the Channel, tended to wipe the slate clean where classroom hostilities were concerned.

Nevertheless it seemed as though there would be no fishing trips with the two boys for the time being. As for Céline, now that he had quoted her words to such devastating effect, he hadn't found the courage to speak to her again. So when the holidays began Adam found himself confronting the not very cheerful prospect of being thrown entirely on his own resources for the duration. True, he would have Beethoven, Bach and Debussy for company, but he wasn't too hopeful of their capacity to compensate for flesh and blood companionship entirely.

He passed the first days of the holiday quietly: sleeping late, reading, practising the cello, and doing the daily milk walk. The milk walk consisted of a pleasant stroll through the village lanes to the largest farmhouse of the community at afternoon milking time. He carried an aluminium can with a tight-fitting lid that swung from a metal drop-handle. In the milking parlour Madame Lepage, who took charge of the milking, would fill it direct from the cooling vat with a giant ladle. It was still so fresh that its warmth heated the aluminium can and ran slowly up the metal handle until Adam could feel it in his fingers.

Sometimes there was cheese to buy too. Madame Lepage made her own white, creamy version of *fromage de Langres* in the farm kitchen. She would turn a whole cheese out like a cake from its tin onto a board when a customer called for one, allow the little residual trickle of whey to drain off for a moment, then wrap it carefully in waxed paper and present it with both hands outstretched, like a Christmas gift.

The Lepage family had been good neighbours from the moment of Adam's arrival in the village, ready with offers of help and full of local information and rural wisdom. Grand-père Lepage, although well into his eighties, had cycled round with a scythe over his shoulder - resembling Old Father Time so strongly that no-one thought it necessary to comment on it - and had mown the long grass at the front of the house on their very second day, without having to be asked. Then a week later he had arrived without scythe or bicycle and announced to Hugh, who opened the door, something that sounded like, *"Chef et le chef, allez."* In response to Hugh's uncomprehending silence he had added, for clarification: "You take me in the car. *Bon?*"

At that particular moment Jennifer had the car keys. Hugh asked her for them. She naturally asked him why he wanted them. He was going off with the old man, he explained. Why, she asked? He didn't know. Where, then? He couldn't say that either.

Adam decided to jump in the car too, attracted by the idea of a mystery tour. They did not go far. Just to the farm where Grand-père proudly showed them, standing in an outbuilding, a new sawing-horse. What he had actually said, it appeared, was, *J'ai fait le chevalet.* Well, as Hugh said afterwards, how was one expected to know vocabulary like that?

Another time Grand-père had shown them with equal pride the alembic still, all burnished copper boilers and pipes like an early railway engine, with which, for a small consideration, he made damson brandy in

51

the autumn for those villagers who had damson trees on their property - that was nearly everybody - and who took the trouble to press and ferment the juice... which these days was not quite so many. He was the only person in the neighbourhood who had the right to do this legally, he explained. When he died though, his licence would sadly expire with him and not be renewed or transferred to anyone else in this modern age of motor-cars, EU regulations and supermarket shopping. His longevity then was something in which the whole community had an interest. He was cherished by all and cosseted in every household whose threshold he crossed.

For those first few days of the Easter holidays Adam found himself envying the tranquillity of Grand-père's existence and imagined himself living into a golden old age on the plateau, somehow inheriting Grand-père's mantle of venerability together with his alembic still and the licence to use it. But only for a few days. Then the lack of stimulation, the lack of youthful company and livelier pursuits began to bite. He missed the infuriating Thierry and his puppy-dog Christophe. He missed Michael. Missing Michael during term time was only a distant murmur of missing, now it became again a real rush of longing. There was more than sex between them. He had never been more conscious of the fact than now. They shared such a lot, so much experience, so many thoughts and feelings. Then there was Sean. He always missed Sean, even in his presence, because he never actually *had* Sean, in the sense that they were not actually close friends. Much as he treasured Sean's mere existence Sean had never become part of him the way Michael had. But now he ached with desire just to see him again, just to be in the same room as Sean. Yes, he missed Sean these days more than ever. And then, finally, he had to admit it to himself: he missed Fox.

He had told himself that Fox was in the past. He had decided just a week ago never to see him again. But that decision was beginning to be a difficult one to hold fast to. A part of him, the part that included his sexual longings and imagination, dreamed wistfully of an idealised faunlike existence with Fox, wild and randy among the greening woods. Another part of him, wiser and more circumspect, warned against the dangers of more folly. Too much emotional reliance on one, clearly unsuitable person. The chasm that existed between their different backgrounds, aspirations and understanding of the world. Discovery. This last was the most chillingly frightening of all. He had seen television news items about court cases in Britain. Accusations of child abuse, the public exposure - in lurid detail - of unsuitable relationships, slanging matches between rival sets of parents. How it might play out in France he could only speculate grimly.

As usual, he compromised with himself in the end. He would still not seek Fox out. But of course it was silly to imagine that he could avoid their paths crossing. On this unpopulated upland they were practically neighbours, living less than two miles apart as they did. So if they ran into each other Adam would have to play the situation by ear. Which might not absolutely have to mean cutting Fox dead. Surely Adam was old and intelligent enough to handle the situation. It might be possible even to resume a sexual relationship. It wasn't the end of the world, after all, if Fox imagined he was in love with Adam. Adam would make it clear that he could not return the compliment and they would both find a way to live with that. Thousands of people all over the world had to do just that. For example, Adam was in love with Sean and Sean didn't reciprocate that. It didn't seem to pose a problem for Sean, though.

Adam's strategy was not to be tested yet. As the days passed, his solitary rambles by bike and on foot resumed their previous range but they still gave him no sightings of Fox. He seemed to have gone to earth all of a sudden. By degrees Adam began to find the continuing no-show first irritating then frustrating. He wanted an opportunity to put his action plan to the test. He also found himself running conversations with Fox in his head, though their conversations in real life had up to now been extremely limited in scope. Then he began to imagine that he glimpsed him, satyr-like and half-clothed, among the trees in the forests and through the gaps in the hedgerows that divided the fields. When this had happened for about the third time Adam found himself almost unthinkingly unzipping and hauling out his stiffening cock, then masturbating boldly in the open field where he stood, as if, by doing something that Fox had told him he did himself, he could charm the fugitive creature to his side.

One day he found himself walking along the road to Perrogney. "Well, what a surprise," he said to himself - out loud, as if to make the lie to himself more persuasive - "I'm halfway to Perrogney. Might as well walk round by that old farm down there." He thought a little later that he had never tried so blatantly to deceive himself before and had to ask himself why it had become such a necessity now.

A stony cart track with a thin centre-line of grass wound downhill from the lane between two barbed-wire fences. A huddle of roofs rose above the crown of a hump-shaped pasture. Blue wood-smoke climbed peacefully into the windless air. A two-stroke engine puttered at a distance; the top half of a grain elevator was in view; hay-bales were being loaded onto its top end by someone in the dark doorway on the upper floor of an old stone barn.

Adam had no intention of following the lane round and entering the farmyard in full view, surrounded by the inevitable barking dogs as if he were a salesman. Instead he adroitly vaulted the barbed-wire fence, placing his two hands on the top of a post to take some of his weight, then ran across the pasture to the shelter of a line of trees. From there he approached the farm, moving from trunk to trunk each time the man at the top of the barn - the look-out in the crow's-nest - disappeared inside to fetch out another bale of hay. His absences grew slightly longer each time, as the dwindling stockpile receded away from the doorway.

At last Adam stood just ten metres behind the back of the farmhouse, yet raised almost roof-high by the steep contours of the ground, with a view down and across the yard itself, of the buildings that surrounded it and of a small vegetable plot beside. With ducks foraging in and around a muddy stream, hens respectfully taking the long way round the dogs that lay snoozing in the yard, and with a litter of unsightly receptacles and redundant hardware scattered about, it was a scene familiar from nearly a millennium of literature and paintings, yet relatively new - and sadly unfamiliar before this year - to Adam with his modern upbringing in the English suburbs.

Standing in the yard, taking the hay-bales off the bottom end of the elevator as they descended, and stacking them on a small cart attached to a tractor, was a middle-aged man. He looked quite sane and normal at this distance. He had all his clothes on for a start. His only unusual feature was the leather helmet he wore on his head. Reminiscent both of a rugby scrumcap and of an infantryman's headgear circa Agincourt, it featured especially hefty ear-muffs and a stout chinstrap. No doubt it was a godsend on achingly cold winter mornings. But today was warm and spring-like. Perhaps the rule about casting clouts before May were out was applied with particular rigour in the capricious climate of this high region.

Adam supposed, for want of any evidence to the contrary, that the man he scrutinised was Fox's father. A little way off, on the far side of the vegetable plot, a woman was moving to and fro among beehives. She was taking off lids, bending over and peering briefly in, businesslike and unfussy. She wore no veil and carried no smoke-gun, as far as Adam could see. She was a short stumpy creature in gumboots, wearing a nondescript apron over a mud-coloured skirt. She had long brown hair which fell to her shoulders where it finished raggedly, evidently not having been trimmed for some considerable time. Was this Fox's mother? he wondered, with something of a frisson. Everybody had a mother, of course, as he had realised with the same frisson when hearing the story of Beowulf at school and reaching the point when the mother of the slain monster, Grendel, came toddling out of the foggy fens to take her revenge. Even monsters had mothers then. Though Fox was no monster...

Adam peered up at the doorway high in the stone wall of the barn where the half-seen other man was still loading bales in the gloom. Could that be Fox himself? All that could be seen was a pair of brown hands which, seen from this distance, could belong to anyone. Suddenly, his task presumably complete, the unseen person stepped from the shadows and climbed onto the elevator himself, crouched down on it and descended slowly to the ground. Adam could see just enough to see that it was a young man who might have been Fox's brother but was clearly not Fox himself.

At that moment Adam found himself suddenly and comprehensively surrounded from the rear by a small army of ragged children and two - though it seemed for a moment more like twenty - barking dogs.

Alarm lasted only a second while Adam spun round and the children called the dogs to heel. Embarrassment lasted longer. He had difficulty in following the chatter that ensued. He picked out some words such as *spy* and *prisoner* and though not intimidated by a posse of children whose ages ranged from twelve down to four, he knew that any explanation of what he happened to be doing there - even supposing he could think of one - would be totally unconvincing to such an audience, especially when delivered in a funny accent like his own. He was dimly conscious of having seen the two eldest children on the school bus.

"Seen you on the school bus," claimed one of them in sudden triumph.

Suddenly Fox appeared at his elbow, to his intense surprise ... and relief. Here was Fox, ready to take charge and sort out the situation. "Let him alone," he addressed the children. *"C'est mon p'tit-loup, mon copain."* My kid, my mate. Adam took all the nuances of this public announcement on board and was touched.

"You don't have any mates," said one of the younger children, aged perhaps seven, with the withering honesty of that age. There was laughter from one or two of the others.

"You're so wrong," said Fox. "I have now."

"You're crazy, Sylvain."

Sylvain. So Fox had a name after all. He was not just a fantasy figure, a woodland faun, but a human being with a family and all the humdrum paraphernalia of human existence that went with it.

Adam was suddenly very conscious of being in two strange situations at once. First, he was surrounded by a group of unfamiliar children and dogs: a situation in which he felt extremely uncomfortable, though hardly threatened. And then, he was in the company of Fox, now Sylvain, and discovering that he had never wanted to be in anyone's company quite so much before in his life. He was on the point of calling out childishly to Sylvain something along the lines of: *take me with you*; only Sylvain spared him the embarrassment by doing just that. He put an arm on his shoulder in a hearty sort of way, propelling him forward with it just as he had done on their first meeting when he wanted to show Adam the daffodils, and said: *"Allez, viens"*. He marched Adam right at the wall of little brothers and sisters that faced them, and the wall fragmented, scattered and vanished, dogs and all, at their approach. He kept his arm around Adam's shoulders even after the children had gone. "Now," he said, "it's just you and me."

They made a few more purposeful strides together in silence and then stopped with one accord as it dawned on them both at the same moment that they did not know where they were going. Sylvain turned and looked cautiously into Adam's eyes, not taking his acquiescence for granted and said: "I've got some damson spirit up in the barn. Do you want to try some?"

"In the barn? How do we get there? On the elevator?" He imagined them riding up together on the grain-loader he had just seen in operation, in full view of the farmhouse.

"You're joking. Someone has to start it up and switch it off at the bottom. We couldn't stop it once we'd got to the top. Attract attention, that would," Sylvain said seriously. Then he paused. "Mind you, my folks don't mind who I bring back and anyway, I do what I want. So..." There was another pause while he reconsidered this bit of bravado. "No. I've got a better idea. There's a way round to the back of the barn. No-one'd see us if we went that way."

They tacked across the pasture, keeping below the crown of the field, descended into a spinney and then came out at the stream a little below the place where the farmyard ducks were paddling. From here they circled slowly upwards, screened from the farmyard by trees. From time to time Adam's gumboots slipped and slithered where spring-water made the ground unexpectedly boggy. "Don't stagger around like that," said Sylvain. "You really will attract attention." Adam giggled. Had Sylvain told him to beware landmines and sniper fire he would hardly have been surprised.

At last the climb levelled out and the going became easy. The back wall of the barn stood dead in front of them now and grew suddenly huge as they approached it across the final stretch of meadow, blocking all the other farm buildings from sight. Then they were standing beneath its rough stone wall. There was no access to the barn at this level. Adam

56

stared up. Near the top the wall was pierced by a line of vertical slits like the loopholes of a medieval castle. There was also an arched doorway, closed after a fashion by a pair of decaying wooden doors.

"Up we go," said Sylvain, and before Adam had time to say, "How?" he had grasped a metal cleat that was cemented into the wall at shoulder-height and begun pulling himself up something that Adam had not noticed: a ladder of iron staples embedded in the wall. When he had gone up only two steps he turned back to Adam. "Someone who climbs trees as well as you do isn't going to have a problem with this, *quoi?*" He permitted himself a grin for the first time since his encounter with Adam among the children.

Soon they had pushed open the rickety doors and were inside a large attic space which would have seemed ill-lit but for the brilliance of the spring sunshine forcing its way through the loopholes and under the roof-tiles, and lighting up an open area that might have been the roof-space of a gothic cathedral, all timber-vaulted and with nothing to furnish it except a few broken bales of hay and straw. Sylvain pointed towards a small untidy pile of them. "Have a seat."

He lifted the corner of a loose floorboard nearby and pulled out from under it a clear glass bottle about three-quarters full of colourless liquid. He held out the bottle towards Adam who took a small, suspicious swig and handed it back. They ended up sitting on the floorboards, facing each other, boots just touching, with straw-bales at their backs. They were close enough to pass the bottle from hand to hand without leaning forward.

There was an awkwardness now as both of them were obliged to remember the circumstances of their last parting just over a week ago. Sylvain dipped a toe into the tricky waters first. "And the cello? How is it going?"

Adam smiled. "I've done a lot of work on it since the school term finished. I love music and I hope it'll be my work one day. But, *tu sais*, music isn't the only thing." He pulled a fistful of straw from the bale nearest him. "You need people, too." Then Sylvain smiled too, a smile of grateful relief, and Adam realised that their brief exchange had conveyed everything that needed to be said, at least for the moment. Sylvain realised this too and silently handed Adam the bottle.

It was the first time Adam had been fair and square on Fox's territory. It was also the first time he had had damson brandy out of a bottle. *"C'est bien, non?"* Sylvain said. Adam nodded agreement, though it felt like firewater going down. Perhaps drinking that kind of spirit required practice. Still, once the initial shock was over, it did leave a lingering plummy aftertaste in the mouth which, a few seconds later, suffused the nose as well and then the whole head. He nodded again, this time with a little more conviction. He thought, suddenly concerned, that without a glass it was difficult to know how much of the stuff you were drinking and was anxious as to the effect it might have on him. There was something to be said for the bourgeois convention of drinking vessels.

"Did you ever go to school?" Adam asked suddenly. He would have liked to try out the name Sylvain, but was shy of doing so just for the moment.

"Of course. At first I did. But it didn't seem to agree with me after a time and I stopped going."

"Didn't people make a fuss about that?" Adam asked. He himself had never even considered playing truant; the repercussions among his parents and teachers would have been too traumatic just to contemplate.

"*Ah, oui*. Official people used to come round and write things down. In the end the doctors said there was no point my going on with it - with school, I mean. So that all worked out nicely."

"The *doctors* said?" Adam had never heard of long-term truancy being prescribed as a medical treatment before.

"They though I'd be more use, and learn more, on the farm."

"And were they right?"

"*En quelque sorte*. But they found that too much work didn't suit me, either."

"I can sympathise with that," said Adam, enviously wishing that the medical profession might have made a similar discovery about himself. "And so here you are." He thought for a moment and Sylvain passed him the bottle again. After giving his system another shock with the fiery liquid he went on. "But can you read and write?"

Sylvain frowned, fearing a challenge. "I can read what I need to. I can write what I want. My name. Notes and messages." He brightened. "I can take telephone messages and write them down all right." A thought struck him. "It's remembering to give them that's difficult." He felt at his pockets. "I don't have a pencil and paper on me or I'd prove it. I'd write something specially for you."

Adam felt strangely, disproportionately, flattered. "Another time," he said.

"Of course I couldn't write a book," Sylvain went on, almost to himself. "At least I don't think I could. Mind you, I've never tried. But if I could, I think I'd like to write a book about blue sky."

"About blue sky." Adam couldn't stop himself from repeating the words. *Sur le ciel bleu*. He found the idea unaccountably touching. Yet before today if anyone had announced a project so absurd he would have laughed in their face. As it was he found himself wondering in all

58

seriousness what such a book might actually be like, and over how many pages the idea could possibly be sustained. He gazed at Fox and heard himself saying earnestly: "I hope you do write it. It will be a most beautiful book."

Sylvain leaned in towards him, caught his hands in his own and kept on moving his face towards Adam's. *"Embrasse-moi"*, he said. And so, quite unexpectedly, Adam found himself for the first time kissing a man who was not his father.

The sensation shocked him in its intensity. The longer you sustained the moment, he found, the longer you wanted to sustain it. And it was not only that. The feelings that had been building up in him over the last week without finding either form or expression burst upwards and out of him in a great exhalation of breath that came as powerfully as any orgasm. And as he tore his lips away from Sylvain's just long enough to let it out, he discovered that his great sigh carried words upon its warm current, almost accidentally, it seemed, as leaves are borne on the autumn wind. *"Je t'aime, Sylvain,"* Adam heard his own breath whisper.

"Eh moi, je t'aime aussi, Petit-Loup," said the other.

"Je m'appelle Adam." They had introduced themselves at last.

Now that they had discovered each other's lips they found themselves unable to tear them apart again for some time, but knelt up against each other and clumsily unbuttoned and fumbled their trousers down around their knees. They brought each other off in this position as if they feared the manoeuvre required to get themselves lying down might have involved too much risk of separating their mouths.

Afterwards, Adam did look down for a moment, anxious lest Sylvain might follow up his performance with a waterspout as on the last occasion, but nothing of the sort occurred. Adam wondered if Sylvain had deliberately made an effort to conquer his old habit. If so, he thought, it was quite a tribute to him and a real, if quirky, token of love.

Only then did they lie down together, on a drift of straw, clasped in their shared stickiness and snoozing lazily. The damson brandy, no longer required, lay neglected at their side. A little later they came a second time and after that Adam said that it was really time he had to go. Sylvain did not try to stop him. They arranged to meet the following day and chose, with grave symbolism, the spot in the woods above Courcelles where they had first set eyes and hands upon each other.

It took Adam about half an hour to get home. Sylvain had shown him a short cut across the fields that kept him away from prying eyes from the farm or anywhere else. He didn't feel at all drunk: the quantity of damson brandy he had consumed had not been so very great after all. But he was unsure of his head for spirits and apprehensive as to whether there might be some after-effect that had yet to manifest itself. To be on the safe side he practised walking in a straight line along the edge of the roadway, once he reached it, pretending that the demarcation line between grass and tarmac was a tightrope. But he had no problem.

Arriving at the house he found Hugh already returned from work, which surprised him a little. He had quite lost track of time.

"You went for a long walk," his father said, mildly surprised himself.

"I ran into someone from school." Adam told himself that this was not a lie. There was an archaic use of the expression *from home* that meant *not at home*. Stretching a point, Sylvain could be said to be someone *from school* in that he had once been to school but didn't go there now.

His father frowned very slightly. "Have you been drinking?"

"He had a can of beer with him. We shared it." That was a lie and Adam was cross with himself. He had a healthy dislike of telling untruths and tried to tell himself that when he did lie it was in order to spare the feelings of others rather than to get himself out of a tight spot. He didn't really feel that the present case gave him any such justification. Instead he found himself wondering how long his luck would hold.

"Well at least you shared it," said his father. He was still frowning, thinking perhaps that the smell on Adam's breath didn't quite match the explanation of beer, but deciding not to challenge it. "I'm not happy about you drinking with friends in the daytime but perhaps it's better than doing it alone. Now hop upstairs and clean your teeth before your mother gets in and catches wind of you."

Glad to have got off so lightly, Adam did as he was told and made a mental note to buy a breath-freshener spray next time he was in the town.

SIX

When Adam set off for his rendezvous with Sylvain the following day he realised that he had entered a new phase of his life. He dared to imagine that this held true of Sylvain too. Yesterday's kiss had transformed them both into different people. Under the tree from which Adam had dropped into Sylvain's path, to their mutual surprise, just a month ago, Adam now encountered a more self-assured young man than he had had met back then. No longer in muddy, zipless, trousers, Sylvain wore blue denims, admittedly ancient, faded and with a modish slit at one knee, but looking freshly laundered and clean-on that day. The holed dish-cloth of a sweater had been replaced by a striped shirt - again old and without a collar, but clean and seeming actually to have been ironed - which was rolled up to Sylvain's elbows and showed off his now familiar brown forearms: they were attractively muscular without being threateningly over-developed. A leather belt and lace-up working-boots completed the outfit. When he saw Adam his face relaxed into a confident smile of welcome. No longer a wild man of the woods, he looked exactly what he was: a boy in love for the first time in his life.

They kissed when they met, standing up and fully clothed, like people who cannot remember a time when they were anything less than lovers. True, the next thing they did was to force a hand down each other's trousers in exploratory fashion. (Adam, who had experienced a tiny twinge of regret that Sylvain had grown out of wandering the woods with his flies wide-open, felt compensated by the discovery that his maturing sense of sartorial style had not taken him as far as wearing underwear.) There was an unspoken agreement between them that there was no hurry today. Their sexual appetites could be left in a delicious state of salivating anticipation for a while longer. After enjoying for a few seconds his squeeze of Sylvain's semi-awakening cock and the tickling brush of his pubic hair on the back of his hand, Adam withdrew his hand and a few seconds later Sylvain followed suit.

Sylvain put a hand on each of Adam's shoulders and looked into his eyes. "Where shall I take you today?" he said. "What shall I show you?" Then he answered his own question. "We'll go down to the western arm of the Mouche lake. See the frogs. I'll show you the nest of a *litorne*."

They set off exactly as they had done a month ago, leaving the track in the direction of the clearing where the daffodils had been. And there they still were, a little past their best perhaps, but even now able to surprise the eye with their yellow sparks of light among the shadows.

Yellow was to be the colour motif of that day, not to say of that month. For March had gone out like a lamb, leaving the white wood anemones fading to pink and wilting, and April was in. Sylvain had said that the new month would turn the fields the soft colour of Chablis wine, though Adam had yet to see this happen. But they made their way today along a woodland track that Adam hadn't found before and it took them to an unfamiliar side of the forest. And little by little, as they neared the wood's edge, the sunlit open country beyond gleamed in at them with increasing intensity until the trees thinned out into a realm of lemony light.

The wood stopped then and so did they. *"Cou-cou,"* said Sylvain, and laughed. Adam wondered if he was being obscurely teased, but then Sylvain bent down and picked one long flower-stem from which five brimstone flower-heads sprang. It was these, multiplied by thousands and then by hundreds again, that gave the meadow its sudden new wash of colour. "We call it *cou-cou,*" he explained. "It comes just a day or two before the cuckoo bird." It was simply the name for cowslip in that part of the world.

The meadow fell away a little, then climbed towards the motorway which formed its eastern boundary. They waded through the yellow, wind-ruffled surf of flowers, surprising bumblebees and yellow butterflies as they bounded along. Sylvain knew a tunnel under the motorway embankment which was used by the farmers and their tractors and which brought them out above the western arm of Lac de la Mouche. The lake was invisible as yet; there was still half a mile of woodland to climb down through. But the wood was not dense, and sunlight splashed down upon its bridle-paths and clearings. Here too the white carpet of March's windflowers had given way to high-gloss yellow stars of celandine and the occasional magical firecrack of daffodils.

Adam could not remember a moment when he had been happier. He could not remember another time from which he had looked back and thought: no other moment has been as good as now. He could not remember - because he had never done so - saying to himself: I am as happy as I can ever be, because I am in love.

He looked sideways at Sylvain, wondering whether to share this insight with him now or later. Then, conscious that they were both at least partly preoccupied with picking their way among outreaching branches of saplings, and negotiating stray tree-roots and the odd dead bramble with their feet, he decided that later was the more sensible alternative.

At last their downward sloping path opened out onto a flat expanse of grass that had been cropped so short by rabbits that it was almost a lawn. You could have played bowls on it if it had been a bit flatter. This clearing was a long crescent, its outer curve formed by the woods, its inner one the shore of the lake. It was a place of total seclusion whose regular visitors were normally only birds, insects and frogs. And in the still sunshine their voices only were to be heard. Like a small park, the grassy clearing was scattered with a few well-grown trees. Tussocks of bramble and rush grew around their trunks, enmeshed in eruptions of suckers that were just coming into full leaf, some way in advance of the cautiously budding crowns above them, and it was in one of these thickets that Sylvain showed Adam what he had promised: the nest of a fieldfare, just a foot above the ground, in its own private fortress of bramble thorns. The hen bird was sitting as they peered cautiously down. Her yellow bill and ash-grey head, her russet back, all seemed startlingly bright for such a gloomy recess. She moved her head infinitesimally and looked up at them with one eye, but sat tight, unflinching. They let her be and stole quietly away.

They did not go far. Sylvain abruptly turned to Adam and embraced him. As if responding to a cue they unbuckled each other's trousers and released the erections that had materialised almost instantaneously, as if by magic. Then when Adam eased Sylvain's jeans down his now familiar furry thighs he discovered a new aspect of his situation. All that was Sylvain: all that muscle, hair and wind-tanned skin, all that warmth and energy, all that vibrant life was now a part of him. Part of Adam. His Own Flesh. The discovery overcame him and he felt dizzy with it, felt like fainting, felt like sobbing. Sylvain seemed similarly overcome. He clutched at Adam's buttocks and pushed his cock hard against his crotch. To Adam it felt, had looked, more massive than ever it had seemed before. And Sylvain asked him, in a broken voice: *"Puis-je t'enculer?"* Very politely. May I fuck you? Not just 'can I'.

Adam had supposed for some time now - perhaps a year - that, if he found out, or decided, that he was really gay, this moment would occur at some point in the exploration that was his life. He gasped involuntarily, like someone plunging into a cold sea, and thought both, God I'm young for this, and, why not now? And then thought, better get it over. So he said yes, but in the nettle-grasping spirit of someone who accepts the necessity of a painful rite of initiation rather than out of real enthusiasm or desire. Sylvain drew Adam down to the ground where they tussled lightly for a few moments, Sylvain seeming unsure whether to turn Adam on his front or lay him on his back, and Adam uncertain which way was correct and waiting to be shown. In the end Sylvain decided to take him from the front but was then confronted by the immovable (in the suddenly short time that remained to him) obstacle of Adam's gumboots which prevented his jeans from going any further than his knees and pinned his legs together at that point as effectively as any chastity belt. Sylvain by then had run out of time and, still on hands and knees over Adam, came spontaneously, his semen raining down on Adam's bared chest in hot staccato spurts. A few seconds later and Adam had followed suit with only minimal prompting from his hand. Then Sylvain threw himself down on Adam and they rolled together on the rabbit-bitten grass in a wet and warm embrace, laughing.

When they felt ready to they continued their walk. They followed the lake to the end of the grassy crescent and then continued along the water's edge by its fringe of trees. Adam was happily surprised to find the euphoric feeling of that spring afternoon in no way diminished by the all too early climax of its purely sexual element. Rather the reverse in fact. Perhaps there was more to sex than people gave it credit for. At least this seemed to be the case when you were in love. With Michael, once it was finished it was finished. You mopped up and then went on discussing Kant's Critique or whatever. Adam put his hand, trusting and childlike, in Sylvain's and Sylvain clasped it with a joyful tightness. It was as if an electric current flowed between them and Adam knew that there was no need to speak - neither of European philosophy nor of anything else.

The west arm of the lake grew narrower and finally dwindled to nothing more than a ditch which was crossed by an old brick bridge that carried a narrow lane. This brought them round to the opposite shore which they followed for a mile or so along the lane. The banks were well wooded on this side too. And although there was the possibility of the odd car surprising them round a bend - even a car driven by someone who might know one or other of them - their hands stayed tightly clasped together. The danger added an extra dimension to the experience. Then suddenly the silence was broken by a loud crack behind them, a short swishing sound and a thump. They turned, startled. A large tree branch lay just ten metres behind them, nearly blocking the lane. Ten seconds earlier and they would have been flattened beneath it. Adam let go Sylvain's hand. A superstitious dread stole up upon his happiness, a sudden storm cloud crossing the sun. Was the hand of God to be discerned in that suspended sentence? A warning tempered with mercy … subject to certain conditions of course. Adam thrust the idea behind him, turned the double heat of his mind and heart against the baleful chill of the cloud. He told himself that God - if he existed - really would move in more mysterious ways than this, would not conceivably employ such

64

schoolteacherly unsubtle tactics, and certainly not when dealing with a creature of Adam's intellect and sophistication.

By the time Adam had mentally wrestled with all this he had physically run back with Sylvain to the fallen branch and started to wrestle with that too, hauling it out of the path of traffic. It wasn't all that easy: it was both heavy and awkward to handle. But once they had manoeuvred it off the carriageway it tumbled down the bank with a satisfying somersault, coming to a final stop in the undergrowth a few metres below them, just above the lake shore. When they walked on again, this time it was Sylvain's hand that sought the comforting clasp of Adam's fingers.

At last the lane brought them round the curve in the shoreline where the two arms of the lake became one and there a whole new vista swung into view. Christophe's house was clearly visible on the opposite shore, its beige paintwork and orange roof tiles catching the sun among the distant trees. Further round, the top of the dam showed as a thin line dividing the stacked up waters of the foreground from the distant hills beyond. And a few moments later the rooftops of St Ciergues appeared, climbing picturesquely up the western slope; among them was the lakeside bar where Adam had gone with his schoolmates after his last fishing trip and been obliged to drink shandy. As they got nearer Sylvain began to head for the bar quite purposefully, though pragmatically he let go of Adam's hand as they approached the centre of the hamlet. Adam hung back, suddenly anxious. Sylvain sensed this and said: "Don't worry. You're with me."

"I can't go in there with you. They know me there. My father's site office is just two hundred yards away. If he sees me, or if someone tells him…" He tried to reduce the impact of this betrayal of his love. "He won't let me go drinking with my friends in the daytime."

"Well," said Sylvain, "I can go in and buy the drinks and we can drink them in the garden."

"There's nobody else in the garden," objected Adam. "We'd be even more conspicuous if anyone in the site office looked in our direction."

Sylvain stopped, trying to think what else they could do next. But before he could come up with anything, the solution presented itself in the unexpected form of an old green Peugeot pick-up which came bouncing along the road from St Ciergues towards them shrouded in its own micro-climate of smoke and dust. Sylvain stepped out into the road and waved at it with both arms until it stopped. He turned back to Adam. "It's our van," he explained. "Get in."

So Adam found himself clambering into the front and only passenger seat of the truck, which he had to share squashed up with Sylvain, and

65

being introduced to Sylvain's brother, Jean-Paul. This was the man he had seen loading hay-bales onto the elevator just the day before. He looked quite like Sylvain, seen at close quarters, though his features were a little firmer and there were lines around his mouth. He was also a bit more solid in terms of muscle. This could all be put down to the fact, Adam thought, that he was probably two or three years older, and he found himself deciding - he who had never considered that even a twenty-two-year-old could be sexy before he met Sylvain - that Jean-Paul was also quite attractive in his way.

"Can you take us to Perrogney?" Sylvain said quickly to his brother. "To the *Licence Quatre*. The kid doesn't want to drink with his enemies and he has one or two who go drinking at St Ciergues."

Jean-Paul nodded and grinned. He seemed to find nothing out of place in the idea that an English teenager should want to hole up in a rural bar where his enemies didn't hang out, nor in that his brother should be taking a foreign school-kid out drinking in the middle of the afternoon in the first place.

"I'm on my way back to the farm myself," he said. "It'll only take me a minute out of my way to drop you off." He turned to Adam. "You like the country way of life, *non*?"

Like a video on fast rewind, the last hour of their lakeside hike ran backwards outside the car window in a couple of minutes, then they turned uphill and wound their way by a back road into Perrogney village. Here all was silent. The ancient houses of roughly rendered stone had a brooding air about them as they slept through the afternoon and from their blank facades half-shuttered windows peered like old cynics who had seen all of life pass before them. They stopped outside one particular cottage. In one small pane of its front window was pasted a flyblown notice. It read, simply, *Licence IV*.

The truck drove off and left them. Sylvain pushed open the cottage door and Adam followed him inside. He found himself in a narrow room which nevertheless ran the full depth of the house towards a window into which the late afternoon sun was slanting. A refectory table ran halfway down the length of the room with half a dozen chairs on either side. Beyond, towards the window, stood two smaller tables, square, with four seats at each. On the left was a short bar counter that jutted a short way into the room and behind that a door that led into the more private recesses of the house.

For the moment they were the only people in the room. Then the door behind the bar opened and an elderly man appeared. Without showing any sign of surprise or curiosity about them he said simply: *"Qu'est-ce que je peux vous servir, messieurs?"*

66

Without consulting Adam Sylvain ordered *deux demis* and a moment later they were sitting opposite each other at the refectory table with two glasses of draught blonde beer in front of them.

None of the individual parts of the experience was new to Adam. He had shared cans of beer with friends in England, sometimes had a small glass with his father at home. Being in bars was nothing new either: there was his occasional glass of shandy with his French friends and before that, soft drinks in pubs in England. Sitting eyeball to eyeball with Sylvain was hardly new either, even if his perception of Sylvain as the object of his love, like his knowledge of his name, was a mere twenty-four hours old. But now all these elements came together and he found himself in the middle of a new adult experience that comprised all of them and created something much greater than the sum of all its parts.

Conversation seemed in order, but Adam found himself suddenly tongue-tied. He looked into his glass of golden beer and watched the bubbles rising. He tried to follow them back to the beginning of their mercurial progress upwards through the sun-coloured liquid and failed to see where they started from, or how, or why.

"They come from nowhere, stream up like chains of beautiful jewels and then disappear for ever." Adam was startled to hear his exact thoughts articulated out loud, the more so as it was not he but Fox who voiced them.

"That's what being in love is, I suppose," Adam thought, and was again startled, this time to find that *he* had voiced the thought out loud. He had meant, thinking your lover's thoughts. But Sylvain seemed to realise this and showed no surprise at what might have seemed a strange non sequitur. Suddenly Adam found the presence of the table between them irksome, likewise the hovering innkeeper, and he found himself wishing he could have Sylvain's company without any context at all, without any of the accidents of everyday life - clothes, furniture, work, other people.

Especially other people, Adam decided when, at that moment, the front door opened and two specimens of the genus walked in. Adam recognised them vaguely. They belonged to another farming family of the plateau. And because the population density thereabouts was marginally lower than that of Saharan Algeria (a statistic treasured by the local population and brought out to astonish visitors on every possible occasion) the new arrivals recognised Adam too and gave him a curt nod of greeting. As for Sylvain, they clearly knew him slightly better, since they greeted him by name, although with a hint of guarded surprise in their voices, as they looked around them, uncertain whether to join the two boys at the long table or to form a separate party at one of the small ones. In the end they joined them.

"It's not often we see you out with company," one of the men gently ribbed Sylvain. "Are you celebrating something?"

"Nothing in particular," Sylvain replied gruffly.

"It's a Wednesday afternoon," said Adam. "Why not celebrate that?"

The two men looked at him. One, who was wearing a tie - not around his neck but as a belt to keep his trousers up - began to nod his head slowly and started to smile. "Here's a cocky one," he said. "Though there's nothing wrong with that. You have a funny accent though. Where do you hail from?"

It was amazing, thought Adam, how a centimetre of beer could loosen your tongue. Within a few minutes he was chatting away with the two countrymen about his father and the dam repair project, discussing the timing of the cattle's imminent release from their enclosed winter quarters and their turning out onto the pastures, and had even started on the subject of favourite French wines ("You know what he sells here," said the one with the tie, "*C'est la merde*," at which the innkeeper managed an uneasy laugh) before he realised that Sylvain was taking no part in the conversation but had withdrawn into a state of silent communion with his beer glass. He was immediately filled with remorse. How could he have been so insensitive as to let his thoughts slip away without Sylvain, the lover whose being filled his heart? He stretched out his foot under the table and caressed the side of Sylvain's calf with the toe of his gumboot. Sylvain came to with a pleasurable jolt, his face relaxed into a smile and he giggled.

"He's funny, your friend," said the man who was not wearing a tie (he had braces), not appreciating the reason for Sylvain's sudden laughter. "Bring him again." They had only called in for a quick glass of wine each, and now they drained them and stood up to leave. Their transport could be seen outside the window, or at least part of it could: the upraised front loader of a tractor, with strawy cattle-dung hanging off the tines. As they turned to leave the bar, one of the men turned back to Adam. "Hope you can put a firework up this bloke's arse." He indicated Sylvain with his thumb. "Nobody else has ever managed to."

Sylvain gave a surly valedictory growl that might have been "*au revoir*," or "*fous le camp*." It was impossible for anyone to tell.

When they had gone, Sylvain said: "Arseholes. Fucking arseholes. All of them."

"Sylvain," said the innkeeper, mildly reproachful. "Don't talk like that. They're your own flesh and blood, those two. And if they're no better than you are, they're certainly no worse." He turned to Adam.

68

"We're all one family up here, you know. For centuries we've gone through everything together. *Ah oui*. All the same flesh and blood."

"Come on," said Sylvain, noticing that Adam's glass was empty like his own. "Let's go. Got to get you home." And he paid, which seemed strangely to restore his good humour, for he gave the *patron* a cheery *"au revoir,"* and then they left.

"We need to find a place where they don't come," Sylvain said once they were outside. "Not your enemies, not mine. We need a place that's just for us."

Sylvain's words made Adam's skin tingle. He had heard people express similar sentiments in films, read them in books, but nobody had ever said them to him before. He had never imagined how wonderful it could be to hear them in real life - addressed to him.

Of course it couldn't happen in real life, exactly. He hadn't yet started to imagine, even in his wildest moments, that Sylvain and he could actually go off and set up home. It would have to be a place in their hearts only, he thought.

"In my heart we're always together. We always will be," he said. Sylvain was visibly moved and, although, they were in the nearest thing to a village centre that Perrogney offered, could not restrain himself from pulling Adam's head towards him and giving him a quick, strong kiss on the lips.

SEVEN

The following day brought with it two surprises. The weather had done a back-flip during the night so that Adam awoke to see his ceiling the spooky white of winter mornings and when he went to the window to check, sure enough, the garden, the lane and the fields lay under a seamless white blanket of snow that stretched to the farthest horizons. The fall itself had stopped, but the sky was still leaden and overcast with spent cloud.

And when he stepped out of the back door, first thing after breakfast, there was the second surprise. The cuckoo, harbinger of summer, was calling, calling, calling, across the white wastes. Was it his imagination or was there a hint of puzzlement in the bird's voice, cuckooing obsessively over the snow?

Later in the day he talked about this with Sylvain. They had met in the woods as arranged, not in the T-shirts and rolled-up sleeves of yesterday, but in overcoats, scarves and sweaters. It was not really an afternoon for al fresco love-making, but they had done it all the same, albeit in a rather perfunctory fashion, standing up and without exposing any more naked flesh than was strictly necessary. "Yes," said Sylvain, buttoning himself up. "We call it cuckoo snow. It comes the same time every year" – he looked around him at the inch-deep blanket – "though not usually as much as this. But it's the last snow of the year, *P'tit-Loup*, I promise you. And it won't stay long. Two days and it'll be warm again."

Sylvain was right. The snow had gone by lunchtime the following day, thawed by strong sunshine, and the day after that was positively hot. The cuckoo continued to call, and Adam fancied that the note of hysteria he thought he had at first detected vanished from its voice. Meanwhile its namesake flower nodded its head again in the pastures where it bloomed in ever greater numbers until all the fields around were a soft yellow-green billowing sea.

By now there existed a routine for Adam and Sylvain of days spent together, a routine as heavenly as the celestial journeys of the stars, the routine of lovers. Adam and Sylvain, Sylvain and Adam, Adain, Sylvam, Sylain, Advam.... Adam tried their two names over and over on his tongue, spoonerised and anagrammed them in every possible permutation, as if he could make them into the one single name that identified the one, conjoined person that Sylvain and he had now become.

It no longer needed to be said that they would spend all their free time together - most of the daylight hours. They only had to arrange a time and place to meet and then it was a matter of discovery as to where their subsequent roamings of the plateau, sometimes by bike, sometimes on foot, would take them. As the days passed they found themselves fording streams deep in the *vallons* at Vieux Moulins, crossing the high plateau towards Chameroy, descending the vertiginous corkscrew road to Noidant-le-Rocheux, and striking upwards towards the water-tower on its lonely height from which the rains divided into their northward flow towards the Channel and their southward path to the distant Mediterranean.

Wherever they went they made love. Often twice. Occasionally more. They enjoyed each other in the deep recesses of the woods. They were no longer shy of stripping naked together beside the fast-flowing streams. Under lowering cliffs they would lie whole afternoons in each other's arms, between each other's thighs. Even in the open fields up on the windswept heights. Sylvain had made no further attempts to penetrate Adam since his first rather comical failure beside the lake and Adam wasn't forward enough to try to adopt a dominant role in his sexual relations with Sylvain, six years his senior. It seemed to him, trying to keep a mental hold on what was normal for a boy like him and what was not, somehow part of the natural order of things that the older, bigger and stronger of the two should have the first test-drive down this potentially two-way street of pleasure. They just continued with what they had been doing up to now, and found the many variations that they improvised on its basic theme perfectly satisfying for two young people as much in love as they were. Adam even found an additional opportunity for pleasurable contact. When they were walking (this was not possible on bicycles: Adam did try but without success) he would encircle Sylvain's waist with his arm and reach his hand into his lover's pocket. The pocket linings in two out of Sylvain's three pairs of trousers were worn to rags. He thus had direct access to Sylvain's sex, still charmingly a stranger to underpants, which he would fondle like a semi-rigid comfort object as they walked.

They met few human beings on their travels, though other creatures there were in plenty. Everywhere field crickets scolded them from the grass roots and, when searched for, could be seen, black, shiny and fat as miniature moles, reversing down into their burrows until only their two long antennae protruded from the ground. Swallowtail butterflies haunted the reedy river margins, and the cuckoo called incessantly.

Sylvain found the nests of all kinds of birds and showed them to Adam. He had a country boy's knack for finding them: the basketwork platforms of moorhens' among trailing branches just above water level with their cargo of eggs, the semi-basement wigwams of willow warblers with entrances no wider than your finger, the treetop hideaways of owls. They got to know as an individual the white and sandy wheatear that bobbed and whistled on his fallen tree-trunk just outside Noidant. They greeted him as if he were a personal friend, with laughing ça-va's, and he appeared to greet them in the same spirit, even if the reality was simply that he was impatient for the arrival of his mate from Africa. Adam brought his father's bird book with him sometimes, then Sylvain would find the appropriate colour plate and give the bird its French name, Adam then pencilling it in alongside the English one.

Down in the depths of the valley at Noidant they discovered, in the front room of a house, a small bar that neither of them had come across before and which - even better - was unknown to anyone who knew either of them. This gave them a special sense of relaxation and privacy, then, as the days passed, almost of proprietorship. This would be the place "where *they* don't come, a place just for us," the place that Sylvain had wished for when they had run into neighbours in the bar at Perrogney. There was even a terrace, a metre wide strip of riverbank outside the back entrance, where two minuscule tables perched unsteadily, with two metal chairs at each, and one red sunshade with Martini written on it which would never stand straight and always threatened to descend and engulf unwary drinkers and their drinks.

Out here they could be quite alone: the *patronne* stayed within and no other customer ever arrived to take the second table. They would sit over a glass of bright beer and talk, or else not talk, as the mood took them. Occasionally a kingfisher would arc across the stream like a blue spark; more often they would only hear his whistle at a distance. Sometimes they varied their drink - usually just the one and that one drunk slowly - experimenting once or twice with whisky (the *patronne* raised her eyebrows expressively but said nothing - French law allowed Adam beer but not spirits, even if it was Sylvain who ordered) once with Campari *(mon dieu!)* and more often, and less experimentally, with a glass of wine. "Was I your first?" Adam asked suddenly, during one of these lazy afternoons of riverside, dappled, sunshine.

The question surprised Sylvain a little. "Why do you want to know?" he asked.

"Because I want to know you, know you better, I mean. Mainly." He paused then found himself trying but failing to repress a smirk. "But also

I'm curious. About sex … and other people." He paused again. "Is that so shocking?"

Sylvain responded slowly. "No. But I'm not used to talking about things like that. I don't know if I know how. How to find the right words, I mean."

Adam smiled a little nervously. "Then I'm not the first. Since you say that, you must have something about which there is something to say".

"Your French sounds a bit too posh today." It was the first time Sylvain had ever found fault with it.

"Sorry."

"You aren't the first. You're the second." He paused for thought. "Not counting… uh…never mind. You're the first I care about. The first I've ever told: I love you. Satisfied?"

"Very," said Adam. "Otherwise I wouldn't dare to ask about the other one - or two - or one and a half."

Sylvain suddenly relaxed and smiled. "OK. I'll try to explain."

"You met my brother, Jean-Paul. Handsome, isn't he? Well, you could say he was the half - of the one and a half. We used to play with each other in bed when we were little. Nothing wrong, was there? But then he grew big and hairy and wouldn't let me touch him, touch him in that way I mean. Of course he knew what might happen: that he would lose control and come, and shock me and… uh …embarrass himself. And soon after that he got interested in girls and that was that. That was all it was." Sylvain looked uncomfortable for a second. He batted the problem subject over to Adam. "Did you have a brother?"

"Did? No. I'm an only child. You know that. But I always was. I never had a brother in the past either. I think I'd have told you if I had."

"Maybe. Maybe we've had better things to talk about," suggested Sylvain.

There was a silence as they both considered this and wondered if it were true. Then Adam picked up his glass, which was nearly empty, and slowly turned the last drops around the bottom of it while peering intently into it as if with great concentration. "And the other one?" he said.

"How to say this… It was a man who came to the farm on business quite often. He was quite young - for a man. And nice-looking. He was slim. He had a good head of hair and he smiled … you know … he smiled with his eyes. He used to talk to me. When I was about fourteen he used to play a game with me where he'd try to get his hands into my pockets to see what I'd got in them. I enjoyed it. Of course I did. When it came to my trouser pockets, well, they were always old, like they are now."

"There were holes in them, you mean. Like now."

"Just the same. It's the same game that you play with me."

There was a moment's silence while Adam took the connection on board. "And, as you say, you enjoyed it."

"Once I'd got over the surprise that he was interested in me in the first place."

"And where did you... I mean, where...?"

"Around the farm," said Sylvain coolly. "In the pig-shed or the big barn. Like with us now."

"And you? Did you do anything to him?"

Sylvain rolled his shoulders slightly as if the memory made him physically uncomfortable. "Once or twice, yes."

"And did he... Did you both..."

"Come? Yes. Once he knew how ... how agreeable I was, he got braver. He started to take mine out and I'd come in his hand. Just once or twice I undid his *braguette* and, how shall I say, returned the compliment."

Adam was both appalled and thrilled. "How long did it go on then?" he managed to ask, discovering as he spoke that his mouth had gone quite dry.

"I don't know. Maybe five years. I was quite grown-up when we stopped."

"You stopped the thing?"

"His job changed. He stopped coming to the farm."

"And now? You feel bad about it?"

"Should I? I just thought it was the sort of thing that happened. Of course it wouldn't have been right of him if I'd been like the other kids. But I was always different. And he was kind to me. Always gentle. We liked each other." He paused for thought, perhaps struggling to find the interpretation of events and feelings that would least worry Adam. "But it wasn't like being in love, of course," he went on. "I can say that now. I know now - I didn't know then - what it is to fall in love. And I only know that now because of you. But all this time I've never thought before about you before."

"Pardon?" said Adam.

"I mean, before me. I mean, I never thought much about who you were before you met me. What you did. About you and other people maybe. Not bright enough, I suppose. Not the right kind of imagination."

"A different kind," said Adam gently.

"But I'm not your first either. *Quoi?*"

"I wonder," said Adam, "if just for once we could have a second glass of wine."

74

Sylvain took up the suggestion and went inside to order. While he was away Adam reflected on the fact that Sylvain's brief summary of his previous sexual experience had both made him jealous and given him an erection, but that at the end of the story, when Sylvain talked about loving him, the erection had died while the jealousy had remained. He found himself wondering, with a coolness that he was surprised to find in himself, if the same thing would happen when, in a minute's time, he told Sylvain about himself and Michael.

It did. Having had a moment to collect his thoughts, and encouraged by Sylvain's almost too obvious eagerness to hear them, Adam found himself narrating his early exploratory adventures with Michael with much brio and in colourful detail. Very quickly they were both displaying bolt-shaped outlines in their trousers, though frustratingly unable to do more than look at them because of where they were. "But it was the same as with you," Adam finished. "Michael and I were never in love together. Only friends." Though he wondered if, in equating his experience with Sylvain's, he was doing justice to his relationship with Michael. They really had cared for each other, after all, and for his own part at least Adam still did. And it was something between equals too, not something foisted by an older person on a kid who wasn't ready yet to know what was right for him. Something in this line of thought began to make him feel uncomfortable. Sylvain himself was an older person as far as Adam was concerned. He dropped the thought-line at once and picked up another one. For some reason he had not mentioned Sean nor even wanted to. Why not? He didn't want to pursue this either. He looked down at himself and across at Sylvain. They were both still rock hard and almost shivering with repressed desire and excitement. He gulped the last of his wine. "Let's go," he said, and quickly reached out his hand to touch the tense outline in Sylvain's trousers for half a second. "I think we need to do something about this."

On another of those magical days they were cycling along the high lane between Mardor and Ormancey. It was a sunny afternoon, not quite as warm as most days were around that time, and there was something of a wind on the heights. Sylvain suddenly stopped and pointed upwards. *"Regarde!"*

Adam looked. Two birds were wheeling together high above them. A buzzard had evidently strayed into the airspace of a sparrow hawk, or at least into what the sparrow hawk considered to be her own airspace. The buzzard, a dark silhouette nearly as broad as a tea tray, was trying to maintain a dignified course of slow spiral ascent in a thermal, pretending that the sparrow hawk was of no greater annoyance than a gnat. But the sparrow hawk was not to be ignored. A female, all grey and white stripes like calico and about the size of a table-napkin, she charged at the buzzard, dived down on it from out of the sun, and reared up unexpectedly from below, swerving away only at the last instant when the threat of a potentially fatal collision had forced it to alter course. For some minutes this dogfight continued overhead, a struggle between strength and agility, between mass and energy, between the dark silhouette and the lighter one through whose wings and tail the light of the sun shone in regular curving stripes.

Then at last it was over. The buzzard decided it was hardly worthwhile continuing to stake its claim to that little part of the air for what had now become simply a matter of principle. With its whole body expressing its contempt for its miniature attacker it turned away and glided downward in a long glorious sweep towards the distant trees.

It never made it. Perhaps its concentration wasn't perfect; perhaps the wind caught it off guard at just the wrong moment. Its high-speed swooping flight arrested suddenly as if someone had hit the pause button and it dropped, in an undignified vertical tumble, head over tail, to the ground. It took Sylvain and Adam a second or two of gawping astonishment to realise that it had struck the telephone wire that ran high beside the road.

"Come on," said Sylvain. He laid his bicycle on the verge and went jogging off towards the bird. And Adam who, on his own, would probably have left well alone and tried to forget the injured victim, went trotting after. They found the buzzard standing on the ground, holding its head up proudly and frowning, but with one wing half open and trailing. "I should have gloves," said Sylvain. "To catch a thing like that you need them. Plus a leather hood to slip over its head."

"I didn't bring one with me," said Adam. "Silly me. Should have thought."

"Give me your hanky anyway," Sylvain instructed. "Better than nothing."

"It's a bit of a mess still." Adam got it out reluctantly. Since Sylvain rarely carried such a thing on him, not having many pockets to keep one in, Adam's hankies were a permanent mess these days, having as they did to do duty for them both.

Had the bird decided to run it might have got away from them but all its instincts were to fly. At Sylvain's approach it simply turned away and thrashed its wings against the ground. To Adam's surprise Sylvain had no difficulty in dropping the handkerchief over its head, then seizing the bird around the shoulders and expertly folding it together in the right way as if it had been a carelessly discarded map. And just like a map, it

76

seemed so small now, clasped in a pair of hands. No longer a flying machine the size of a tea tray: just a poor bewildered bundle of feathers and still dangerous claws.

"Now what?" asked Adam.

"You hold it," said Sylvain. "Keep it down on the ground so it can't get its talons to you. I'll knot the hanky around its head then it'll be calmer." So Adam found himself for the first time in his life in charge of a live buzzard that wriggled warmly in his hands, and feeling surprised at how calm he was managing to be himself.

Although they were both in shirtsleeves, Sylvain had luckily taken the precaution of bringing a pullover - the old one with the holes - which he had tied round his waist. He now wrapped this twice round the bird so that it was effectively strait-jacketed. Impressed, Adam did not repeat "now what" but waited, this time, for Sylvain to tell him.

"Et maintenant?" said Sylvain.

They carried the bird back to where their bikes were lying by the threadbare hedge, and discussed the feasibility of various plans. Sylvain would cycle one-handed with the buzzard under one arm. No, they would take Adam's bike only; Sylvain would perch on the crossbar, cradling the patient, while Adam steered and pedalled. These might have been reasonable solutions for a journey of a few hundred metres but they were a mile from the nearest house let alone anywhere else and there were steep hills, down and up, to negotiate in every direction. And where were they going to take the buzzard anyway?

For the second time in a fortnight their predicament was eased by the appearance of a car arriving along a lonely road. Adam flagged it down. Its single occupant was a local farmer but a stranger - at least to Adam. But he seemed not at all put out by the sudden interruption of his journey by two boys and a buzzard. He took in the situation even before it had been explained to him. "You'll be wanting to go to the vet's." he said. "Those bikes'll go into the back. Boot won't shut but I've got string. Tie the handle up with."

Adam was too surprised by the whole sequence of events to try to make conversation in the car and neither Sylvain nor their phlegmatic driver seemed to think it necessary. After a few minutes they pulled up outside a house in St Martin, the village next to St Ciergues, down by the dam. "You'll be all right now," said the driver, unlashing the boot of his car and handing out bicycles like Father Christmas. Then he got back in and went on his way.

"I know the vet who works here," said Adam, suddenly recognising the old stone house they stood in front of. "His wife teaches music. She's a friend of my mother. We've had them to dinner."

"I know him too," said Sylvain, "but it's his assistant we've come to see." Sylvain nodded at the door with his head - the only part of him available to point with. "Ring the bell."

The vet - it was the young assistant who came to the door - seemed taken aback to see them, a reaction in sharp contrast to that of the farmer who had given them a lift. In fact, Adam thought later, his face had registered something close to alarm. "You'd better come in," he said, when Sylvain explained what they had come about.

Once inside, he was thoroughly businesslike and without fuss examined the damaged wing. He was a good-looking man, Adam noticed. He was beginning to show a few grey hairs at the temples, it was true, but he had a sensitive face and hands. While Sylvain held the buzzard's head and legs he felt carefully at the damaged wing. "I think we may be lucky," he said coolly. "If I'm not mistaken it's a simple long-bone fracture. The radius in the fore-wing. There are two bones there and the other one, the ulna, will work as a kind of splint provided we help it along a bit."

He left the bird in Sylvain's hands while he went to fetch some simple bits and pieces. There was a plaster-impregnated tape which he moistened and then wound around the bird's lower wing. Then he folded the bad wing tight against the bird's body and wound a bandage round both wing and bird. Finally he found - remarkably, Adam thought - exactly the kind of leather hood that Sylvain had wished for up on the heights and slipped it over the bird's head. To Adam's mortification he held the now redundant but still wet handkerchief out towards both Sylvain and himself, wordlessly inviting one of them to claim it. "It's mine," said Adam and felt himself turning red as he held out his hand to take it. Sylvain could not suppress a smile as the thing changed hands. He had been carrying out his ancillary role, all this time, in a manner that looked almost as professional as the vet's. There were other skills, thought Adam, besides playing the cello.

"I've got cages at the back," the vet said when he'd finished. "I'll keep him in one of those." He seemed more relaxed with them now, though his manner was still businesslike and his voice serious. "He'll have to have the hood on most of the time, of course. It'll be about ten days." He paused. "Well then, so who's going to volunteer to feed him?"

"We hadn't thought..." began Adam.

"Frankly, I should be charging you four hundred francs just for setting the wing." The vet sounded peeved.

"It's not our buzzard, though," protested Sylvain.

"I fully realise that. But this practice isn't meant for everyone to bring in every lame wild bird they find. Surgery time costs money. I don't just

78

mean me. There's more important work to do, that's all. OK. I'm not going to charge you." He smiled at Adam as though for practice and then for rather longer at Sylvain. It struck Adam as a very gentle smile, quite at odds with his demeanour up to now. The word that came to Adam's mind was ... tender.

"That's decent," mumbled Sylvain gruffly. "And we'll come and feed it if you like. Every day. Satisfied?"

"Can you get dead mice? Chicks too, if there are any."

"Won't raw liver do?" Sylvain argued.

"Not all the time. It needs something with feathers or fur on. Very fresh."

"OK," said Sylvain. "I'll do my best." He grinned round at Adam then back at the vet. "Adam here's a great mouser." It was the first time Adam had heard Sylvain make a joke.

"It's a deal," said the vet. "Only," he adopted a weary tone, "please don't bring me any more." He smiled again and gave a little chuckle that sounded almost sad. Then, to Adam's great surprise he reached out a hand, not to shake Sylvain's but to rumple his hair. Adam was even more surprised to see that Sylvain didn't back away but bent his head towards the brief caress. It was only then that Adam realised who they had come to see.

Until now Adam had successfully concealed from his parents the nature of his long walks and bike rides. Occasional vague mumbles about meeting school friends here and there had helped prevent any parental unease developing over his spending such long days in totally solitary pursuits during the Easter holidays. But once the buzzard had become a fixture at the vet's - not two kilometres from where his father worked - and visiting it occupied a regular slot in his daily schedule, he felt it prudent to divulge some part of the truth of the situation, pragmatically diluted with one or two unavoidable fibs. He said that he had been with Christophe when they found the buzzard, that a young man from one of the farms (no, he hadn't caught his name) had stopped by and helped them get it to the vet's, and that he would be going there once or twice over the next week or so to see how it was getting on, the young man from the farm having offered to help feed the creature. This story would serve quite well, he thought, should anyone spot him with Sylvain in the vicinity of the dam over the next ten days. The only thing that could blow a real hole in it would be if either of his parents ran into Christophe or his family and asked about it. On that score he would just have to keep his fingers crossed.

Fortunately Sylvain was as good as his word in supplying mice and chicks - he had some help from the cats on his family's farm - and even came up with the raw liver as well for the days when mice were unobtainable. Their daily schedule needed only minor adjustments: they would meet at the back of the vets' surgery in St Martin, feed the rather sulky captive, and then start their rural wanderings from there. Adam was relieved to find that their arrival in St Martin usually coincided with the young vet's absence on his rounds among the farms. His reason for this feeling of relief found its most succinct expression in the saying: two's company. When they did meet him once or twice everyone behaved correctly. That is to say, they were polite and friendly but not too friendly. Their conversations were short and to the point. After a phrase or two about the weather they exchanged a few remarks about the progress of the bird and that was that. Adam did learn the vet's name, though. It was Pierre. The three always shook hands formally on parting. Adam never saw him ruffle Sylvain's hair again, but he made as sure as he reasonably could that he was always present at their meetings. They did, also, once or twice encounter the older vet, the occasional dinner party guest of Adam's parents and then he was glad of the little tissue of half-truth he had woven for their benefit and peace of mind.

Their routines continued: their relaxed drinks beneath the Martini sunshade beside the stream in the haven of Noidant, their unrestrained lovemaking in the heart of nature with the glories of spring unfolding day by day around them. Adam found himself occasionally wondering about Sylvain and the vet and the buzzard. "Don't bring me any more," the vet had said. Was this because Sylvain had brought him wild birds before, the way a cat will bring wild things to its owner as a wordless expression of devotion? Could that be why the farmer who gave them the lift showed no sign of surprise at the nature of his sudden errand? And Adam realised that wonder was all he could ever do, that however well and however long he might know Sylvain, there would always be some questions that could not be asked, and their number might grow, not lessen, with time.

EIGHT

Adam was startled to find his mother energetically cleaning out a spare bedroom one evening and then going round the whole house with a vacuum-cleaner and as much cleansing, scouring energy as if a visit from the Pope were to be expected. "You can't have forgotten," she said in answer to his puzzled question. "Tomorrow's the day Gary arrives."

"Gary Blake?" He had forgotten all about him.

"Sometimes I think you haven't taken in a single word that's been said to you all holiday," said Jennifer. "I don't know where your mind's been all this time."

"What time's he coming?" Adam tried to express a normal seeming degree of interest.

"Early afternoon, I think. Anyway, he'll be here when you get back from school."

Adam's jaw fell open.

"It's the *rentrée* tomorrow," his mother reminded him teasingly. "Don't say you've forgotten that as well."

But he had. Not only forgotten the start of the summer term but also managed to forget that it would ever start. He had projects to complete in geography, in physics and in *langues vivantes*. They were due to be submitted in the morning. He had not even begun. "Oh my God," he said, and rushed headlong to his room.

"Don't say 'God' like that," Jennifer's voice floated up the stairs after him.

The return to school was a major upheaval at the best of times. This time, having literally forgotten all about it - and being in the middle of the mightiest experience his emotions had ever engaged with - to say nothing of being expected by Sylvain tomorrow at the vet's to witness the return to liberty of the buzzard patient, and not being able to tell Sylvain that he couldn't make it, and uncertain how and when he could contact him again...

Adam experienced this *rentrée* as an unprecedented clash of worlds, a collision of forces on a cosmic scale. In the safe privacy of his bedroom he first sat on his bed in silent trembling shock, too overcome with the surprise of what tomorrow signified even to cry. Then he composed himself and put his mind to the practical problem of his unstarted holiday projects for the school. There was no point even attempting anything tonight. Tomorrow he would have to beg for an extension, on bended knee if he had to. And after that he did the only thing he could think of that would give him any solace there and then. He picked up a biro and his *bloque-notes* and wrote a letter to Michael. The letter was long. It needed to be. It told of all his deeds with Sylvain and all of what he felt. Only afterwards, when his heart was safely sealed up in the envelope and he was in his bed, did the tears flow quietly down his face.

But the dreaded return to school the next morning proved unexpectedly painless. Although he set off feeling like a soft-shelled prawn forced to swim through storm waves breaking onto rocks, so heightened was his sensitivity, his actual arrival presented him with nothing at all that was painful or fearsome. To his great surprise Thierry greeted him with unfeigned pleasure and seemed genuinely disappointed to have seen nothing of him over the holiday. He did not appear to remember - or at least chose not to - that they had quarrelled and come close to blows the last time they had met. Adam was learning the lesson that the things you said to people and regretted immediately afterwards were seldom remembered for as long or with such crystal clarity by the people they were addressed to as they were by yourself.

Christophe too seemed to have forgotten how unpleasantly Adam had turned on him on the same occasion, and met him with smiles. "You might have to cover a white lie of mine some time," Adam said to him. "About a buzzard. I'll explain another time."

"A buzzard? You're crazy, Adam - though what's new? *Ouais.* Just tell me what to say and who to. I'll back you." Christophe laughed and their friendship seemed quite restored.

The unaccomplished holiday homework presented little difficulty either. Adam was given a two-week extension for one task and a three-week respite in the case of the others. He received the strong impression that his teachers would have preferred it if he had forgotten about the projects entirely and it even crossed his mind that perhaps they had forgotten too.

Only one seismic change had occurred during the Easter break. Céline had met a man two years older than herself, the eldest son of a wealthy paper manufacturer and wildly handsome with it. She would no longer be the focus of competitive strife among her male schoolfriends.

Adam found himself slotting back into his French school for his third and last term with less difficulty even than he had at the start of his second. More than that, he found that he was now quite positively accepted by his peers. The holidays had transformed him, by some strange alchemy of time, from a weird foreign creature that represented some obscure threat into a new personage that, despite its funny accent,

82

had something of luck and magic about it like a talisman. People who had never even looked in his direction, let alone spoken to him, were coming up and asking him how he was. There was talk of tennis games and summer evening barbecues. He was conscious of the irony that, just when his growing certainty about his sexual orientation was forcing him to see himself more and more clearly as an eternal outsider, his schoolmates were choosing this moment to open the gates, haul him in like the wooden horse of Troy and deck the city from end to end with festive greenery.

Not until he arrived home that evening - driven in his mother's car and fretting because he had found no way to contact Sylvain that day - did he give a thought to Gary Blake. But when they got in, there he was. From Jennifer's talk of him Adam had expected him to be something of a drooping lily: someone in the Chopin mould, with sensitive features, delicate limbs and wearing a halo of melancholy. Adam was relieved to find the reality somewhat different. Gary was a trim, fit-looking man who positively radiated energy. Although some grey could be seen in his hair if one looked closely (Adam did) the general impression he gave was of someone rather more youthful than his mother and very much more so than Hugh. His bright brown eyes wore an amused twinkle that was perhaps a permanent feature; time would tell. He was not as tall as Adam, which came as a surprise. Adam was not yet used to the idea that adults might be smaller than he was. His growth-spurt had only begun during the last year and he had yet to catch up with its implications. He still had a perception of himself as a small, rather skinny boy, while the reality - which was what other people saw - had become something very different.

"So, the famous cellist." Gary extended a businesslike hand. "Last time I saw you was…"

"I know," said Adam. "My christening."

"I'm sorry," said Gary. "We do say the most stupid things once we've passed the age of thirty. You must forgive me."

Adam smiled, so it could be presumed that he did. "I've seen you on television in England sometimes. Only I don't remember it very well…" Adam stopped in confusion. He had meant to be nice; it had just come out wrong.

"Touché," said Gary. "It *was* rather a long time ago."

Jennifer made quite a fuss over dinner that evening. She 'set the little plates on top of the big ones' as the French say, and quite literally do. In honour of Gary's arrival and also to console Adam for what she guessed were the rigours of the *rentrée* she came up with a colourful vegetable terrine, a *filet de boeuf en croûte* and a chocolate mousse which came after, not before the cheese. (Jennifer had quickly adapted to the French order of courses.) There was red wine: Morgon, from the Beaujolais region a little over a hundred miles to the south. Adam was just awakening to the enjoyment and knowledge of wine, thanks in part to his father and in part to his visits with Sylvain to the bar at Noidant-le-Rocheux. He regretted that this new appreciation was developing towards the end of his stay in France rather than at the beginning. He doubted whether wine of the quality he was getting used to would appear quite so regularly on the table once they were back in Britain.

Gary was a charming and amusing dinner-table companion. He was enthusiastic in his praise of Jennifer's cooking, and full of gratitude for the invitation to come and stay with them all in the first place. The peace and quiet was exactly what he needed, he said, in order to finish his commission for the Avignon festival. There was a deadline and he was afraid that, in the bustle of Paris, he would never have met it. "You can stop concerts and cancel lessons all you like," he said. "But unless you physically remove yourself some hundreds of miles they never let you alone. And I'm far too soft to say no to people." Adam looked at Gary and wondered if the self-deprecating claim were true.

Gary smiled back at him. "I'm sure I'll be spending quite a lot of time just walking in this wonderful countryside you've found to bury yourselves in. Even driving up here this afternoon was an eye-opener. I've never been to the region before. Do you know what they call it in Paris? *La Champagne Pouilleuse*, the louse-ridden corner of the Champagne. They don't know what they're missing. It's beautiful."

Adam was startled by the idea of Gary at large in the woods and meadows that he had come to think of as the private domain of Sylvain and himself. This must have shown itself on his face because Gary immediately looked at him and said: "I suppose you feel a composer should spend all day crouched over the piano with sheets of manuscript paper blowing about all over the room. Did you see that film about Mahler?" Adam thought he had. Certainly Gary's picture had chimed exactly with his own idea of how Gary should spend his day. It fitted his own schemes very well, Gary's presence in the house giving cover to his own intended absences in the company of Sylvain. Gary roaming the plateau at the same time as Adam and his lover would rather upset his tidy plan. Still, he was sure that things would work out somehow.

Gary continued. "It was Brahms, you know, who said: 'If you want to compose you should go for long walks in the woods.' But, as usual with Brahms, not being there to hear him say it, you can't be sure whether he said it with a smile or with terrifying Teutonic *ernst*. Do you compose?"

"No," said Adam, sounding quite shocked by the idea.

Gary laughed. "It's not such a terrible thing to do. All players should compose as well as play. I know your mother doesn't, but she's excused because she had you instead. But you should. Even if you find your best audience is the waste-paper basket."

"I don't think I have a talent for it. Even though I do enjoy long walks in the woods." He had tried, feebly, to be witty but immediately regretted it.

"Perhaps we could take a walk together sometimes," Gary responded smoothly. "You could show me the best ways to go." But Adam thought he detected for the first time a hint of diffidence in his voice, as if a brush-off by a sixteen-year-old boy might actually be wounding.

Adam was gentle enough, on a good day, to try to avoid hurting people, even by accident. "Yes, why not," he said brightly, but then quickly steered the conversation back to music.

Next day Adam thought about explaining in advance that he would be late home from school but decided against it. As a tactic it would only set a precedent. He would simply be late, and as he intended to be late every afternoon for the foreseeable future it would be better to establish the fact brazenly and without explanation from the start. Easier to concoct a reason from time to time if anyone thought to ask him than to have to produce phoney explanations up front on a daily basis.

The time bubble that he planned to allow himself every day between school and arriving home was to be set aside for Sylvain. However he was still uncertain as to how to engineer their first meeting when he stepped off the school bus at the bleak little crossroads just outside Courcelles. There were three possibilities, one agreeable but time-wasting: to wander the woods and hills randomly until his path and Sylvain's might fortuitously cross; it could take weeks; he ruled it out as being pointless. The other two were both stark and unappealing: walk up to the front door of Sylvain's family's farm and knock on it, or call on Pierre the vet on the off chance that he might know something about Sylvain's movements. After a half-minute's indecision during which he watched the bus trundle away in its permanent trail of brown smoke, he decided on the last option. He had taken the precaution of cycling to the bus stop that morning and concealing his bike on the far side of the hedge. Now he retrieved it and set off down the road that wound past Lac de la Mouche towards St Martin, conscious that at any moment he might pass his father coming the other way in the car. But there was no alternative; the off-road walk would have taken over an hour.

Arriving at the vets' surgery he took a deep breath and knocked. It was Pierre who came to the door. He looked slightly surprised to see Adam but greeted him with a smile nonetheless. "We were expecting you yesterday," he said. "As it was we had to say good-bye to the buzzard without you."

"It was the *rentrée*," said Adam. "I'd forgotten all about it."

"That's what I guessed," said Pierre with a half-smile. "Anyway, I drove Sylvain back to the spot where you found the bird and let her go."

"And?"

"And that was that. The break had mended well. She flew off a bit slowly at first - the muscles will take a little time to rebuild their strength - but she flew straight and well. She didn't look back or anything; animals aren't like that."

"And Sylvain?"

"Yes, I guessed it was him you wanted. When I brought him back here he got straight on his bike and rode home." Pierre caught sight of a stricken look on Adam's face and his tone softened. "I did explain to him that it was the *rentrée* and that that was why you hadn't turned up. He does know. But I can't tell you where he is now except to state the obvious: presumably at home. He didn't think to leave a message for you with me and neither did I think to ask if he wanted to leave one."

There was then a sudden silence as they both realised that the conversation had come to an end and that there was nothing further to say unless either of them decided to begin a new one. Adam imagined for a crazy half-second that the next thing to happen would be for Pierre to dip his hands into Adam's pockets, and for another crazy half-second he felt absurdly cheated that he didn't. Then he came back to life. "OK then, I'll look for him at home." He turned rapidly on his heel, mounted his bike and fled away without so much as an *au revoir* or a backward glance. Just like the buzzard.

It was too late now to ride all the way to Perrogney. That would have meant going all the way back to Courcelles and then going half as far again beyond it. Besides, having nerved himself to the encounter with Pierre, he wasn't sure if he could face a cold call on Sylvain's family quite so soon afterwards. Meekly he cycled home - where his disappointment was slightly tempered when he found the atmosphere lighter than usual, his mother picking vegetables in the garden, Gary, clad in shorts, cutting the grass rather inexpertly with the motor-mower and both of them laughing.

But the next day was Wednesday which meant there was no school in the afternoon. Usually there was a choice of sports, besides club activities of all kinds, and then, most weeks, there was Adam's cello lesson with M. Rocharnaud. As it happened, M. Rocharnaud was not expected this week though Adam's parents were not aware of that. They would not question his staying in town till late afternoon while he in fact took advantage of his freedom to make his couldn't-be-put-off-any-longer journey to Perrogney in search of his lover.

Without Adam's noticing, the fields had changed colour during the last week. The pale yellow of the cowslips had melted away and, just as Sylvain had predicted, everything had become a haze of shimmering blue. There were scabious and wild chicory, wild columbines, orchids here and gentians there, forget-me-nots and strange blue daisies, and in the thin grass on the heights the pasque-flower's cobalt trumpet blossomed along the ground. Adam had decided to walk to Sylvain's home. He was apprehensive enough about the visit as it was. He simply could not see himself turning up brazenly in the farmyard on a bicycle. It was with an effort of will that he turned off the public lane and onto the cart track that would take him the last half-mile. Then when he was just halfway down the track his heart sank to hear the sound of a vehicle clattering along behind him, apparently taking the flinty drive in top gear. He refused to turn round until the truck came to a stop beside him. Then he had to. It was the same pick-up in which Sylvain's brother had given them both a lift to the bar at Perrogney. And the same driver. The tension and embarrassment of the moment melted away as Jean-Paul leaned out through his open window and said: "Adam, *non*? Looking for Sylvain? I'll give you a lift."

A bone-shaking thirty seconds later they came to a halt in the farmyard right in front of the main door of the house. Adam was too surprised by the eventual suddenness of his arrival to know exactly how he felt, though nervousness was certainly a big part of the emotional mix. It was strange to think that you could have had sex with someone who was then a virtual stranger without more than token qualms, yet that the walk up to their front door should be so much more alarming. But at that moment the house itself with its flat, no-nonsense frontage of grey stone and blank, black windows began, in spite of itself, to look oddly welcoming. The front door, which appeared to have been painted a colour previously unknown to art or science, so nondescript was it, stood open and Adam, suddenly emboldened, walked eagerly forward, shoulder to shoulder with Jean-Paul while the latter called his brother's name: *"Sylvain, c'est ton jeune copain, Adam."*

Adam's triumphal entry into the house unfolded as if he were stepping into a dream. He was at first in a whitewashed hallway where piles of egg-boxes jostled for room, and barely kept their balance, on a windowsill, and where the floor was banked up with old leather boots, paraffin heaters and cardboard crates. Then, following Jean-Paul who pushed open another door, he had just time to glimpse a living-room that looked, for the split-second that he had time to observe it, to be furnished entirely with newspapers and dogs, except in places where dark corners of chestnut furniture and shapeless areas of grubby upholstery appeared like the visible peaks of mostly submerged icebergs. But then a door in the opposite wall flew open, Sylvain bounded into the room and, all in the same moment as the dogs rose up and began to bark, was at Adam's side, spinning him round with a hand on his shoulder, saying "*salut*" to his brother and to Adam, "*Allez, viens*, we're going to feed the pigs." And Adam found himself propelled back out of the house and into the yard.

"But not just yet," Sylvain continued, practically frog-marching Adam across the yard. "Up to the top of the barn first." Adam let himself be led. Into a dark doorway then up an unfamiliar rickety stair and then into a place he recognised: the churchlike roof-space where they had once drunk damson brandy and Sylvain had changed his world with a kiss.

There was brandy under the floorboards still. The level in the bottle seemed unchanged since last time. They had a couple of swigs each, while Adam noticed an agitation, a sense of urgency, about Sylvain that he hadn't seen before. "Sit down," he said, and as soon as Adam had obeyed, unlaced his trainers and roughly pulled them off. It was clear to Adam what was coming. Sylvain stripped him naked from the waist down before undoing his own belt. He was so excited, Adam noticed, that his cock already glistened with wet. Then he threw Adam face down on the broken straw-bales and, after the briefest of anointments with a moistened finger, entered him with three sharp thrusts.

The force and the surprise of it caused Adam to bang his chin upon a wooden object half-hidden in the straw. There was a jarring sensation and a crunch and Adam felt something in his mouth like broken oyster-shell. So this is what it's like, he thought.

It was over very quickly. He felt Sylvain swell inside him, felt him come. He'd thought it would hurt and was surprised that it didn't. Perhaps it was only painful if you fought against it. Though ("ow", he said) it did hurt when Sylvain pulled himself out. "You should have come out more slowly," he complained. They were his first words to Sylvain for half a week.

There was another new experience to come. Sylvain said, very gently, "Sorry I hurt you," then rolled him round and took his hard cock in his mouth. A moment later and Adam felt himself unloading hotly, urgently, inside Sylvain's uncomplaining cheeks.

The whole experience had surprised both of them, despite the fact that Sylvain had clearly done some thinking about it beforehand, and once they had pulled apart they spent some time simply looking at each

88

other in wonder and doing nothing to return any kind of order to their general state of dishevelment. Then Sylvain reached forward again and kissed Adam long and hard. Next he gave Adam and then himself a restorative swig of damson spirit. Only then did he say, "Dear God, I missed you," and Adam, by now quietly crying, managed to articulate, "I missed you too," in a choked pianissimo.

They recovered themselves and their clothing slowly, in between hugs and caresses. "Let's have a look at your mouth," Sylvain said, once it became possible to talk of practical matters. "They're all there," he said reassuringly, once he had carried out a cursory inspection. "Only the two front ones are a bit shorter than usual."

"Merde," said Adam. He had been proud of his top front teeth. With the pronounced gap between the centre two they had given his smile a winsome photogenic quality throughout his short life. He felt them with a finger. He was appalled by the changed sensation, by the sharpness of the broken edges.

"It's not as bad as it feels to you," said Sylvain. "You imagine you've lost half of two teeth. I promise it's only about one tenth. Where can we find a mirror?" He looked around them, not very hopefully.

"Later will do," said Adam. "Tell me about the buzzard." He was interested to hear Sylvain's account of the end of the bird business, but he was even more concerned about Sylvain having spent time in Pierre's company without Adam to chaperone him. How quickly jealousy could germinate in a new relationship.

Sylvain dutifully related the story, much as the vet had done, though his version was more detailed, and coloured by his tender feelings both for Adam and for the creature they had rescued together. But Adam was still uneasy. Had Sylvain's new sexual adventurousness come from nowhere or did Pierre somehow have something to do with it? He decided to be bold. "Did you and Pierre ... do anything together?"

Sylvain looked shocked by the question. Then he burst out laughing. "No," he said. "Of course not." He paused and looked thoughtful. "Maybe he would have liked to in the end, but he knew better than to ... to make the attempt. He could see as clear as day that I belonged to you now. *Ça se voit, tu sais.*" The explanation made perfect sense to Adam. He was relieved and happy and the broken tooth was at once forgiven and forgotten.

They really did go and feed the pigs then. The animals lived in a spacious if ramshackle apartment, divided into half a dozen separate pens, on the ground floor of the barn. Sylvain showed Adam how to open the meal-sacks by pulling on the white thread which then came ripping out of the paper in one piece with a satisfying purring sound. The meal was tipped into a wheelbarrow which Sylvain then trundled back and forth, measuring the meal into troughs with a scoop while Adam poured on water to make a mash. The pigs' heads usually got into the trough in advance of their dinner so that the oatmeal cascaded onto their necks and ears, to be licked off by their neighbours and finally rinsed down by the water from Adam's bucket. The snuffling of the pigs crescendo-ed into hoots and shrieks as the wheelbarrow approached each pen and then became submerged into the general squelching and slurping as snouts engaged with supper.

It was time for Adam to go after that. It would take him over half an hour on foot and he didn't want to be so late as to attract comment. He took his leave of Sylvain with a smoochy kiss - he was getting good at those - and with a very practical arrangement to meet the following afternoon, and every school-day, by the rainbow springs down in the *vallon* ten minutes after the arrival time of the school bus. Then he began the long trudge up the farm track, leaving Sylvain sorting out some minor problem with a door-latch on one of the pig pens. But he had only put one bend in the track behind him when he heard the sound of the pick-up rattling up behind. He turned round and was astonished to see Sylvain himself at the wheel. The truck skidded to a halt on the sharp flints. "Get in," said Sylvain.

"I didn't know you could drive."

"Of course I know how to drive." They were jolting up the track even faster than Jean-Paul had driven down it. It did go through Adam's mind that knowing how to drive and having a licence were two different things but he did not pursue the matter. Once in the lane they continued to bounce along towards Courcelles at a speed that made Adam tense up every time they approached a bend and then breathe a small sigh of relief at the discovery, as each bend opened out, that nothing was coming round it. Then Adam said, "This'll do," a little way before his parent's house came into sight. "Too many questions if you drive me right up to the door." Sylvain showed no sign of slowing down until Adam added: "Unless you're kidnapping me, that is." At which Sylvain laughed and stamped on the brake so hard that Adam was lucky not to arrive at his front door via the windscreen. Sylvain gave Adam a rapid kiss while grabbing simultaneously at his crotch. Adam squirmed his way out of the car. *"A demain,"* he said.

"A demain, Adam... hein?" said Sylvain, grinning with delight at the unexpected brilliance of his wordplay. Then he shot backwards, turned rapidly in the mayor's driveway just as the startled mayor himself emerged from his front door to take his dog for its evening promenade, and headed for home.

To his relief, Adam's lateness was passed over without comment. Jennifer was talking to Gary in the kitchen while they prepared food together. They seemed so much at ease in this situation that Adam guessed that they had often made meals together in the past. It was funny how he had never tried to imagine his mother's life as a student beyond the few anecdotes and memories she had chosen to share with him. He put his head round the door just long enough to establish his presence, then retreated to the living-room and took out his cello. It would be the first time he had played the instrument since Gary had arrived and he began to practise the Beethoven A-major sonata in a spirit of something like defiance, hoping to be heard, and at the same time not heard, by Gary. But once he had begun he was surprised by the confidence, not to say boldness of his playing. One or two days away from the routine of practice could do you good, he told himself.

A little later Hugh returned from work and dinner was ready. Then, a few minutes into the meal, Jennifer suddenly called out her son's name in a stifled shriek. "Adam! Your front teeth! What on earth have you been doing?"

"Oh," said Adam. His mind was such a swirl of impressions - reunion with Sylvain, two new kinds of lovemaking, a new take on Beethoven - that he had all but forgotten the little dental accident that had occurred along the way. He had given no thought to providing a convincing explanation. "I was... er... fighting."

"Fighting?" said his mother. "Why? Who with?"

"You, fighting?" queried his father, unable to keep a hint of admiration out of the surprise in his voice.

"Not real fighting," Adam backtracked. "Just a friendly scuffle with Thierry. Over a chocolate bar. Fooling around." He was astonished at the circumstantial details he managed to dream up under the pressure of the moment. "It was only in fun. Just an accident."

"Well, just wait till I see Thierry," said Jennifer more calmly. "I'll have a thing or two to say to him. It's quite spoilt your smile. You look like a pirate."

All this time Gary had said nothing but had been staring at Adam with a fixed expression that somehow gave him the feeling that Gary was fascinated by the change in Adam's appearance, that he did not believe a word of his explanation, and that he had quite a shrewd idea about the real circumstances. Of course Adam might have been imagining all this. Then Gary said, "But a very handsome pirate," and immediately earned Adam's gratitude by turning the conversation. "I liked your way with the Beethoven. I had no idea you would play with such maturity and with such technique. Would you like to play it through with me after dinner?"

Quite coolly Adam answered, "Yes, why not?" though in fact he was quite overwhelmed by the thought - flattering, daunting and exciting in equal measure - that he was going to play Beethoven with someone who bestrode the concert platforms of the world and whom Thierry listened to on CD... Thierry. Oh dear. Here was somebody else now whom he had drawn into a lie in order to protect his relationship with Sylvain. And this was far worse than merely implicating Christophe in the rescue of a hawk. Thierry was going to have to take the flak from his mother, the next time they met, for breaking his shop-window teeth. With an effort Adam came back to Gary's offer. "I mean, I'd really like to. It would be..." he struggled to find a word "...an honour." He meant it.

"Are we excused the washing-up?" Gary asked facetiously at the end of the meal. Adam was glad that no-one had tried to make a concert out of the event. His parents sensibly, almost conspiratorially, withdrew into the kitchen and left the performers to it.

Adam found the piano part and handed it to Gary who sat down with it at the upright Pleyel, checking with experienced fingers that the pages would turn easily when he wanted them to. Then he gave Adam his tuning 'A' and, without fuss, they began. Adam experienced a momentary pang of nerves at the thought of the gulf that separated them in terms of musical prowess and achievement during that initial lonely moment when the cello plays the first unaccompanied phrase, but it melted at once in the intensity of the experience that began to unfold when Gary joined in with the piano's answer.

The quality of Gary's playing seemed somehow to seep into Adam's. It was inspiration by osmosis, if you liked. Adam found himself quite simply playing better than he had ever played before, better than he had ever imagined that he could play. His rows of notes joined up into a single stream of sound, a song pouring from his heart as spontaneously as if he had written the work himself, a spring gushing from the rock like the spring in the *vallon* where the rainbows had darted like butterflies and the butterflies had shone like rainbows on the day he had first discovered the humanity, the heart, of Sylvain. This sharing of a work of art, this dividing it up and putting it together at the same time, with just one other person, was as wonderful, as magical almost as... He had to thrust that thought aside while the sonata continued; it was all too confusing, too much on a day on which so much had happened, a day which had given him so much to think about, so much to feel and take into his heart ... and, in addition, blessed him with the features of a handsome pirate.

92

The sonata finished. Adam put down his bow. He was in a state of near-shock, having found himself on a plane of existence that yesterday he had not known existed; he was the pirate captain of a great new ship of dreams, the weaver of musical spells in glorious partnership with Beethoven and Gary Blake, and not only all this but he was also physically intermingled now with Sylvain, their bodies mutually penetrated today as if to underwrite their penetration of each other's hearts.

Adam's parents crept out of hiding in the kitchen, murmuring their appreciation of what they had just overheard. His mother's face in particular expressed what she was too tactful to put into words: as a musician herself she recognised the change in Adam's playing and knew that, whatever had occurred to make it happen today, it was a wonderful and profound change and one that could never be reversed.

Hugh had the very practical idea that they should all have a drink after that, and this was a relatively unusual experience for Adam too. He did not usually get included in general rounds of post-prandial alcohol at home. He was thus elevated to the status of adult and professional cellist in addition to everything else that had happened to him that day by the simple action of his father in handing him a brimful glass of red wine and he felt as he might have felt at an after-concert celebration at the Festival Hall.

"One day you must do the D-major," Gary said. He moved back to the piano and without bothering to find the appropriate page in the score, launched into the opening bars of the piano part, with its two peremptory questions and its haughty condescending answer, a limpid descending waterfall of notes. Adam was on such a high that the beautiful shock of it nearly made him cry aloud. Gary broke off as suddenly as he had started and came back to rejoin the family among the easy chairs. Adam discovered that there really were tears in his eyes and turned his head away, momentarily cross with himself. He did not want Gary to see them. He rather suspected him of conjuring them on purpose.

A moment or two later the telephone rang, which startled everybody, cruelly breaking the mood of the evening. Hugh went out to the kitchen to answer it. "It's for you," he announced to his son. "From England. It's … um … Michael."

NINE

Adam rocketed out of his chair and into the kitchen. He picked up the phone and heard Michael say without preamble: "It's half-term in a few weeks. We've got a whole week. Could we come and stay for a few days?"

"We?"

"Me and Sean," said Michael matter-of-factly. "Or should that be Sean and I? There's cheap ferry and coach tickets on offer."

"I suppose so." Adam's mind was a flurry of questions and half-perceived complications. Sean and Michael together? Whatever had happened? Michael whom he'd had sex with, shared secrets with, and Sean who made love to him only in dreams. Could they conceivably have become an item in Adam's absence? The thought made the blood rush to his head. "I'll have to check with Mum," he said and then used the necessity to go and consult her as an opportunity to catch his breath. Returning to the phone a moment later he said that it would be fine and added as an afterthought that he was really pleased about the idea. They talked dates and bus times for a minute or two, then Adam remembered something. "I posted you a letter a few days ago. You won't have got it yet."

"*Au contraire*," said Michael, "I got it this morning. And I still think you're mad. Even madder than ever."

"Oh well, then, yes," said Adam. "You've realised. So I may as well tell you that I'm now a pirate captain."

Adam fell into step with the new rhythm of his days. There was school, the bus home, the dive down from the bus-stop into the *vallon* to be met by Sylvain, lovemaking of one kind or another in their old secret place on the grassy spur where the cliffs fell away on three sides, the trek back home where he would arrive looking as though butter wouldn't melt in his mouth, then cello practice, family dinner, school homework and bed. Things were made easier by the putting back of dinner time by half an hour or so since Gary's arrival, perhaps by unspoken agreement between Gary and Hugh - who did not have so very much in common - to shorten the social conversational part of the evening that lay like a slightly awkward piece of terrain to be traversed between the end of the meal and bedtime. This gave Adam a little more time with Sylvain each

94

day and made the lateness of his arrival home less noticeable than would otherwise have been the case.

Saturday saw a slight change to the schedule. Adam arrived home from school in time for lunch and then made his excuses and went to meet Sylvain in the early afternoon. But they could not make too long an afternoon of it; Sylvain was wanted back on the farm to help castrate some bull calves and so Adam found himself back home at about four o'clock. There Gary was sitting in the garden, at a table covered with sheets of manuscript paper which he had weighted down with two half-bricks. The tactic was only partly successful and the breeze was picking up the corners teasingly and making the pages difficult to write on.

"I've had enough of this," said Gary when he saw Adam. "I'm off for a stroll. Care to join me?"

Adam accepted Gary's invitation. Gary was not to know what Adam had just been up to and that his middle-aged companionship would therefore be exposed to cruelly close comparison with the recent sensual, sexual proximity of Sylvain. Gary put on a jacket over his shirt, Adam, very deliberately, did not. They turned left. "Towards Noidant?" said Gary.

"Why not?" Adam was quite willing to go where Gary wanted. Having had sex within the last hour he was anybody's friend.

"Are you planning to be a professional?" Gary asked once they had gone a little way along the road.

"Professional what?" asked Adam, startled.

Gary guffawed. "Professional cellist. What on earth did you think I meant?"

"Yes, I suppose so. I'm going to go to music college anyway. At least, if they'll have me."

"I don't think there'll be much doubt about that," said Gary seriously. "Not if you continue to play the way you did with me on Wednesday."

Adam heard the words and could barely believe them. Above them a red kite rode high on the wind. "Thank you," he said. "Thank you very much."

"Of course," Gary went on, "you are a man in love."

Adam literally stopped in his tracks. His left foot which he was about to lift and place in front of the right one refused to budge. Gary had to stop too. "Why do you say that?"

"I'm not really very clever. It's not one of the privileges of age to know what young people are thinking. But I heard it in your playing. As clear as day. So I'm sorry if it's a great big secret but if you want to keep it that way you'll have to give up music I'm afraid. Don't tell me you've played like that from the beginning."

"You're only guessing," said Adam sulkily. "You can't possibly read all that into the way someone plays a cello."

"Really?" said Gary archly. "But I'm truly sorry if I'm wrong, and even more sorry if I'm right and I've upset you by bringing the subject up. It was very insensitive of me. We'll talk about something else. Tell me, what's your opinion of Schubert?"

"No." Adam put one foot in front of the other. "I don't want to talk about Schubert. You're quite right, of course. I am in love. And for the first time. You can laugh if you want to." Gary did not. "Well, one and a half times, I suppose."

"Whatever does that mean?" Gary did laugh now, not unsympathetically.

"It means, I suppose, only once with someone who loves me in return."

"And once with somebody who doesn't?"

"Does that make sense?"

"Perfect sense. Am I allowed to ask their names?"

Adam frowned. Their road was winding down towards Noidant. Soon they would pass the tree-trunk where the wheatear bobbed and whistled.

"I shan't mind if you don't want to tell me. It's only a standard question in this kind of conversation, a cliché if you like, like talking about the weather."

"You think 'girls' names', don't you?" said Adam through tight lips. "You might get a shock."

"If they were boys' names, you mean? I don't think so."

"Well, they're both boys, so there," said Adam in the defiant, petulant voice of a small child. "One happens to be in England, the other's in France. I won't tell you their names. You might meet them."

"Wednesday night's telephone call?" Adam was silent. "Sorry," said Gary. "No business of mine."

But Adam was somehow flattered by Gary's curiosity, and played, flirted with it almost, like a fish nosing at an angler's bait.

"You could be right," he said. "But that would only be the half-a-one. The other's right here in France. He lives just a mile away."

Gary's eyebrows rose in spite of himself but Adam could not stop himself now. "He's beautiful," he said aggressively. "Handsome and... strong. Natural. A man of nature... I mean a boy..."

After a moment's doubt, for he was afraid the gesture would make Adam either angry or tearful, Gary put a hand very lightly on Adam's shoulder. "Relax. You don't have to say any more. I'm not judging you, or him. And I'm not asking any more questions. I shouldn't have begun this conversation."

"Have you ever been in love with more than one person at the same time?"

"Yes, as a matter of fact," said Gary, glad that he had steered the conversation past the dangerous shoals its course had led it to. "It's not an unusual situation to be in. Especially when you're young. And if you really want to know, I think you should enjoy the experience as much as you can. Maybe that's dangerous advice to give a teenager, and very immoral. But though you may fall in love a few more times in your life, those times won't be *that* many."

"Why do you say that?" asked Adam, startled into taking an interest once again in someone other than himself.

Gary broke his stride for an instant. In the pasture below them the wheatear called. "The voice of experience, that's all. And there's no reason at all why you should take any notice of it. In fact, come to think of it, I'd like you to forget I ever said it."

"You're younger than my mother, aren't you?" said Adam slowly as if carefully assembling a complicated piece of forensic evidence.

"Yes. I went to the Academy when I was fourteen. She was already nineteen or twenty, like most of the others. She was a bit like a mother to me. Only a little bit, mind. She wasn't that much older."

"You were a child prodigy, then."

"Something like that, yes."

There was a pause while Adam wondered whether he dared ask his final question. He did, but in a quiet and halting voice. "Gary? – Are you gay?"

"Yes, Adam, I am," said Gary slowly. "I'm not sure that your father would put up with me around your mother if I wasn't."

"Does he know, then? Does my mother know?"

"Let's say that they both know and don't want to know. Will that do?"

"But they put up with you around me."

There was a silence for a moment, broken only by the whistles of the lonely bird, bobbing up and down and flaunting his white back on the dead tree-trunk beyond the fence.

"Yes, they do, don't they?" said Gary, as if surprised by a thought that had not struck him before. "Perhaps they think it's possible to be gay and also a gentleman. What do you think?"

***

These were the weeks of blue flowers and fields, the weeks that comprised the last part of April and early May. They would be followed, according to Sylvain - whose projected timetable nature had followed punctiliously up to now - by a few more weeks of brilliant yellow-gold before the poppies took over everything in mid-June and brought the colour sequence to its glorious end, turning the landscape into a sea as scarlet as arterial blood. Adam did not want to think so far ahead. Some time after the end of June would come the end of term and his return to England. And that meant... His mind balked at the thought. It was still a long way off and anything might happen before then. He sailed on a broad untroubled sea, clear to the horizon. There was no sign now of the precipice beyond, no sound as yet of the roaring of the waters as they crashed fuming into the abyss that lay beyond the edge of his world.

There was something more immediate to deal with though. Half-term and the impending arrival of Michael and Sean. Of course Adam was delighted that his old friend Michael was coming, though he welcomed the news of Sean's turning up with him with more complex emotions. He was surprised, even flattered, that Sean should want to come, but also a little alarmed. He couldn't guess at his reasons or at what his relationship with Michael now was; these things would not become apparent until they both got here. But there was the problem of Sylvain. Michael knew of Sylvain's existence. At a pinch Adam thought he could cope with a meeting between the two of them, provided it could be well stage-managed. But that would only be feasible if Michael were coming alone. A social gathering that included Michael, Sylvain and Sean was out of the question. So far as Adam knew, Sean didn't know that he was gay. Adam himself hadn't been certain the last time they had seen each other, after all. He might be shocked, would certainly be baffled, to find Adam having an affair with a full-grown farm lad. He might accidentally blurt something out to Adam's parents or, if he met them, his French schoolfriends. The risks were too great. Adam would have to find a way to keep his different lives apart for the duration of this testing time. One thing was certain, though. He would not be having sex with Michael. Quite apart from the presence of Sean in the house, severely limiting the practical opportunities as well as disorienting Adam's emotional compass, the simple fact was that he was Sylvain's lover now and that was that.

Adam continued to meet Sylvain daily after school; they made love in the sunshine with total abandon as if without a care in the world. By some miracle nobody caught them out. Gary could guess, of course, what kept Adam occupied after school, but he didn't know who or exactly where, and he never asked. He and Adam occasionally went for walks together, once even drinking a beer together under the Martini sunshade at Noidant, but their conversations remained tethered to safe, although usually interesting, subjects and did not stray again towards matters of relationships and sex. They talked about musical form: Adam said he couldn't see the point of fugues; they were like nothing in nature, he said. Gary said he would see what he could do to make him change his mind. They talked about musical child prodigies. Gary had been one - "Well, half a one," he qualified. Adam said that he knew *he* wasn't one. "You're very lucky," Gary said. "To not be one and to know that you're not one is the best possible combination." Adam's face had fallen slightly. "That doesn't mean, though," Gary added, "that you're not rather highly talented," and was rewarded with the sight of Adam's face brightening as if the sun had come out over the landscape. Sometimes Gary would indulge Adam by playing the piano parts of his cello pieces, and once or twice, just for fun, Gary would take them through a Mozart piano trio, playing as much of the violin part as his hands could manage in addition to his own piano part and humming the rest, while Adam sight-read the rather minimal contributions that Mozart had written for the bass instrument.

Not until three days before the arrival of Michael and Sean did Adam get round to squaring the event with Sylvain. Unable to find a solution to the impending problem, Adam at last decided, reluctantly, to tell him a lie. "I'm going to be away for a few days." He saw Sylvain's face fall like a child's and, seeing it, felt a stab of pain. He had to stop and recover his composure before going on. "It really is only for a few days. I'm going to England. They're having a short holiday at my old school. They want to see me." At least most of the detail was true.

Sylvain's face crumpled. "You won't come back," he said baldly.

Adam did what he had to do: took Sylvain's head in his hands and kissed his face all over, stroking and tangling his fingers in his hair. He cursed Michael just then for fouling up his lover's idyll, for robbing him of the person who was his whole world and for forcing him to lie to him, to the one person to whom he wanted always to be true. "I am coming back," he said, his voice resonating in his chest in a sort of growl he had never heard before. "I'm coming back on Sunday week. We'll meet at the usual place at three o'clock. In any case we still have tomorrow and the next day before I have to go. But I will come back. I promise. And I won't leave you again." The growl in his voice had modulated upwards into a wail. "I'll stay with you for ever." Then it was Sylvain's turn to take over the role of comforter.

***

Once again it was time to get a room ready. There were four bedrooms. At the front, Adam's and next to it a spare one that had become Gary's. Behind Gary's lay Hugh and Jennifer's. This one was spacious and had its own bathroom; it looked out over the garden and the countryside at the back. Behind Adam's bedroom lay the bathroom that had once been all his. Now he shared it with Gary and would soon share it with Michael and Sean as well. The last bedroom was at the back, beyond the bathroom, and it, like all the others, opened off the gallery that ran round three sides of the living room like the circle in a theatre. This arrangement gave the living room double height - there was an enormous picture window at the rear, garden, end - and also gave a certain amount of distance between all the bedrooms except Adam's and Gary's. It was the back room, unused till now, that was going to be prepared for Michael and Sean.

Jennifer asked her son to help her with it. He went in first and put the light on. Although it was only dusk outside the room was in pitch darkness as the outside shutters had been kept closed to keep the windows clean through the storms of winter. Adam walked across the room to open them. First you had to pull the windows inwards, then you reached through to unhook the shutters from their fastenings. But this time, as he pulled open the glass panes, Adam became aware that something was not quite right. In the dark space - a sort of box formed by the windowsill and surrounds, the shutters and the glazing - something was hanging. Something like ragged brown curtains or half of a dead doormat. And as he looked at it, it began to fall into shreds, disintegrating before his eyes into countless moving, flying fragments. Which buzzed.

Adam turned and ran towards his mother, standing uncertainly in the open doorway. He pushed her through it. "Get back," he shouted, panic-struck, and followed her through, almost in one movement, slamming the door behind him. They almost tumbled over the gallery rail together into the living room beneath.

Alone of all the bedroom doors this one had a small pane of frosted glass set in it and through this could hazily be seen the glow of the electric light that hung from the centre of the ceiling - Adam had had no chance to turn it off again - and around it a blizzard of insect silhouettes whirling in disoriented fury with the noise of a fighter squadron as preserved on the soundtrack of an old newsreel. Bees were beginning to crawl out under the bottom of the door. Adam stepped on them. "Mum," he called out, "get a wet towel from the bathroom!" And she did. Adam laid it along the bottom of the door like sandbagging. Only then did Jennifer and he feel safe enough to breathe.

100

Madame Lepage, when telephoned for help and counsel, took the information very much in her stride. Swarms behind the shutters were a common occurrence among the plateau villages. Was there a quantity of comb? Adam thought yes, though he had only looked for about a quarter of a second. Well, Mme. Lepage knew a family who kept bees on their holding and who would probably be willing to take the swarm off their hands... to speak metaphorically, of course. She would set things in train, ring them back later and, with any luck the beekeeper would arrive in the morning. For tonight, nothing could be done; they would just have to sit tight and try to ignore the roaring sound behind the bedroom door as well as the sinister lighting effect that played through the frosted glass. Adam found himself hoping that the bee-keeping family would not be Sylvain's and then, perversely, that it would.

It was. Nor was there any question of Sylvain's mother arriving alone to take charge of the situation. She came, her husband came, Jean-Paul came, two urchins, Nathalie and Dominique, came with a large dog called Milou, and Sylvain himself came. He knew exactly where he was, of course, but seemed ready to handle the situation with a certain amount of streetwise nous. To Adam he said, "So this is where you live," in the hearing of his brother but not of Adam's parents. He mostly avoided Hugh and Jennifer but managed to find himself in the same place as Adam as if by chance whenever they were not around.

The weather had somersaulted back to winter in the night. A gale was blowing and the rain lashed down. It was a perfectly foul Sunday morning for dealing outdoors with half a cubic foot of disgruntled insects. Hugh repeatedly expressed his grateful amazement that the funny family had turned out at all. First an attempt was made to prise the shutters open from the outside with a long-handled pruning-hook wielded from ground level. But the fastenings were sturdy and would not give. Next, Sylvain's father went up a ladder, at some risk to himself, and tried to force the shutters with a crow-bar. It looked as though the shutters would be reduced to matchwood before either the hooks or staples let go their rock-fast hold.

There was nothing for it except to approach from the inside: into the bedroom, then an arm thrust through the squatters' hive itself to open the shutters in the normal way, as had been Adam's original errand last night. This task fell to the plain, squat little woman who was Sylvain's mother, and she accepted it without a flicker of expression of any kind. Up the stairs she went, Adam showing the way and Sylvain following, trying not to show his delight at this extraordinary opportunity to explore the inner sanctum of his lover's home. "Are you sure you'll be OK?" Adam asked when they reached the door behind which the many-headed monster still roared. Sylvain's mother gave a curt nod, opened the door and disappeared inside, shutting it courteously behind her.

Adam and Sylvain looked at each other on the gallery. They were close enough to kiss, and both wanted to, but since people were scattered all over the house and garden, and they themselves were in full view from the living room below and through the picture window from outside, they did not.

The door reopened. Sylvain's mother reappeared. "The shutters are open and the light is off," she announced matter-of-factly. "But the window must stay open for today as the room is full of bees. I'll come back later and shut it when I take the swarm away."

"How many stings did you take, Maman?" asked Sylvain.

"Just four," she replied. Adam watched in frozen wonderment as Sylvain unceremoniously but expertly removed them from her cheek and forearm. Her face remained a picture of serenity while this was going on, and Adam had time to notice that for all its plainness it had nevertheless the same full lips, the slightly upturned nose and the lustrous brown eyes that had first drawn him towards her son.

Dealing with the swarm took up most of the rest of the day. No music was composed, no cello practised, lunch was a scratch affair. The combs were torn down from the window embrasure and placed rather messily in a spare hive, thoughtfully brought along by Sylvain's family, in the garden below. There were rainwater and honey and sticky doomed bees clinging to everything. But miraculously, as the day went on, more and more of the bees in the window and in the bedroom behind it, scenting the presence of their queen in the new hive, transferred their allegiance to it. At last Sylvain's mother went upstairs and closed the window. The battle for the spare room had been won, the territory reclaimed, though at a cost of many hundred small lives.

And the mess. Jennifer looked despairingly at the bedroom. There was wax everywhere in smears and little broken crumbs. There were dead and dying bees. There was mud on the floor. Above all, there was honey, in minute amounts it was true, but simply everywhere. "I can't possibly get this clean before your friends arrive," Jennifer said simply. "It's only for a few days. They'll have to go in with you."

Sylvain admired the bathroom when it was his turn to use it. "I've never had a bath," he said. "We always had showers where I live."

This gave Adam an idea. He put his hands on Sylvain's shoulders and looked gravely into his eyes. "Here's a promise then. When I come back from England we're going to have a bath together, right here."

"Your parents...?"

"When they're out of course," said Adam, laughing at the idea.

102

TEN

Strictly speaking, Adam's French school did not have a half term holiday during the summer term. But this year two public holidays had somehow got crammed into the same week in May and so had the feast-day of the obscure local saint whom Adam's school was named after. Given that most organisations in France took 'bridge' holidays on a Monday or Friday whenever a public day off occurred on a Tuesday or Thursday, the school had bowed to the inevitable and so Adam found himself with a week of freedom that coincided with the official half-term of his British friends.

Hugh drove Adam into Chaumont to meet the coach on which they were arriving early on Monday evening. It was a tense drive for Adam. What would his friends look like after nearly a year? What would they be like? Would they even recognise him after so long a separation? Teenagers could change so much - or at least develop - in that length of time.

Change or develop. Was there a difference? Adam and Michael had argued so strenuously over this semantic distinction one afternoon about a year ago that they were both ready to cry with frustration when neither would give in. Adam made the assertion that people never changed, they simply developed; Michael said that, on the contrary, human beings were capable of real change. They had kept up this argument for a punishing two and a half hours until Adam (they were in Michael's bedroom) slammed out and went home angry and exhausted. That was the trouble with Michael, he thought. You had sex listening to Wagner and then wrangled over something pointless for the rest of the day just for the sake of it. How much better, how immeasurably more wonderful it was with Sylvain.

It was a shock to see the two boys tumbling off the coach together. Sean, who had towered over Michael and Adam a year ago, now seemed stocky and compact at Michael's side. He still had his blond cornfield of hair, though, and the cornflower eyes that went with it; after a moment's reflection he was still unmistakeably Sean. Michael, in contrast, was now tall, spare and gangly; no longer the petite, skinny figure he had cut when Adam was last intimate with him (not counting what had happened at Christmas, but on that occasion Adam hadn't actually seen him). He was looking good. Adam thought for the first time that he stood a chance of actually being handsome one day. But it was Sean's beauty that really captured his imagination at that moment. Intensified by a year's absence and by a year's progress on the road to adulthood, Sean's appearance - which was also the window through which his sweet-natured personality projected itself without distortion - made Adam's pulse suddenly race. He understood for the first time that the expression *a heart-throb* was more than just a cheap figure of speech. To be in the physical vicinity of Sean was to be on the receiving end of a barrage of... of what? Pheromones? Charged atomic particles? Cosmic rays? Here in Chaumont. Sean was here in Chaumont-sur-Marne. It was hard to believe.

Michael and Sean stared uncertainly around them for a moment or two before they spotted Adam. Then they rushed over to him, rushed back again for nearly forgotten backpacks in the luggage hold, then there were shoulder-claps and pulled rib-punches, jokes and hallos, and much surprise that Adam - who seemed unaware of this - had grown some four inches since they had last set eyes on him.

Then there was a sudden silence as they all looked at each other with something like wonder at meeting old friends in such new, or at least altered, shapes and sizes. What other, less visible, changes might have taken place over the same period of time?

It was Michael who broke the spell. "What happened to your front teeth? Have you been scrapping?"

"Something like that," said Adam, feeling awkward. He didn't want to say more, especially with Sean and his father there. Perhaps Michael sensed this because the next thing he said was: "Sean got off with a bird on the ferry."

"I did not," Sean returned with weary good humour, then turned to Adam. "He still enjoys winding people up." He sounded a little conscious of his marginal seniority and of the presence of a real adult in the person of the until now ignored Hugh.

Getting into the car Adam took a seat at the back, leaving the other two to sort themselves out. Michael cheerfully got in beside Adam's father and Sean, with an easy smile, took his place with Adam in the back. Sean spread his legs innocently wide so that his knees touched Adam's... whose own legs were spread equally wide in a pretence of nonchalance in which innocence played no part.

"This is just so beautiful," Sean said, looking out at the landscape beyond the car window: at the winding trout-stream that was the River Marne in its optimistic bubbling youth; at the forests that flanked the road; and then as they headed up towards the plateau, at the meadows which were now a golden blaze of buttercups in the slanting evening sun.

104

"Last week it was all blue," Adam said. "It changes every month. It's now in its second yellow period." He did not say who it was who had alerted him to the glories of the coloured seasons.

"Then it has turned quite gold from grief," said Michael for Adam's benefit. Quotes from Wilde would be lost on the others.

Adam laughed and seized the moment to put one arm along the back of the car seat behind Sean's shoulders as if they were in the back row of a cinema. He found that he had a hard-on and only restrained himself with an effort from reaching out to check whether Sean might have one too.

Arriving at their destination the boys fell out of the car like puppies and without invitation embarked on an immediate tour of the garden. If they had been equipped with tails they would have wagged them. They hadn't guessed quite what Adam's new home would be like and now that they actually saw it, the place far exceeded their modest imaginings. "You never said there were peacocks," said Michael in wonder.

Over dinner and until long afterwards the new arrivals excitedly relayed news from the school in England. Anecdote followed anecdote in a bewildering litany. There was a story about a tedious cricket match that came spectacularly to life when someone called Frank split his trousers in two while taking his guard at the wicket. ("And we could all see he had nothing underneath.") There was the duel that Sean had fought with another friend in the street using imaginary fencing foils and during which the friend died so convincingly that passers-by alerted the emergency services. Then, during the mock exams someone had told Morsehead (Who? Adam tried to remember a Morsehead) that his afternoon paper had been switched to the morning; this was just as he was arriving at school on the stroke of nine in the morning; Morsehead had looked like having a stroke himself until someone kindly told him it was only a joke.

Michael himself had read a paper to the sixth form about Nietsche but (in Sean's words) "nobody in the school had heard of him and the discussion afterwards didn't even begin." Michael had been left with egg on his face and a thirty-minute period to fill. "What did he do?" Adam asked. "He told jokes of course," Sean answered.

There was little that the three adults could do to get a word in edgeways while the flood of stories ran its course, though Adam noticed that Gary in particular was attending to them quietly with a look of mild amusement on his face.

There was another story (which Adam enjoyed) about a notice that appeared one day on the staff-room door and which read: *Arselickers Anonymous. Crawl Right In.* The perpetrator was never found.

Then there was something about a character called Stupid Squirrel who had apparently taken to doing his exam revision sitting on a first-floor outside windowsill, wearing an old fringed lampshade on his head. Adam couldn't remember who Stupid Squirrel was, or even if he knew him.

These stories had the perverse effect of making his old school seem more remote and strange rather than bringing it back into focus for him. Till now he had felt very close to the place, as if he had never gone away. Now he saw that it had become a new and different place, a venue where unfamiliar dramas were being played out by a cast of unknowns. He realised for the first time that his life here in France had become more real than that other one across the sea. Once again he had the impression of worlds colliding, with unforeseeable results.

It was bedtime before either Jennifer or Adam had a chance to explain the emergency sleeping arrangements. Adam told the story of how the spare bedroom had come to be spangled with droplets of honey and littered with dead bees. They all trooped in and had a look, Sean and Michael nodding their heads and for the first time since their arrival, unable to think of anything to say.

There were two beds in Adam's room. Someone would have to make do with a sleeping-bag on cushions on the floor. Jennifer suggested they toss a coin to settle it and then quickly retired and left them to it. Adam had already imagined what would happen next. Sean would be the gentleman, the unselfish guest, and volunteer to sleep on the floor; Michael, the spoilt youth would accept the offer of the second bed without even a pretence of protest, while Adam would occupy his own bed as a matter of right. But, as usually happened when he expected something - Adam had recently become aware of this - what actually happened was the completely unexpected. Sean said: "Nobody has to sleep on the floor. I'll tuck in beside Adam, if he'll have me, and Michael can have the other bed to himself." This bombshell was delivered totally straight and apparently innocently, without a hint of knowingness or innuendo.

Adam could hardly believe what he had heard. Did Sean have any idea that Michael and he had - or rather, used to have - a sexual relationship? Adam supposed now that the answer must be no, but this was hardly the moment to ask. Sean did seem to have answered the unasked question about himself and Michael though. Clearly there was nothing of that nature between the two of *them*. Sean's proposal was accepted with *sotto voce* polite noises, both Adam and Michael trying to hide from him their very real astonishment. And if it occurred to Michael, momentarily, to pipe up and assert a prior claim on Adam as a

106

sleeping partner, he must have buried the idea at once because he said nothing at all to that effect.

All in turn visited the bathroom and began, rather self-consciously, to undress. Adam had taken to sleeping without pyjamas since he had begun his affair with Sylvain. He wasn't quite sure why; it seemed somehow to be part of the natural evolution of things. Both the visitors had brought pyjamas with them; they now hesitated as to whether to wear them or to do without. In the end no-one wanted to be the first to reach into a rucksack and drag forth effete nightwear and so nobody did.

Sean took his clothes off with his back to the others. Adam saw that the naked Michael had a substantial erection which he made no effort to hide. He had one himself and didn't dare to let Michael catch his eye. Instead he hopped quickly into bed before Sean could see it. He didn't trust himself to look at Sean when he finally had to turn towards him to get into bed too. Adam did not know how he would have coped were it to turn out that Sean had a hard-on too.

As it was, the night was one of the most excruciating torture. Every accidental brush of Sean's body against his own - and in that single bed these occurred constantly - racked up Adam's state of desire to a never before experienced degree. He felt like a musical instrument being tuned up to an unimaginably high pitch. He dared neither to caress his unwitting torturer, asleep and oblivious beside him, nor to try to give himself relief by hand. The latter idea seemed vaguely sacrilegious; besides, it would have been cringingly embarrassing were Sean to wake up. Then he thought miserably that he would almost certainly have a wet dream, something that would be all too obvious to Sean in the morning even if he were not - horror of horrors - literally bespattered at the climactic moment.

By some miracle, morning came without Adam having done so first. Sean was the first to saunter off to the bathroom to shower. At which Adam took immediate advantage of his absence to leap out of his bed and into Michael's, whereupon they both came explosively the moment their two bodies touched. It was quite unnecessary for either of them to explain why. Sean returned unexpectedly soon from the bathroom to discover them still lying in the same bed, though both on their backs and as nearly non-intertwined as the narrowness of the bed permitted. They looked as caught-out as they felt but Adam had the presence of mind to brazen the situation out rather than to leap absurdly back into his own bed. Sean stopped for a second, then he just smiled and shook his head. "You crazy pair," he said.

It was not until after breakfast that it dawned on Adam that what had taken place would have some bearing on his relationship with Sylvain.

To put it more simply, his conscience woke up. Before the weekend he had told himself (he had hardly needed to: it had seemed so obvious back then) that he would not be having sex with Michael during his visit. He had never imagined finding himself in the situation he had been in last night. Every morning for nearly two months he had woken to the thought of Sylvain and the image of his face. But not this morning. For there Sean had been with his flesh and blood face, warmly breathing, in the place where he had never even dared to imagine it, on the pillow beside him. The last thing he had meant to do was to rush into bed with Michael, throw himself upon him and ejaculate on his chest. But he had done exactly that. And not because he wanted Michael, but because he had been driven mad with desire by the proximity throughout the night of Sean. You crazy pair, Sean had said. He had been right. In a way that Adam had never anticipated, this morning had dawned on a crazy world. Well, let what had happened stand as a warning. Tonight he would make sure that the sleeping arrangements were different. Let the others do as they liked; he would have his own bed to himself. What had taken place would not be allowed to happen again.

The three boys spent most of the morning in the garden, part idling and part working on the one task that Adam's parents had asked of them: namely to clean out the window embrasure where the bees had nested. There were waxy remains to be scraped off the stone surrounds and the shutters and the window-panes to be polished. As for the inside, the bedspreads and floor-carpets were to be collected by the cleaners' van while Gary had very decently volunteered to clean the floor. The general mood was rather subdued. Sean and Michael were a little tired after a long day's travelling, and all three of them were preoccupied with making their own private sense of what had occurred in the bedroom earlier.

They livened up as mid-day approached. They took the rare bus into Langres to be shown the sights by Adam and by the time they had had a small beer and a sandwich each at the Café du Jardin, the three of them had rediscovered their extrovert ebullience of the day before. In the Café - which was the smartest hangout in the town and *the* place in which to be seen - they ran into Thierry with Christophe's sister Monique and were all invited to a barbecue which was happening the following day at Christophe's place on the shore of Lac de la Mouche. Adam was quite relieved that things were happening that would occupy their time and save them from the kind of otherwise pleasurable rambles around the plateau that might bring them into contact with Sylvain. He also had reason to be grateful that, since they had become lovers, Sylvain had abandoned his routine of cycling past the house first thing in the morning. Adam's bedroom would have shown unmistakeable signs of occupation at getting-up time, not just by one naked boy who was supposed to be in England but by three of them.

Adam took his friends on a circuit of the ancient ramparts which commanded impressively plunging views of the valley on three sides. He was able to point out with a proprietorial air the remains of the funicular railway that had once permitted a speedy if vertiginous descent to the mainline railway station far below. He showed them the small white chapel on its grassy mound that had been built in thanksgiving for the town's narrow escape from invasion during the First World War. And he told them how he had once looked down from this height upon the backs of three jet fighters as they skimmed the forest in a high-speed training dash up the valley.

It was not until later in the day, back in the garden, that Adam and Michael had a chance to catch up on things that they felt could not be discussed in front of Sean. For example Sean himself. (Sean at that moment was sitting under a damson tree a little way off and engaged in animated conversation with Gary, who was unsurprisingly delighted to have his peace and quiet dispelled by the arrival of two further puppyish teenagers, of whom one at least had the looks of a nearly full-grown god.)

"Well, is he or isn't he?" Adam wanted to know. "And – just checking, because after last night I'm pretty sure the answer's no, but - are you and he by any chance an item?" Seeing a look of incredulity cross Michael's face he added: "I'm so out of touch, remember. Don't forget I haven't seen either of you since September."

Michael giggled. "Except Christmas."

"You know what I mean. Anyway I didn't actually see you, if you remember. You were on the other end of a telephone line. I simply meant that in that long a time anything's possible."

"Yes, maybe," said Michael, "but not that possible. Sean still claims to have a girlfriend, though we never see her. But there's certainly no sign of him going the other way. Pity, really. Unless you count last night, of course. What *was* all that about?"

"Nothing, I think," said Adam. "You know what happened, or rather didn't happen and then did. He's a big innocent in some ways, I sometimes think."

"He's certainly innocent of me. We haven't done anything together. He's all yours if you can persuade him."

"I don't intend to do that," said Adam sternly. "I would have tried to once. I mean, if he'd ever behaved like that before. But I wasn't kidding when I wrote and told you I was in love with Sylvain. I'm not doing it with anybody else."

"That's not the impression I got this morning," said Michael.

Adam looked down and stared with apparent fascination at a small beetle wading through the grass they were sitting on. "That was an aberration. I suppose it's as well you brought that up. Because I want you to know that I don't think I should have done what I did. It's not going to be repeated."

"If you say so." Michael sounded slightly disappointed, but only slightly. He also sounded unconvinced that Adam's high-minded resolution would stand much testing.

Adam looked up again. "Are you seeing anybody else?" He asked broad-mindedly, more eager to change the subject than anything else.

Michael looked a bit sheepish. "There was somebody a couple of times. Remember Richard Sargent?"

"The one you used to call Little Beau Creep? Surely not!"

Michael winced. "Oh he's alright. He's grown up a bit now. And physically too. It was only a couple of times after school anyway. No big deal." He sensed an opportunity to shift the discomfort back to Adam. "Not like your wild loony of the woods at any rate, who you're so serious about. Thought we'd have met him by now. What's happened to him?"

Adam had to explain the whole story: how he felt he could have let Michael but not Sean meet Sylvain, and how he had pretended he had gone to spend half-term in England. Michael looked at him with an expression of pitying wonder. "You really are mad, aren't you? You've got this thing big."

Sean's turn for a private chat with Adam came a little later. It was just before dinner and Michael had gone indoors to be nice to Jennifer in the kitchen. Sean began by asking about the climate on the plateau, about the fauna and flora and the economy of the region. Adam couldn't remember him talking like this before. But eventually he took the plunge and asked the question he had really been wanting to. "You and Michael. Do you... you know... do you actually...?" He couldn't quite manage to finish.

Since Adam and Michael had stared, horror-struck, at Sean out of the same bed earlier that day, their tummies still wet from their extremely brief encounter, there seemed to Adam to be no point in denying it. "Yes," he said but then, for a whole complex of reasons, amended it to: "I mean we used to."

Sean gave a little chuckle that wasn't meant to be audible. Then, apparently changing the subject, he said: "Don't you get lonely out here?"

110

"Yes," Adam admitted. "At first it was quite hard. But I've made friends, sort of, at school. You met two of them for yourself and you'll meet more of them tomorrow."

Sean looked at him with a slight frown, an expression he had rarely treated Adam to, and said: "Michael was saying something about you meeting up with some strange guy in the woods." Then he stopped abruptly.

Adam was torn between embarrassment - because Sean knew - and feeling flattered that Sean was so curious about him. He decided to answer more or less honestly. "Don't get judgemental. He's twenty-two. And we've been having sex together." He found he could not say to Sean: *and we're in love.*

"Wow," said Sean. Then: "To be honest, I never saw you as the type to be having an adventurous sex life, if you like. But there you were, doing more and going farther than any of us. Good luck to you, I suppose."

"You're not off me on account of it all being gay, then?" Adam was naively surprised and ready to be wounded.

"No. If that's the way the cookie crumbles, so be it." Then Sean looked closely at Adam. "I wonder if I can guess how your teeth got broken."

Again Adam felt the rush, the knock off balance that whatever it was that Sean radiated delivered to his system. "I was being fucked," he said, astounded to hear himself pronouncing the words - to Sean of all people - and in his parents' garden.

"You're quite a guy," said Sean in a tone that Adam dared to imagine sounded almost admiring, maybe even envious. Then they both looked at each other in thoughtful silence until a shout from Michael summoned them indoors for dinner.

After dinner Gary was persuaded by Michael to play the piano. To Adam's astonishment - and slight pique. He had never presumed so far as to ask the great man to play a solo. He felt it was tantamount to asking a doctor to diagnose some ailment when he was in your house as a dinner guest. Fools rush in, he thought smugly. But Gary was surprisingly amenable to the idea. Adam was even more surprised when he sat down gravely at the little piano and launched into a bravura performance of Chopin's Grande Polonaise. It was the piece with the fitness-testing and spectacular octave passages in which the pianist's left hand becomes a blurred jack-hammer for whole minutes at a time. Adam knew that Gary had not been in regular practice for several weeks now and, knowing what a holiday from such practice meant, suspected strongly that he had abandoned his composing earlier in the day when everyone was out and secretly put in some time at the piano to work the piece up. At any rate the performance had an electrifying effect on his audience. Sean in particular was leaning forward in his chair, his expression frozen, his mouth open in astonishment. Adam feared at one point that the piano would break.

When he had finished Gary turned to his gobsmacked audience and accepted their very vocal appreciation with a quiet smile. They begged him to play something else and he hesitated, explaining very reasonably that he was not sure how he could follow what he had just done. In the end he decided to play some Chopin waltzes, going up to his room to fetch the music and then playing them from the score while Adam volunteered for the honour of turning the pages. The atmosphere had changed subtly from concert hall to family fireside.

"I never heard Chopin properly before," said Sean afterwards. "At least I never listened properly. And certainly never played like that - and at a distance of five feet."

"Could you play something else - just a nightcap, you know?" wheedled Michael. Gary laughingly said, no, of course he wouldn't, and then changed his mind. There was a piece he was thinking of including in his next season of recitals once he started playing again in the autumn. They could hear him try it out, if they wanted, and tell him what they thought. He would have to play it from the score, though. Of course everyone said, yes, they wanted to hear it, and Adam was despatched upstairs to fetch what Gary called the 'dots'.

The piece turned out to be Liszt's shimmering transcription of Schubert's Erl-king. Gary explained the story for the benefit of those who didn't know it before he began, quoting some of Goëthe's text in German and English. Then as he played the story came to life. They heard the drumming hooves as the lone horseman gallops through the night, saw the rainswept landscape of fen and gnarled alder trees, heard the bewitching voice of the Erl-king himself as he tries to lure the rider's boy away from his father with promises of music and banquets in an unseen other world. The Erl-king's tone becomes more menacing. *Ich liebe dich, mich reizt deine schöne Gestalt* (I love you, your beautiful form excites me) *und bist du nicht willig, so brauche ich Gewalt* (and if you're not willing, I'll take you by force.) By the end, when the hoof-beats first race and then crash to a stop with the sinister spirit's victory, child dead in father's arms, Adam's hair was prickling on the back of his neck. Looking at his friends he guessed they felt the same sensation. Nobody spoke for a moment and when Gary looked round for his plaudits none came. In the end he had had to break the spell he had himself woven by a laugh. Then they all talked about ghosts until it was

112

decided by general agreement that it was bedtime. The three adults went first and the boys followed up the stairs a minute or two later, Adam going first. Halfway up, he jumped, startled, at the touch of a hand on his shoulder and was then very surprised to feel a gentle kiss on the back of his neck. This must be one of Michael's jokes and Adam spun round to have a laugh with him. But Michael was nowhere to be seen. It was Sean whom he found himself facing, Sean who had kissed him. He had to repeat that thought to himself in order to believe it. Sean had kissed him.

Sean looked somehow changed, no longer his confident laid-back self. There was a note of vulnerability in his voice as he said: "Can I sleep with you tonight? I mean, not just like last night, I mean..." He couldn't finish.

Adam knew what he meant. Knew but could not take it in. Did Sean have any idea how Adam felt about him? How he dreamt about him and entertained him in his most private fantasies. How he would never have dared to ask Sean the question that Sean had just asked him because he knew it was a dream that would never come true. And now Sean, imagining that he exposed himself most painfully to a rebuff, was diffidently asking *him*. The mountain was begging to be allowed to come to Mohammed. The roasted chicken was pleading for permission to land in his mouth. He just stood and stared and Sean stared back looking more miserable by the second. Then Adam slowly enfolded Sean in his arms and said, "I'd like that very much, Sean," marvelling that he managed to get any words out at all, let alone make a coherent selection, while Michael emerged from the downstairs loo and started up the stairs below them.

ELEVEN

As Jennifer drove the three boys over to Christophe's barbecue the next morning under a sapphire sky, Adam was still on an almost unimaginable high. His memory of last night was crystal clear and he ran the details over and over in his mind, partly to savour their sweetness repeatedly while they were still fresh, and partly in the way that he would memorise a piece of music so as to preserve it in his memory bank for ever.

Michael had not been slow to sense the new state of things between Adam and Sean when he joined them on the stairs, and he had made his own way to bed with no more than a minimum of acerbic comment. Adam had a strong sense of action replay as he waited in bed for Sean to join him, though this time his eyes were wide open and focused on those new parts of Sean - the hard and furry parts - that he had not seen before. In bed together they had both been overcome with nerves. Adam could hear Sean's teeth chattering just as he felt his own uncontrollable shivering, but somehow that shared reaction had helped to relax them as they lay tense, side by side like two guardsmen on some bizarre horizontal sentry duty.

Adam was determined not to be the first one to make a move. Maybe Sean had had the same intention. But at last Sean did move. He put an arm over Adam's chest. And Adam, with an involuntary audible intake of breath that cruelly made public his emotion, seized it, briefly kissed the back of it and then drew it down to where he most wanted it to be. Then with his own hand he began to explore Sean.

Sean was nearly without hair on chest and stomach but his pubic fur was soft and thick as a fluffy animal. Adam automatically assumed, on the strength of his knowledge of Sylvain, that anyone older and bigger than he was would have a correspondingly longer dick and was slightly surprised to find that this was not always the case. Sean's was thicker than his, especially around the base, but slightly shorter. Adam wasn't quite sure whether he was reassured by this discovery or not. At any rate Sean had a comfortingly heavyweight pair of testicles, the size and feel of large plums, to set it off.

If it had momentarily crossed Adam's mind that Sean would masterfully turn him over and fuck him noisily while the duvet slid to the floor and Michael looked on in awestruck silence, the idea vanished

114

pretty quickly. Despite the hardness and size of his muscles Sean was surprisingly gentle in bed and, perhaps less surprisingly, relatively unadventurous. Perhaps he was inhibited by Michael's presence in the next bed. Only the sudden wetness of his fingers alerted Adam to Sean's rather quick ejaculation, but at least Sean was gentleman enough to make sure that Adam came too a few seconds later. Then for the rest of the night they had snuggled close together - though there was hardly much choice for Sean there - and Adam had the sublime experience for the first time in his life of waking in the morning with someone else's arm around him - and of it being Sean's.

The car crossed the bridge - the frogs' bridge, Adam now called it - at the head of the lake and began to nose along the eastern shore. Here Adam noticed the alder trees, now in full leaf, with their twisted branches, that grew by the water's edge and he thought back to the spooky Erl-king whose beguiling voice had seemed so real in Gary's playing last night. *...und bist du nicht willig, so brauche ich Gewalt.* It was just a fairy-tale, of course. You couldn't really be spooked away from your parents and friends. Certainly not in the broad light of day. There was nothing at all sinister in the landscape they travelled through now.

Adam found himself scanning the far side of the lake as the dam came into view, a thin line framing the edge of the water. Was there a lone figure cycling along the top of it in silhouette? Adam couldn't be sure. For a moment his heart ached for Sylvain. He would explain to Sylvain about last night, he would have to. Sylvain would understand. No he wouldn't. Why should Sylvain understand when he, Adam, didn't understand himself? For comfort he reached out to Michael who was next to him in the back seat and laughingly tousled his hair.

It had been Michael's turn, earlier that morning, to leap into Adam's bed as soon as Sean had - obligingly first again - headed out to the bathroom. Adam had pleasured him with a mixture of feelings. Michael did not bother to pull the duvet over them so that their activity was very much in Sean's face when he returned from the shower. Michael had actually grabbed at his hand and boldly suggested that he join in. "I'd rather not," Sean had replied rather crisply and then pointedly ignored them while he got dressed. The atmosphere between Michael and Sean had been a little tense at breakfast, although they had enjoyed a novel treat in the form of golden honeycomb salvaged from the wreck of what Adam called 'the beehive in the bedroom'. Adam had had the feeling that he alone was flying above the weather, flying without understanding the mechanism that had propelled him into the stratosphere. Yet somehow he had achieved it. He had slept with Sean.

They arrived at Christophe's house. The dogs barked as usual and overhead the kites banked and yawed in the jewelled air. All was the same as before and yet nothing was. (Although there was one change in the garden: the swimming pool excavations had been started but come to a halt as a result of some unforeseen difficulties with the subsoil; a massive unsightly mound of flint and clay filled a quarter of the garden but no-one, young as they all were, was ill-bred enough to notice.)

Adam would have liked to spend the whole time shoulder to shoulder with Sean, in a public parade of new-loverdom. Perhaps people would not ask them directly, but they would ask each other - Is that Adam's boyfriend, then? Must be, I suppose. Didn't know he was that way, but seeing the two of them together, like that... Mmm, quite a catch, *n'est-ce pas*?

This little daydream was punctured, however, by Sean himself who wandered off with great self-assurance to talk to the girls at the party in a language of which he had mastered only a few words. Perhaps he needed to re-establish his heterosexual credentials for his own peace of mind.

Céline was there with her new man. It was the first time Adam had seen him. Yes, he was handsome, no doubt about that, even if it was always relatively easy somehow to attribute good looks to the heir to a small industrial empire. But his looks were nothing, in Adam's eyes, compared to those of either of the two men he loved: neither of the absent woodlander, Sylvain, nor his conquest of the previous night, Sean, who was wonderfully present, his fresh complexion glowing like a light among the bright female butterflies that quickly surrounded him.

Adam had to make the best of it. He decided to feel flattered that the man he had been to bed with was the star turn among the girls. It vindicated his taste and enhanced the value of Sean's desire to sleep with him. For not only Céline but all her girlfriends were flocking around the blond cricketer with his tongue-tied French and were emboldened by his beauty to try out their own shy English.

For a time Adam lost sight of his other friend too. Michael seemed to hit it off well with Christophe and the two wandered away together, apparently finding much to say to each other, though in which language Adam could not tell. He found himself for a time in the company of Thierry who had taken on the role of *chef de barbecue* and was hovering over the red-hot embers and roasting-racks with impressively long pikes and tongs like a demon in a medieval depiction of the Last Judgement. "You haven't spoken to my mother lately?" Adam asked him.

"No, why?"

"Well that's probably for the best. On the way here she was saying that if she saw you she'd give you a piece of her mind."

116

Thierry looked puzzled. "What am I supposed to have done to her?"

"Not to her, to me. And 'supposed' is the operative word. See my front teeth?" He curled his upper lip like a dog.

"*Mon Dieu*, how did you do that?"

"I told my parents you did it."

Thierry's eyes bulged. A sausage burst with a hissing sound a tongs-length away. He took no notice. "You *what? Why?"

"Because I couldn't tell them what really happened. I had to tell them I was scrapping with someone. And you're the biggest person I could think of. Verisimilitude, *tu comprends?* You will back me on this won't you?" And he dodged behind a group of people as Thierry seized a trident-sized toasting fork and lunged in his direction.

It was after the food and drink were finished and the party was beginning to wind down around mid-afternoon when Adam finally caught up with Sean, though in fact it was Sean who had decided to come looking for Adam. He took Adam by surprise and plonked himself down on the grass next to him. Then he came to the point directly. "We shouldn't have done that last night."

"Oh," said Adam.

"You see," Sean went on, "I accept that you and Michael are gay, and you're still my mates and it's no problem. But I'm not. In spite of last night. That was a... an..."

"An aberration," supplied Adam. The word was fresh in his mind.

"Exactly. Not that I didn't enjoy it. And I'm glad it was you." Sean took hold of Adam's hand - it was only an inch away from his own - and gave it a squeeze. "But let's forget it. Can we?"

"Sure," said Adam, trying to feel adult about it. "Let's just forget it." But he kept hold of Sean's hand, and Sean was too kind to withdraw it.

The jewelled day had faded like the dream it obviously was. The Erl-king's promised treasures disappeared in smoke. Sean had been the substance of Adam's romantic fantasies for nearly half his life and of his sexual ones for nearly three years. Now the unattainable had been attained. He had shared a bed with Sean and they'd had sex. And it had been initiated by Sean, not forced on him by an over-eager Adam. Sean began it. Sean had actually asked him... And now Sean said 'let's forget it.'

"Now I've hurt you," said Sean softly. "I'm sorry. I do love you, you know." That was too much. Adam broke free from Sean's handclasp and walked off across the garden, explaining unconvincingly that he had to go for a pee.

He was still in a chastened mood when Michael found him again a few minutes later. He was afraid Michael would want to talk to him

117

about Sean, and his heart warmed to him when he found that he chose
not to. "Your French friends are a weird lot," he said instead. "Quite
nice, though. The one doing the cooking is like a young version of
General de Gaulle. *La France, c'est moi.* That kind of thing. But he's
right about one thing. We both agreed that you're absolutely mad. He
told me you'd told him you'd told your mother he'd broken your teeth.
And that you wanted him to go along with the story if she asked him. I
mean, come on man! He was really pissed off about that, I can tell you."

"I know," said Adam.

"Well, why did you?"

"I don't know," said Adam, though he did. Now that he had come
down from his Sean-induced, sex-induced high he regretted his earlier
silliness.

"If you go on like that you'll have to spend the whole of the second
half of your life apologising to your friends for what you said to them in
the first half. That is, if you still have any friends left to apologise to."

Adam grabbed at Michael's wrists and wrestled him to the ground,
though not without an effort. Michael had toughened up a lot in the last
year.

"Tell you one thing, though," Michael said calmly, looking up at
Adam through the trellis of their forearms. He had no objection to being
sat upon by his friend. "I'm surprised you haven't had young Christophe
yet."

"Christophe!?"

"Why not? He's rather cuddly, don't you think? And clearly prefers
boys to girls."

"You're kidding."

Michael gave Adam as pitying a look as anyone could manage in
such a pinned-down position. "Don't tell me you haven't noticed. He's
mad for Thierry for a start - much good that'll do him - and he's also a
little bit in love with you."

"Jesus," said Adam. Then: "He didn't tell you all this, did he?"

"No, of course not. But I could tell." He put on a singsong voice that
might have been meant to be Micky Mouse. "I know when people are in
love. I ain't stupid, you know. I don't have to have everything spelled
out for me. And I tell you what…" He had abandoned the silly voice by
now, or perhaps it had abandoned him. "When it comes to people falling
in love, like baby-face Christophe you know, people do make *the* most
in-ap-*pro*-priate choices."

Adam released his friend from underneath him and allowed him to
scramble to his feet.

The atmosphere at bedtime that evening was more than a little tense, though not from any animosity or jealousy between the three of them. Almost the reverse, in fact. Sean, decently, set out his position first. "Look, I really don't care what the two of you want to do. I really don't mind. But it was a mistake my trying to join in, so count me out, OK? And I don't mind sleeping on the floor if that's more convenient."

Then everyone tried to outdo everyone else in gentlemanly sentiment and self-sacrificing gesture. Michael assured Sean that he wouldn't have to sleep on the floor but could have 'his' bed. He, Michael, would sleep with Adam - if, of course, that was what Adam wanted. Adam answered that that would be no problem and tried to explain to Sean that he quite understood his not wanting to... though he wasn't sure how to formulate the end of that sentence and so abandoned it just there.

In the end Sean had one bed to himself while Michael shared with Adam, the two of them playing with each other until they fell asleep, but quietly, out of sensitivity to Sean's feelings on the matter - whatever they might have been. As for the matter of Adam's disloyalty to Sylvain, well, it seemed a bit late to dwell on that just now after everything that had already happened. The stage of 'avoiding the occasion' was well past; it would now have to be a question of putting things right afterwards. In the meantime, Adam supposed he might as well be hung for a sheep as a lamb.

In the morning Sean did not hurry off to the shower as usual, so Michael went first instead. At which point Sean astounded Adam by calling softly across to him: "Come over here." And amazement notwithstanding, Adam arose without hesitation, his cock doing likewise, and stepped across to Sean's bed. "Give me a cuddle," Sean said, without any of the shyness he had shown two nights ago, and pulled back the duvet to let Adam slip in beside him. They didn't experiment with anything more than they had done the last time but found it vastly more fun for being the more relaxed about it. So much so that they were quite unperturbed when Michael returned to the room to find them loosely cuddled together, quite uncovered, moments after they had simultaneously come - Sean most copiously; Adam, understandably after the night he had already enjoyed with Michael, in rather less spectacular fashion. Michael was wiser this time than to try to join them. He just sat on Adam's bed and stared across at the two of them. "Well, well, well," he said.

They had been invited to go fishing. Christophe had made the invitation the day before at the barbecue. Adam was pleased to find that it would only be a small party. No Thierry (just as well, in view of Adam's behaviour to him yesterday), no Céline (enough emotional cross-currents as things were). Just the three English boys, Christophe and his sister. Michael had never been fishing; Sean had, and was a little inclined to play the expert at first. But once the borrowed rods were distributed - thank you, Christophe's family - and the morning's sport got under way, a pleasantly calm and peaceful atmosphere prevailed which, for Adam at least, was a blessed relief from the turmoil that seemed to reign everywhere else, without and within.

They caught a respectable number of roach and then, to everyone's surprise, one quite large pike which had to be killed with an accurate tap from a stone - Christophe expertly obliged here - before it could do permanent damage to anyone's fingers. Adam found himself looking at Christophe with new eyes. Michael had been right: he was quite nice-looking in a cuddly, undeveloped sort of way. For the first time ever Adam imagined holding him, undressing him, discovering his hardening little French *bite*... He discovered that he was getting an erection himself. Perhaps the more different people you got involved with, the more people you took an interest in, the more people you could consider becoming involved with and the more catholic your tastes became. It seemed a long time since last Friday when he had promised Sylvain he would stay with him for ever.

They had not brought anything to eat with them; this time there was no Céline to plunge artichokes into boiling water and to provide ready-mixed vinaigrette. They decided to call at the café at St Ciergues for a *casse-croute* before crossing the dam back to Christophe's house. Without Thierry's presence to remind the patron of parental strictures they were served beers, not shandies, with their *croque-monsieurs* and enjoyed a relaxed but quite serious conversation in which they compared French school life with its English counterpart. Adam found himself at half a remove from the discussion, partly because, as the only person present with in-depth knowledge of both systems, he had little to learn, and partly because they were five in number and Sean seemed more than ready to pair off with Monique, just as Michael was with her cherubic brother. From time to time he was called on to translate an unfamiliar idea from one language to the other but he was surprised to see how well, in the main, everyone coped: the linguistic immersion of yesterday seemed to have prised open unsuspected stores of French in the baggage of Sean and Michael; similarly Monique and Christophe turned out to have a greater command of English than they had ever let on to Adam.

It did occur to him that he was more exposed to the chance of an encounter with Sylvain down here by the dam than he had been at any time since his pretended departure for England, but having survived so far and this being the last full day of his friends' visit, he was beginning to feel less cautious, less fearful of being caught out than he had done up till now. True, once they had finished lunch and set off across the dam top to Christophe's place he did feel a little exposed. Still, there was nobody else on the dam itself or in the near vicinity as far as he could see, and he knew only too well that anyone watching from a distance would see only five figures crossing the dam with fishing-tackle; Sylvain would not be expecting to see Adam in such a party and he would not be able to pick him out if he did.

At last they came off the dam itself and turned right along the eastern shore of the lake. There remained just a couple of hundred metres before they reached Christophe's driveway. A movement caught their attention and they saw that another fisherman had just finished his afternoon's sport and was clambering up the bank towards them through the tall, bamboo-thick reeds. He carried his rod in one hand, his net in the other and his bag of bits and baits over his shoulder. His arms flailed once or twice as he struggled to keep his footing on the steep sandy bank. He was dressed rather attractively, as it happened, in blue denims and a loose shirt in a big blue check. Adam was pleased about that; at least the young man had not been shown sartorially wanting in comparison with Sean and Michael who were both dressed in pretty much the same way. Adam noticed this reaction of his with surprise, like someone making dispassionate psychological observations.

Of course that was the only thing he was pleased about. The rest of his mind was overcome with horror. For a moment his eyes and Sylvain's met. Each saw the same beginnings of a smile of recognition and a wave, each saw the other's smile wither and die, saw the wave abandoned in mid-salute. Each saw in the whole figure before him the mirror of his own sudden confusion and pain. But in Sylvain's expression perplexity had the bigger part, in Adam's, guilt. And each heard, a fraction of a second later, as the thunder follows the flash, the sound of a greeting beginning with a spontaneous intake of breath but then choked off and exhaled as something like a grunt or cough.

Sylvain's ascent of the bank halted. Adam was borne along past him by the momentum of his ambling, chattering friends. They continued along the road towards Christophe's, Adam giving nothing away to his companions by any outward remark or sign but feeling inwardly as if a trap-door had opened in the floor of his life to reveal nothing underneath it but the infinite cold emptiness of space.

***

The pike presented a problem when it came to dividing up the catch: it was a question of who would eat what and where. But a solution presented itself quite quickly after a short discussion and a phone-call to Jennifer. Christophe was invited to dinner at Adam's, bringing all the fish with him. Monique would be out with friends and so quite ready to relinquish her share of the fish but driving back later and so able to pick Christophe up and take him home at the end of the evening. Christophe's mother enquired anxiously over the phone as to whether Jennifer had the ingredients for a *beurre blanc*, was relieved to learn that she had, and then reassured the alarmed Jennifer in her turn that Christophe would undertake to do the actual cooking. When they eventually left, Christophe's father - perhaps relieved to have the chance of an evening alone with his wife for once - sent them off up the hill with a fairly generous present of white wine.

Once again the enjoyable now of life - an evening surrounded by friends, with good food and pleasantly more to drink than he was used to, and during which he, as host, was briefly at the centre of everyone's world - shielded Adam from the storms that howled around outside. The charmed and sheltered moment took his mind off the reckoning that had to come between himself and Sylvain, and the reckoning that he would have to make with himself.

It was the middle of May. The day had been hot and the evening had cooled little, even when the sun's fiery disc had given place to the evening star's plain sceptre in the west. The pike had been a *grand succès* with its buttery accompaniment, and Christophe's health drunk in appreciation. Afterwards, by popular demand, Adam had played the cello - nothing too heavy, no Bach, no Beethoven - with Gary consenting to accompany him. The picture window was slid open so that they played to the outside world as well, and once a bat actually flew in and did a circuit of the room before returning to more profitable outdoor pursuits. And after that the four boys drifted outside, managing to smuggle a full bottle of wine out with them plus (somehow) some glasses and a corkscrew, while Hugh and Jennifer and Gary remained inside with glasses and conversation of their own.

Somehow Christophe got lost. One minute he was sitting with the others, the next he wasn't and a moment later Michael also somehow disappeared into the darkness. "Well," said Sean, left alone with Adam under the damson tree, "it seems to be turning into quite an evening."

Adam giggled. He hadn't realised before that Sean was capable of this kind of observation, that he had that kind of I'm-not-as-straight-as-you-think-I-am sense of humour. Perhaps before this week he hadn't.

Maybe it was the company of Michael that had brought it out. Maybe it was... himself.

Then, "It's been quite a day for you all round, though, hasn't it?" said Sean more seriously. And then, in that tone of tender concern that had always been his hallmark and for which Adam had always loved him, "That was your lover, wasn't it, we saw by the lakeside? He's very handsome."

Adam's romantic, histrionic side saw himself throwing his arms around Sean's neck in a relief of tears but of course the real-life flesh and blood teenager did nothing of the kind. He just nodded soberly and said: "That's right."

"You should have introduced us. Why keep him hidden all this week?"

"I thought you wouldn't understand," said Adam bluntly.

"Perhaps you were right," Sean said thoughtfully. "At the beginning of the week, maybe. But not now."

Adam was surprised to find that he was angry. "Are you saying you're gay all of a sudden? Like this morning you were, yesterday you weren't and the night before that you were. What about tonight?" He stopped, shocked. He had never spoken to Sean in this tone before, had never wanted to. "I'm sorry," he said. "I didn't mean that."

"If you're angry with me I don't blame you," Sean said slowly as if with an effort. "You think because I'm older I should know what I'm doing all the time. Mister Cool, you think. And I try to live up to that. To the way you think of me. It isn't easy, though. Perhaps I shouldn't have tried. Truth is, I'm just as confused as you others. I'm not gay though. I do know that. But somehow in my own way I love you. And I mean you. I don't have the same feeling at all about Michael. Work that out if you can. I can't."

"You're different from Michael," Adam heard himself saying. Perhaps it was the wine. "You're softer, gentler, than he is. I mean your personality is." Then he realised that that was not the only thing he meant, and said so. "Yes but also when I, when we... You're more like Sylvain. Sylvain, that's his name. But he's gay - and Michael's gay - and you're not. So work that out."

"Maybe it's just to tell us that stereotypes don't mean too much." Sean took a mouthful of wine and reached his hand across the garden table to take Adam's. He didn't remove it even when the nearby rustle of denim announced the return of Michael and Christophe from the darkest reaches of the garden. They were not holding hands. They didn't need to. Christophe was as transfigured as if Botticelli had snapped his fingers and brought one of his smaller angels to life, while Michael was trying to restrain a smile that wanted to transform itself into a triumphant grin.

It was only after Monique had called by and taken Christophe home that Michael and Adam had the chance of a few words together on their own. They were in the bedroom, perched on opposite beds while Sean very practically collected glasses of water from downstairs. "You could have fun with Christophe," Michael said. "He'll do anything you want him to, that boy. And you can thank me for breaking him in for you."

"I'll bear that in mind," said Adam.

"Tell me though," Michael said more seriously. "Just what the fuck does Sean think he's playing at? All this blowing hot and cold, straight yesterday and straight tomorrow but never straight today. Holding your hand across the table like Heathcliff. It's getting tedious in the extreme... and that's even for me. I hate to think what he's putting you through. I hope to God that Sylvain doesn't lead you such a dance. Personally, my nerves just wouldn't stand it. Still, nothing to do with me, I suppose, since I seem to be completely *hors de question*. Thank God for the consolation prize of Christophe." He stopped. "Seriously. I don't want you to get hurt by Sean. Just because it's the last thing he would ever want to do, doesn't mean he doesn't have the power to do it." There was a long pause during which Adam realised that Michael had never spoken to him like this before: intimate, solicitous, concerned. Michael sounded almost bitter when he started again. "You think I don't care about you really. You think I'm all surface and no heart. You treasure your relationship with Sean but little old me is just something useful to play with. An intellectual sparring partner and a friendly wank."

This was precisely how Adam did see Michael but he was too slowed-down by trying to think after drinking to deny or soften Michael's charge. He stayed silent, looking down, unable to meet his eye.

"Well, it isn't true," Michael said in a voice become suddenly tremulous. "I care about you. More than Sean does. I love you, Adam." And to Adam's horror, Michael burst into tears: the worst kind of outbreak, involving snot and nose-blowing as well.

The sound of Sean's footsteps coming up the stairs forced Michael to regain his composure quickly. Adam scrambled over to his side and gave him a peck on the cheek - something he had never done before - while Michael scoured his face with his hanky. Adam had to get up to open the door for Sean who was balancing three glasses of water like a barman. And when he came in he sensed at once that he had just missed something of a drama and said: "I'm not interrupting anything, am I?" It was a degree of irony which, a week ago, he would not have aspired to.

124

Then, having put down the water, he sat himself next to Michael and said, gently and earnestly: "Would you mind very much if I slept with Adam tonight?"

And Michael, who might have been forgiven for making an operatic aria out of his reply, said simply: "No, go ahead Sean. It may be your last chance, after all."

"I guess you're right," said Sean heavily.

In bed Sean held Adam firmly, intensely. He was choked-up, even nervy, in a way he hadn't been the other times. He put his mouth close to Adam's ear so that his lips tickled the lobe. "When Sylvain fucked you, you know…"

"Yes?" Adam whispered too, though Michael's bed was so close that there was little point. At that range he would have heard telepathy.

"Was it… I mean, did you enjoy it?"

"I… I'm not sure. I suppose, because it was him… I suppose it brought us closer together." I'm going to get fucked, thought Adam, at two arms-lengths from Michael. Dear God.

"Could I… I mean, do you want to fuck me?"

Adam thought his heart stopped for a moment. This was Sean asking him this.

"I suppose so."

Sean said: "You don't sound very enthusiastic." He sounded half amused.

A moment later, once the idea had sunk in, Adam was very enthusiastic indeed - Sean checked the extent of his enthusiasm with his fingers. Then he turned over and offered Adam his sculpted, muscular behind.

"Oh God," said Adam, "I'll come too soon."

"You won't," said Sean without a shred of evidence.

Adam, making the happy and inspired guess that quantities of spittle would be an important factor in the success of the enterprise, applied as much as he could spare, both to himself and to Sean's inside. Then, lowering himself gently and using his hand as a guide, he urged his bucking penis a little way into Sean.

Who gave a gasp. Adam stopped. "Go further," whispered Sean. Then Adam felt his cock, which had never seemed bigger than tonight, sliding inch by inch into his friend as if it were being swallowed. Once or twice he felt the kind of weak resistance you got when you pushed the plunger of the cafetière down too fast, and knew from that experience that then he must slow down.

He had gone as far as he could. His balls and belly met the smooth buffers of Sean's backside. He could hardly believe what he was doing.

He was inside another person for the first time in his life and that person was Sean, the most beautiful, most unattainable person he knew. And straight... Well, at least supposed to be.

Adam shot. He felt as if his life's blood were pumping out of him and into Sean. He felt Sean squirm beneath him, felt his sturdy cock swell in his hand and then felt all the hot and urgent wetness as Sean let himself go. A not insubstantial amount of noise from the other bed indicated that Michael had been joining in the excitement vicariously and was not too shy to let them know.

The morning dawned cloudy. Last night's wine-induced euphoria had dissipated and a pall of uncertainty, of things unresolved between the three boys, hovered over the breakfast table. Sean in particular looked shifty and unwilling to catch anyone's eye. Adam didn't know what he'd expected - or if he'd expected anything at all.

Later Sean cornered Adam. He seemed agitated. "You know last night. We didn't use a rubber. You've been fucked by this strange guy. He might have been carrying anything. You could have given me Aids."

Adam was surprised and stung. "Given you Aids? What about me, then? That'd mean I had it too. Or don't you care about me?" He might have felt and sounded angry, but his feelings for Sean still made that difficult for any length of time. Instead he felt more let down, more betrayed, than ever in his life.

Something of this communicated itself to Sean. "I'm sorry," he said. "I'm scared, that's all." He paused. "And selfish too."

Adam saw with incredulity, and for the first time ever, that Sean looked ready to cry. What a way the week was ending. Awkwardly he reached out a hand and touched his forearm. "Don't be scared. Sylvain's never been fucked by anyone before me. I'm sure of that. He's told me what he has done and who with. So you're safe. So am I."

Sean looked for a moment as he was going to embrace Adam but he didn't. He only turned away wordlessly. Perhaps he really was finding it difficult not to cry.

The journey back to Chaumont in the car was very different from the arrival earlier that week, the mood sombre and reflective. Adam was glad that his mother, not his father, drove them. To the same driver the difference in mood would have been too tellingly obvious. Sean sat in the back with Adam whose one consolation was that Sean kept his knee pressed against Adam's for almost the entire journey. What message this was intended to give was unclear: Sean's face gave nothing away but at least it was certain, after everything that had happened, that this time the contact was intended and not accidental. Then, when the car at last

126

stopped outside the *Gare Routière* of Chaumont, Sean gave Adam's hand a quick tight squeeze, carefully choosing a moment when it would not be seen by either Jennifer or Michael. Then the moment was over. It seemed to Adam that a momentous event in his life had occurred this week, but one whose meaning was as yet completely hidden. And when, standing by the open door and steep steps of the coach, he found himself shaking hands almost formally with his two friends - or rather lovers - he had the strange sensation that the experience, this leave-taking, was actually happening to someone else.

TWELVE

It had been a genuine mistake when Adam had told Sylvain that he would meet him on the Sunday afternoon after the departure of his English visitors. He had either meant to say Friday or had not taken it on board that Michael and Sean would be returning home so soon; he no longer remembered which. In the event he found himself rather thankful for his muddle: it gave him a breathing space between one world and the other, time to compose himself, think through things and - at the purely practical level - decide how he was going to handle Sylvain when they next met, and what he was actually going to say.

Before Michael and Sean's arrival he had mentally run through a variety of scenarios for the week of their visit. These had ranged from having to explain to an unhappy Michael that there could no longer be a sexual relationship between them, through the possibility that Sean and Michael had somehow metamorphosed into a couple, to the rather more likely chance that Michael had outgrown his interest in boys during the previous year - in which case Adam's new attachment to Sylvain would not have posed a problem. Almost the only thing he never dreamed of was the week that actually happened: the reality of five days of frenzied sexual activity and the roller-coaster ride that his emotions had given him. Roller-coaster was hardly an adequate description, though; it had been Ferris-wheel, dodgems and the whole white-knuckle, stomach-inverting gamut of fairground rides whizzed into one. It would be a couple of days before the world stopped spinning round him like a giant centrifuge and slowed to its normal pace.

Sometimes the events of those last few days seemed so unreal as to be almost unbelievable, now that the two boys were no longer around to corroborate his memory of them and that the forensic evidence provided by the bed-sheets had been efficiently destroyed by the washing-machine - which Adam had had the presence of mind to turn to its highest setting when, in an unprecedented access of domesticity, he had stuffed the sheets into it with something like panic even before breakfast on the day of his friends' departure. The only thing that remained to prove to him that it had not all been a dream was the perfume of Sean's body which, despite baths and showers, clung to him enduringly, endearingly, and seemed to him so strong and pervasive, at times attractive and exciting, at others menacing and dangerous, that he found it difficult to believe that his parents and Gary could not smell it on him too.

Hugh and Jennifer, seeing their son strangely lost after his friends' departure, all moping and bereft, wondered together if, after all, they had done the right thing in bringing him to France. But they quickly overcame their doubts by reminding each other that the dam project had only two more months to run and that Adam would very soon be restored to his English milieu for good.

Gary had a shrewder idea about the state of Adam's mind and heart. Apart from anything else, his had been the bedroom next door. During the previous week he had been working feverishly at his composition for the Avignon Festival, perhaps slightly influenced by the pitch at which life was being lived in the adjacent room, and now it was nearly done. He played some of it through on the piano on Friday evening. But even when Adam made allowances for the fact that it was a mere black and white copy of something created for the orchestra's paintbox of colour and effect, he found it disappointingly alien: all jars and jangles. He really could make very little of it and wondered how much this was due to the music itself and how much to the unprecedented state in which he found his nerve-endings.

Gary sensed that the piece hadn't gone down too well with Adam despite the glib compliments that he managed to dredge up when Gary had finished his keyboard demonstration. He changed the subject and said: "Why don't we do the Beethoven again before I leave on Monday?"

"Oh no," said Adam. "I couldn't. I haven't practised for a week. I'm not like you. I can't just pick it up and do it."

"I couldn't once, either, you know." Then Gary smiled such a roguish smile that Adam thought he might have spotted a childishly smutty, though unintended, double-entendre in Adam's last remark. Then he became serious and teacherly for a moment. "That's what practice is for. You've got the whole weekend."

Gary's challenge was opportune. Immersing himself in music and the demands that Beethoven made on both himself and his instrument, Adam was able to create an emotional decompression chamber that might bridge the gap between the turbulent atmosphere of the last few days and the potentially frosty one of his first encounter with Sylvain. He worked hard on the sonata for most of Saturday, not caring whether Gary overheard his trials and repetitions or not. On the Sunday he merely tinkered with it at intervals. He was outwardly quiet that day but mentally focused on the two confrontations that would come later in the day: one with Sylvain in the afternoon, the other with Gary and Beethoven during the evening.

He cycled off towards the *vallon* earlier than the time he had set for his reunion with Sylvain, reflecting uncomfortably that not only lovers 'ever fly before the clock' but also people with guilty consciences. The path was narrow now. Hawthorns had bushed out, and brushed him on both sides with their foaming white blossom with its sweet and sickly scent. You mustn't take it indoors, people said: its perfume was supposed to be reminiscent of death. Bright campion flowers shot crimson sparks along the banks, while where the meadows showed between the trees the first red poppies were opening among the gold, just hinting at the next month's fields of flame

When he arrived at the sleeper path by the springs there was nothing to do but wait. He heard the birds calling quietly in the afternoon warmth, heard the rustles of breeze and insects, but there was no sign of Sylvain. Time passed and Adam sat tensely on the handrail of the bridge, now impatient for Sylvain's arrival, now glad to be able to postpone for a few more minutes the inevitable awkwardness of their encounter. An hour ticked by. Adam got off the rail, slowly and heavily, like someone three times his age. Pensively he undid his fly and pissed without enthusiasm into the thickening mud beside the log path. Sylvain wasn't coming. He zipped up and retrieved his bicycle from its usual hiding place in the undergrowth. It took an age to push it up the flinty slope. It took another age to cycle home.

Gary was waiting for him when he got back. "Come on," he said, "let's go for it. We'll both get nervous if we have to wait till after supper." Adam was flattered by the inclusive 'both'. This time Hugh and Jennifer were invited to be an audience. Adam had fully expected to be nervous, more so than before, but now the time had come he found that he felt cool and almost detached. Was this how professionals felt when they played in public, he wondered?

They sat down, tuned up, and then Adam drew his bow across the strings. The sonata had begun. Here he was, playing it for the second time with a professional - he almost dared to think 'fellow-professional' but mentally slapped his wrist for such presumption. He did not feel the experience in quite the same intense way that he had done the first time. *...never recapture, that first fine careless rapture.* Sylvain would like that line about the thrush; Adam would try to translate it for him sometime. Sometime. When. ...If.

This time Adam felt a greater sense of being in control, of making the music do his bidding, of a greater technical mastery of the piece. And when the performance was finished and his parents very properly

130

congratulated their almost professional sounding son, he felt a sense of achievement that was only partly due to his attainment in terms of the music. He felt as if he had somehow regained control of what was happening in his life and would be able to keep the events of the previous week in a sensible perspective from now on. He felt more ready and able to face Sylvain.

When they had finished supper it was still light outside. Gary said he wanted a breath of fresh air and asked Adam, almost diffidently, if he would come for a walk with him. Adam by now quite hero-worshipped Gary, at least where music was concerned, and said of course he would.

"There's something I want you to hear," Gary explained as they walked along the road past the mayor's house. "I remember you telling me once you couldn't see the point of fugues in music. They were like nothing in nature, you said. I want to see if I can prove you wrong."

They came to the fork in the road and chose the downhill lane towards Noidant, but they hadn't gone far in this direction before Gary made them stop near a wooden field gate. Beyond it lay a narrow strip of pasture just a few metres wide. Shaggy hawthorn hedges, heavy with blossom, edged the strip on both sides and reached across towards their opposite numbers with vigorously growing branches, just as the upper storeys of medieval city houses stretch out and try to touch their neighbours on the other side of the street. The sun's nearly horizontal rays lit the hawthorn leaves like emeralds among their flower heads of laundered lace. Darting rapidly from one side to the other and then disappearing into the dense foliage were small birds, light brown in colour and with a reddish tinge to their tails - the last part of each one to be seen as they plunged into the obscurity of the hedgerows. The shadows grew perceptibly as the sun sank beyond the *montagne*. In a few minutes the birds would have no colour in their tails at all.

"There was once an English cellist called Beatrice Harrison," said Gary. "She lived near Limpsfield in the Surrey Downs. She used to play her cello in the garden at night. Nightingales used to come out of the woods and sing along with her. Isn't that rather lovely?"

"I think I once heard a recording of her," said Adam.

"You may have done. The BBC made several in the nineteen-twenties. Believe it or not, they were the first outside broadcasts that were ever done."

The sun was finally gone from where they stood. It only picked out the crests of the forest further east, beyond the *vallon*. Three long clear notes pierced the still air: the high-pitched whistle of an elfin ship leaving the port of day to set out on a magic journey across the still, deep sea of night. The hairs rose on the back of Adam's neck as the music began. A second bird started up while the first developed his song, subject against counter-subject, just as in the artful fugues that Adam had distrusted up till now. A third voice entered, announcing its arrival with the same three piping whistles. Then a fourth.

Adam and Gary listened in silence for five minutes, hardly moving a muscle. Then Gary said: "Come, don't get cold. It's their party, not ours. Let's leave them to it." He turned and led the way back up the lane.

"That was brilliant," Adam said. "I never imagined…" He tailed off.

"They used to say at college that you didn't really appreciate chamber music until you'd fallen in love with two violinists, a viola-player and a cellist. Only then could you hear all the voices properly. A fugue is only chamber music in a rather formal shape."

"I think you've won," said Adam. "About the fugue, I mean. That really was one, wasn't it? Not as formal as Bach, obviously, but I can see where the idea might have come from." He stopped, unsure what to say next. Now that Gary's departure was imminent he found there were all sorts of questions he wanted to ask him and that he wished he had thought of before. "Did you fall in love with all those instrumentalists?" was what he finally came out with.

Gary laughed. "I'm not sure if I managed that precise tally. Something like it though, perhaps. I took the advice to heart in a more general way."

"Why did you come to live in France?" Adam asked next.

"Was it for music, or for love? Do I read your question right?"

Adam nodded, embarrassed to discover that he was so transparent.

"Well, both in a way. A prophet is never honoured in his own country. It's easier to be someone special in a foreign land, particularly in the field of music. You'd be surprised how exotic a name like mine sounds to French ears. It's also…" He hesitated "…At least this was the case twenty years ago… It was, how shall I say this, easier to be a gay man some distance away from where you grew up." A mouse rustled in the grass verge.

"Did you tell your parents?"

"No. Does that disappoint you? My father died when I was twenty and my mother nine years later. Perhaps I would have told them if they'd lived. But I don't think they'd have taken it well. My brother and sister know, but that's not quite the same."

"One day," said Adam, "I suppose I'll have to tell mine. But maybe I need to be a bit more sure myself."

Gary drew breath to say something, then shut his mouth tight against a burgeoning smile and appeared to reconsider his reply. "I think that's quite wise," was what he finally said.

132

"Of course, it does seem more and more probable that I am." This time Adam could see Gary trying to suppress the smile. "And then, of course I'll tell them."

"Well, be careful," Gary warned. "They may not want to be hit over the head with it."

"I'm sure they'll be very understanding. They're pretty together people."

"I wouldn't bank too heavily on that. D'you know?"

Adam felt annoyed. "Why not? They're OK about you. They let you take me out for walks in the dark... to listen to nightingales."

"They trust me to be a gentleman. I told you that before. Anyway, don't exaggerate the danger. It's only just beginning to get dark and we'll be back indoors in no time. Seriously, though, there is another thing. I am not your parents' only son. You are. The most tolerant and enlightened people sometimes take a very different view of things when it comes to their own children. And that brings me to something else."

Adam groaned. "Don't say that. You're being like a parent now yourself."

"Sorry," said Gary. "I'll try not to do it again after today. Look, I'm not saying to you, do what I did and never tell them. Things were different when I was young. But I do think you should give some thought to the question of when and how they find out, if they're going to. It may not be as easy or as painless as you imagine. And... this is my last word, I promise - if you carry on under their roof again the way you did last week, they will see only too clearly what is happening and you'll have all hell to pay. You've got away with it once, I don't know how. Put it down to your parents' good natures that they didn't get the whole picture, but you can't go on presuming on their ignorance. You've been very lucky, but you won't get that lucky again. When they do find out, it needs to be at a moment of your choosing, not theirs."

Adam had felt himself go hot and cold by turns during this speech. "You knew? You think Mum and Dad nearly..."

"Dear Adam, I had the room next door. I haven't the slightest wish to know what went on exactly, but let's just say you were hardly the quietest group of teenagers on the continent."

Adam still clung at times to the child's perception that activities that were private to him were as invisible and inaudible to the grown-up world as if he had been a leprechaun. It gave him a jolt to have this illusion so comprehensively dispelled by Gary. Still, he was surprised to hear himself say next: "Don't you think Sean's beautiful, though?"

"Well yes," said Gary. "I can't disagree. He's like an Armani model... No, no, that's quite wrong. He's like nothing of the sort. His great quality is his homeliness. If he became an actor - which he won't - he'd play Thomas Hardy heroes or else take a leading role in the next generation of Hovis ads. I suppose I'm to understand that he's one of the two loves of your life." Adam made an embarrassed mumble of assent. "Well, he's a very nice boy. Sweetness is the quality that springs to mind. He had long earnest chats with me."

"About...?"

They had turned the corner into the village and were passing the mayor's front door - which chose that moment to open. The mayor emerged right into their path, complete with dog. He said: *"Bonsoir Messieurs."* They said *"Bonsoir Monsieur le Maire"* to him, Gary taking his cue from Adam, then Adam bobbed down and fondled the dog's ears for a second and Gary and the mayor exchanged a sentence or two about the weather before they all disentangled themselves and went their different ways. "What about?" asked Adam when he had Gary to himself again.

"What about what?"

"What did Sean talk to you about?"

"Oh yes. Mostly about you actually. He was worried about you. Unsuitable liaisons, that sort of thing. I thought about pots and kettles myself but it was hardly my business to say so. *He* was hardly my business - lovely though he is. You know, the most beautiful people are not always the most rewarding people to know, or love. Sorry, I shouldn't be saying this. It's for life to teach you these things, not me."

"You seem to know a lot about love," Adam said, unsure himself if he was being ironic or not.

"It's just a question of time. Wait till you're my age." He paused for a second. "We seem to be being very open with each other tonight. You've asked me a few questions that surprised me and that perhaps I'd have preferred unasked. So here's one for you. What's happened with the other man, the French one? The one you say you love but who somehow vanished as soon as Sean arrived."

"It wasn't like that," said Adam uneasily. "You wouldn't understand."

"No," said Gary softly. "Perhaps I wouldn't."

"He's still around though," Adam said defiantly. "I'm seeing him tomorrow."

"Then perhaps I ought to wish you luck." Gary's tone thawed slightly. "It isn't easy being in love with more than one person." Then he smiled and added: "Don't you think sometimes the hell of being a teenager is actually rather fun?"

134

Adam laughed in spite of himself. They had reached the front gate. Adam put his hand on it to open it and then stopped. It occurred to him for the first time that a man of Gary's age (thirty-eight, forty?) could be, might be, sexually attractive. Not to him of course, but in a more objective sense. True, his face had the slightly leathery, lived-in look that adulthood quickly brings. But Adam could remember seeing him several times in shorts and T-shirt. Though it hadn't struck him at the time he now thought how trim and well-proportioned Gary was, how flat his stomach compared to most people of his age and how almost boyish were his muscled calves and thighs. Just for a moment his imagination surprised him with the image of Gary's fly unzipped (though not by him of course) and...

Then reality returned and surprised him slightly more. Gary leaned towards him, took his head between his hands and gave him a neat little kiss on the lips. "Good luck, my little pirate captain," he said. "And take care."

As if in obedience to some primeval reflex, Adam clutched with one hand at Gary's buttocks and placed the other on the place in his trousers where his erection might be located, supposing he had one. And he had.

Gary took a pace back smartly. "Don't... touch goods that really don't interest you. I'm still your parents' house guest." He sounded startled, almost alarmed.

"You touched me," objected Adam.

"One day, I hope, you will learn the meaning of the expression *a chaste kiss*. Life might then become a little less complicated for you. Here."

Gary fished self-consciously in the breast pocket of his shirt and produced a card. "You won't want my advice again, I'm sure, but if you ever come to Paris and want to play Beethoven or just drop in for a chat you might like to know where to find me."

Adam, still smarting from Gary's rebuff, accepted the card with a starchy thank-you. He thought: people only carry a card in a shirt pocket when they are already planning to give it to someone.

"Come on," said Gary. "Let's go back in and face the grown-ups." He put an arm lightly on Adam's shoulder and Adam did not shrug it off as he pushed open the gate and they walked the last two metres to the front door.

THIRTEEN

When Adam got up to get ready for school the next morning Gary was already on the point of departure. He was bending in under the bonnet of his car checking the oil level, and he wiped his hand on a cloth before shaking Adam's to say good-bye. When he drove off Adam had just time to realise that the house would seem empty without him before the mental din of pre-school preparations drowned out the noise of quieter reflections.

His schoolmates found him somewhat withdrawn and preoccupied and put this down to a *nostalgie* for his home in Britain, brought on by the visit of his friends. Christophe had a more informed insight into this but it was not something he wanted to throw into the general discussion. In fact he was a little shy of Adam at first, as if he feared that Adam might blurt out *his* new secret, but by the end of the first day, relieved that this had not been on Adam's agenda, and pleased that heavy discussions were not going to be engaged in for now at any rate, he had regained his normal trusting, cherubic mien.

Once school was over, Adam had only one thing on his mind: to re-establish contact with Sylvain, whatever might come of it. He didn't imagine that it would be a straightforward business, now that Sylvain had pointedly not kept the rendezvous they had made for the previous day. It would not be easy to go looking for him in a hundred square kilometres of wooded, ravine-cut countryside, and he didn't think he would have the gall, this time, to march up to the front gate of the farm. (Behold, I stand at the door and knock.) How straightforward their old relationship seemed in hindsight: how unthreatening and safe, compared with the unknown territory of their next meeting and beyond. Everything had been so natural, so ... boyish. But Adam had been growing up fast over the last week and he had learned that nothing in life could go back to how it was before: that for good or ill, nothing could ever stay the same.

To find Sylvain he would have to look for him, just as he had done the last time they had lost contact. There was no point trying the vet, Pierre, this time, and he had already ruled out a visit to Sylvain's home. The *vallon*, by the springs and the log sleepers where they should have met yesterday seemed as good a place as any to make a start.

In a studied repetition of the previous afternoon Adam descended the track as far as the springs, went halfway across the log 'bridge' and sprang up onto the handrail, conscious this time that Sylvain had been sitting exactly here (waiting for him?) the second time they had ever met.

A cuckoo called in the distance, the sound fogged by a kilometre of dense foliage. Maybe this was a futile idea. Although there was a chance that Sylvain might pass this way sometime in the next few days there was no reason why this time should be better than another. Adam could hardly camp out here day and night. He gave up trying to weigh probabilities. The sun was shining on him through a gap in the leafage and he pulled off his shirt so that it could warm his shoulders. Maybe after a million years or so it might even turn them brown like Sylvain's. After a few more minutes' idleness he opened his fly as well and inspected what lay hidden there - a tried and tested method of dealing with moments of private boredom. He enjoyed the unfamiliar sensation of the warm sun on that usually shaded region. He was not very large today, had not been in fact since the torrid debauches of the previous week. Adam stroked himself experimentally once or twice but with no response. He realised with a little surprise that he hadn't touched himself in this way since Sean and Michael left on Friday.

A snap of twigs just two yards away and a shaking of the hawthorn boughs. No time to stuff himself back in his trousers. Adam just managed to throw his discarded shirt across his lap, steady himself with one hand on the wooden rail and hope for the best. If whoever it was wanted to peer closely at his crotch... Adam banked on the probability that they wouldn't.

But it was Sylvain. Who would. And did.

It occurred to Adam that, by accident, he had stumbled upon the most disarming tactic he could have used. Had they not first met, after all, when Sylvain was similarly, disingenuously, exposed? Adam slid his shirt away, simply, not theatrically, and let Sylvain take in the sight of him as he was.

Sylvain stopped in his tracks at the beginning of the log path just as, in a reversal of their present roles, Adam had done three months ago. There was a long silence as the two looked at each other, weighing the situation up, looking for clues in face or gesture, unsure who would speak first, unsure what they would say.

Sylvain spoke. With almost infantile directness he said: *"Tu m'aimes plus:"* the three syllable, French, economy version of *you don't love me any more*. He placed a hand on the rail beside him.

Lately Adam had been playing out his high-tension emotional scenes in English. It was with a shock that he awoke to the obvious but forgotten fact that he would have to manage this one in French. He had also forgotten what a child Sylvain still was. In the last week or so, Adam felt, he had outpaced him still further in emotional development and wisdom.

"Mais si," Adam answered, like an indulgent parent. "Of course I do." He looked down at his exposed member and noted approvingly that it was beginning to thicken up as if in corroboration of his last statement.

"You don't," Sylvain insisted curtly. "You told me lies. You kept me away from you. Instead of going to England you had your English friends here."

"I didn't know what to tell you," Adam said uncomfortably. "I didn't invite them, they invited themselves." He was beginning to regret his state of exposure.

"You didn't introduce us when we met by accident."

"I was embarrassed because you caught me out. I..."

"Invited or not, you all had sex together, I think."

Adam turned scarlet. "Whatever makes you say that?"

"If you could see your face... Other proof not needed. But it was the way one of them was looking at you. The blond one, the hunky *beau gosse.*"

Adam was at once fantastically flattered to think that his new intimacy with Sean had somehow been guessable from Sean's behaviour or facial expression and mightily horrified that Sylvain had remarked it. "It was..." (How this word kept cropping up lately.) "...an aberration. A one-off. It wasn't planned. I didn't want to have sex with anyone but you. Only things got confused... I can't really explain." He bent his head and stared at the mud-streaked logs a little way below his perching feet. It was so much easier to be faithful to Sylvain when he was physically present and Sean was not.

"And now they've gone you come looking for me again." Sylvain paused, then added: "Dangling your cock like bait." *(Faire miroiter ta bite comme appât.)* He could not help the ghost of a smirk appearing on his face as the cleverness of his remark struck him, though he was clearly not yet ready to be won over by the mere sight of an incipient erection.

"I didn't think you'd mix well," Adam tried clumsily. "You don't speak English and they don't have much French."

"They mixed with your other French friends," Sylvain chillingly observed.

"They're all only sixteen or so. You wouldn't have the relationship with them that you have with me. We're a one-off too, you and me. Me sixteen and you twenty-two."

138

"I'm twenty-three," said Sylvain. "It was my birthday last week."

Adam found himself wrong-footed again. Placing his confidence in something older than words he slid off the handrail, took the three paces that separated them and slipped his hands tentatively round Sylvain's back. Sylvain didn't pull away, though his face remained impassive. Adam drew himself closer to him till their chests were touching and his rising cock nuzzled at Sylvain's groin.

For three or four seconds they stood so, then Sylvain's defences broke. He put his own arms tightly round Adam and let his lips brush Adam's neck. "I love you, I love you," he said almost without voice.

His intensity melted Adam totally. "I love you too." His own voice broke and spluttered. Then they both began to cry, chokingly, their chests heaving against each other uncomfortably, Adam's tears soaking into Sylvain's loose shirt collar, Sylvain's trickling hotly down Adam's bare neck. Not only tears but also promises came pouring out in the breaking storm: promises that were barely articulated, that overlapped and interrupted each other; promises that were scarcely heard but - for the two of them at that moment - hardly needed hearing.

When the convulsions had died away there was no doubt or discussion about what they would do next. Without another word they turned along the path they had taken when they had first met here, and then taken time and again since. As a precaution against brambles Adam tucked himself back into his trousers but he continued to walk bare-chested, his shirt clutched, along with his school bag, in one hand. He was childishly pleased when Sylvain took his own shirt off too as they went along, his brown torso making a striking contrast to Adam's pale one. From time to time Sylvain dipped his hand into Adam's pocket as if to make sure that what had so blatantly been offered was still really there.

They reached the summit of the path, where the oak tree grew in its grass clearing and the stream could be heard splashing along a hundred feet below. They turned and faced each other. "Your muscles are coming along," said Sylvain, running the flat of his hand over Adam's bare chest. Then, looking each other steadily in the eye, they removed the few clothes they still had on. "Happy Birthday, Fox," said Adam.

Adam did not forget his promise to let Sylvan experience the first bath of his life. A few days after their reconciliation came an afternoon when Hugh would have meetings in Chaumont until late and Jennifer had to make up piano lessons missed during the half-term holiday, returning from Langres around seven. It was by no means the first time that such a thing had happened, but Adam had not previously dared to think of inviting Sylvain to his parents' house in their absence. Now that he had actually been there on legitimate business, on the day of the removal of the swarm of bees, it seemed somehow an easier step to take. Besides which, after his recent failures where truth and constancy were concerned, Adam felt that there was nothing he would not be prepared to do for Sylvain in order to make up.

Sylvain made the whole thing easier by suggesting that he should make his own way to the house from the back, across the meadow and over the low wall into the garden. The only windows that overlooked the back garden were a long way off and anyone seen stepping over a wall could not easily be identified as Sylvain, but could at a pinch be claimed to have been Adam himself in the unlikely case that anyone said anything.

It was a novel experience for them both, alone together in Adam's house. They were both self-conscious as they descended to the cellar to find a couple of cans of beer. This idea only came to Adam because there was quite a quantity down there just now, a present from Gary, and Adam felt sure his father hadn't actually counted every can. They roamed the house as they drank, Adam showing off the appurtenances of his middle class lifestyle a little uncomfortably. But Sylvain was neither curious nor awkward about the unfamiliar surroundings - he had seen some of the house on the bee Sunday, after all. The only thing that caught his interest was Adam's cello in its case, and then he showed something like excitement, insisting that Adam take it out and show it off to him. Adam was conscious of the limitations of time and played him a curtailed version of *Le Cygne* by Saint-Saens, wondering as he did so how this would go down with his untutored audience who stayed standing while Adam played. But Sylvain was quite knocked out by the experience and demanded an immediate repeat, which Adam was sufficiently encouraged by as to deliver without cuts.

They did not sit down until they reached Adam's bedroom. There, once Sylvain had been introduced to Adam's penguin mascot, it occurred to them both for the first time that sharing a bath together was only the second most exciting new thing they could do. Accordingly they undressed and - something that many other lovers take for granted from day one - slipped together into Adam's bed. If Sylvain had any thoughts about this special place being shared by others not so long ago he kept them to himself.

How fast time went. How tempting to ignore its passing and curl up afterwards and sleep. Perhaps it was fortunate that Sylvain retained his curiosity about the experience of bathing, and badgered Adam into getting up to run the taps. It was amusing for Adam to see Sylvain so captivated by the preparations for something so banal, and then jump in with such a careless splash that Adam was momentarily anxious for the bathroom floor. But joining him inside the tub was new to Adam too; he had never thought to try this out with Michael, though it might have been easier a year or two back with him than it was now with a full-grown man. They soaped and stroked each other and laughed and banged their heads on the taps. Then Sylvain could not restrain himself - he apologised simultaneously - from making water as grandly and vertically as a baroque fountain. Adam accused him of saving it up all week, but admitted it was an impressive spectacle. By then the two of them were hard again and had to deal with each other fiercely in the water, an experience with its own fresh surprises for them both.

That might have been the last of the day's novelties so it came as a surprise to find that towelling another person down was quite good too. But at last time weighed in and chivvied them into dressing and clearing up. Sylvain promised a surprise for Adam in return the following day if he would wait just where he got off the school bus in the afternoon. And Adam, squirting breath-freshener in both their mouths, unceremoniously pressed the two empty beer-cans into Sylvain's hands and asked him to drop them in the mayor's dustbin as he passed. A moment later Sylvain had climbed the garden wall and disappeared.

Adam was not all that surprised the next day, after the bus had dropped him at the crossroads, to find Sylvain turning up at the wheel of the pick-up. *"Aujourd'hui on vient chez moi,"* he said. Adam buried his head in Sylvain's warm lap as they drove through the village, not wanting stray parents or neighbours to see him being spirited away. Once he guessed they were safely back in open country he felt able to look up again, but almost wished he hadn't. Sylvain's driving had not improved at all since the last occasion, and the high-speed journey to the farm was just as terrifying as before. At least it was soon over, Sylvain jerking on the handbrake to scrunch to a stop in the middle of the farmyard. "We're going to see your bees," he said as they stumbled out of the car into a spring tide of barking, tail-flagging canines.

There was no way of telling Adam's bees from any others. The new hive among the apple trees looked exactly like all the others and as for the insects themselves... Adam was prepared to take their identity on trust. He permitted himself the trite observation that they seemed to have made themselves well and truly at home. And Sylvain made one of his rare dry jokes: "No signs of homesickness." It sounded slightly better in French.

141

"Come indoors," Sylvain invited, and they turned back towards the house. As they were approaching the great barn a sparrow hawk appeared dramatically against the sky, steering stunningly fast around the corner of the barn roof, terrifying the sparrows that congregated there into disorderly flight. There was a whirring of wings and a chorus of panicked cheeping that almost drowned out the dying squeal of the one that tried to get away but failed. The hawk flicked away as quickly as it had come and vanished towards the nearby copse. As it banked Adam just had time to see the little bundle of feathers that it clutched tightly to its breast in vicelike claws. *Erl-könig hat mir ein Leids gethan.* The chilling music as well as the words flashed unexpectedly into his mind and he gasped involuntarily. "*Ouais,*" said Sylvain, registering Adam's start, "that was quite something. Happens every day though." He put an arm round Adam's shoulder as if to comfort him and was dismayed in his turn when Adam jerked it away with a cry as if the contact had given him an electric shock.

But a few moments later they were both restored by the novelty of finding themselves seated in the room Adam had once before seen briefly, where everything seemed snowed under with torn and muddy newspaper and dogs, Adam experiencing the strange liquorice taste of pastis for only the second time in his life. Sylvain's father had poured the drink in a no-nonsense, hospitable way after shaking the boy's hand. He had met Adam once before, when he had come with the whole family to collect the bee swarm, but that had hardly been a time for social conversation. He showed no sign of surprise now at Sylvain's bringing a sixteen-year-old home with him. His curiosity was exercised only by the fact that Adam came from England. Wasn't that a terribly dangerous place to live, he wanted to know? Didn't they have terrorists on the news and bombs going off all the time? Adam said he didn't think it was as dangerous as all that. Mostly those things happened in London, when they happened at all, and he himself didn't go there all that often. He thought you could live quite a long time in England without much chance of being caught up in something like that. "Really?" said Sylvain's father. It just showed that you hadn't to put too much trust in the media. He indicated the disintegrating pages that lay on the floor and seats around him with a dismissive wave of the hand.

Various children ran in and out from time to time as they talked and Sylvain's mother appeared at one moment. She greeted Adam with a friendly smile and shook his hand but quickly turned her attention to her son. She had quite a litany of instructions for him, concerning clean clothes and some medication or other which she went on about at some length, and something about money that Adam couldn't quite follow, though it was hardly his business. This was a side of Sylvain's existence that he hadn't seen before: Sylvain as a rather disorganised child having to be nagged and sorted out by parents. He saw that it was a measure of Sylvain's depth of feeling for him that he was letting Adam into his domestic life at all and then realised that, for all the differences of their backgrounds, Sylvain's home life was more like his own than he would ever have suspected.

After a few moments Sylvain had clearly had enough. He turned to Adam. "Want to drive a tractor?" His mother protested but his father did not and so he got to his feet, a signal that Adam took to mean 'follow me', and together they left the room.

Adam had been used to changing gear for his mother when she was driving and occasionally his father had let him take the car up and down the driveways of friends who were lucky enough to have them, but the tractor was even more fun. Adam loved the way you simply chose a gear and set the throttle and let the machine find its own speed like a horse. It took the bumps and hollows of the pasture gamely, without protest, like a boat in a slight swell. And it was fun to have Sylvain at his side, perched on the big rear mudguard, steadying himself with a hand on the back of Adam's neck, telling him once or twice to change the control settings as the terrain required. He was quite sorry when the ride came to an end. He couldn't understand now why the sparrow hawk they had seen earlier had filled him with such unaccountable dread.

On the way home in the pick-up Sylvain drove more calmly, although hardly more proficiently. Perhaps his driving skills were better adapted to handling tractors on rough and open ground than to cars on the public highway, Adam thought charitably.

"In my grandfather's time," said Sylvain, "they didn't have tractors on the farm at all. They did everything with oxen. Ploughing, mowing and reaping, hauling logs. Always a pair together in the yoke. My grandfather told me that the two oxen that made a team grew together like brothers, like twins that were born together and made two halves of the same being. Then, when one of a pair died, the one that was left would be unable to eat. He would spend his time sniffing and smelling the harness and the reins that had his partner's scent on them. He was no use for work. Couldn't work alone and wouldn't work with a new team-mate. Just pined, you see. In the end my grandfather would have to take it to the slaughter. You couldn't give space to an animal that didn't do anything. *Triste, non?* It's like you and me." Sylvain stopped the truck just on the edge of Courcelles village. "We'll be like the two oxen one day, won't we? *Les vieux inséparables.*" He drew Adam's face towards him and gave him a thoughtful kiss.

Adam walked the last hundred yards to home. On both sides of the road the fields were changing colour from buttercup gold to poppy red, as if someone were little by little stirring a dish of tomatoes into scrambled egg. And within himself he felt a similarly bizarre stir and clash of emotions: feelings that ran the whole gamut from sunbursts of the greatest rapture to thundershakes of the most extreme disquiet. It was only as he was pushing open the front gate that he realised he had spent an afternoon with Sylvain for the first time ever without making love.

FOURTEEN

How wonderful it was with Sylvain now. No longer spring but high summer. How much better it was with this man he loved and who loved him back than it could ever have become with Sean. Sean blew hot and cold and, despite his recent dipping of a toe into gay waters, did not and could not possibly return the passionate feelings that Adam had for him. And how much better it was than anything he had ever had with Michael, fond of Michael as he was. Although Michael had surprised him during half-term by hinting that he felt more deeply about Adam than he had let on before, as far as Adam was concerned their relationship was still simply a friendship that included sex - not, emphatically not, a romance.

In the space of the few days that followed their visits to each other's houses - which in hindsight seemed charged with huge symbolic significance - the dynamic and the routines of Adam's affair with Sylvain had apparently returned to how things were before the rude interruption of his English friends... his English lovers. But their relationship was different too: paradoxically enriched, it seemed to Adam, by the break that had occurred between them. Adam had hurt his lover but been forgiven by him. Because of this he was loved the more, and gave his own love even more freely in return.

But even as they resumed their rambles in the woods and meadows - those happy, predictable, short stories with their rapturous, sexy, denouements - and even as Adam felt more certainly that now, *this* now, was better than ever, the best now of all time, there began to sound in his imagination the din of the unseen torrent, the world's end, that lay only just beyond his time-horizon. Inexorably his dream ship headed towards it as it sailed across the golden calm. Soon the din would be a roar and then nothing that either he or Sylvain did to stop their ears would be able to shut it out. They would reach the end of their shared existence; their fragile craft would shatter as it plunged from the ocean's edge and spill the two of them, shaking them apart in final, endless, separation.

Six weeks. That was the prosaic truth. Just six more weeks. The end of term was less than a month away and soon after that Hugh's work on the dam would be finished too. Adam and his mother would have to move back to England at the end of July in any case. The owner of their French house would be coming to reclaim it in August. If the dam contract overran, Hugh would have to stay on in a hotel and join them when he could.

How well did Sylvain really understand all this, Adam wondered? Had he fooled himself into believing - as Adam almost had - that the present millpond state of things would last for ever, allowing them to stay suspended in their summer idyll, sailing for ever onwards to where time had no horizon? For some time Adam did not dare to bring the subject up, afraid that even to mention the reality of their forthcoming final parting would bring it closer and cause the dream that they were living in to fall around their heads in ruin.

Then, one Sunday as they sat by the Lac de la Mouche, watching the dragonflies dart and hover above the reed stems, watching the June sunlight shimmer on the ripples at the sandy margin, Sylvain said it. "We'll live here for ever, won't we, Adam? It's sure. I'll never let you go."

It was too direct a denial of the truth for Adam to let it pass. He had been prepared, far too prepared, to kid himself up to now. But he found he could no longer acquiesce in an outright misunderstanding, or a lie, whichever this might be to Sylvain's mind.

"You know that we can't be together always." Adam stared steadily out in front of him, across the sunlit water as he spoke. "I'll always love you in my heart. Always. But you know that at the end of July..." And Adam spelt out in painful detail the departure dates of his family and himself. Sylvain was frowning with displeasure. "You did know that," Adam added gently.

"Then I'd forgotten," said Sylvain crossly. "Can't you get them to change their minds?"

"That's not possible. That's the grown-up world."

"Why should that concern us?"

"Don't pretend to be a baby," said Adam, now sounding cross himself.

"Then *you* should stay, just you. With me. On the farm. Or if they won't have us we could live in the barn. Or out here in the woods."

Although Adam understood perfectly well how ridiculous and impossible this suggestion was, he found his heart quite literally racing at the thought. He could see it so clearly. Sylvain and he living in the woods in blissful wish-fulfilment. It would always be summer. Winter would never come. They would always be young: Sylvain a lithely muscular twenty-three-year-old and Adam (who would nevertheless permit himself a little further physical development) eternally sixteen. In the late evenings he would take his cello out of its case and coax the nightingales into song...

146

He willed the seductive scene out of his mind, simultaneously ready to laugh at its absurdity and in thrall to its powerful attraction...There would be campfires at night, lovemaking in the firelight. They'd cook the rabbits they caught themselves...

"Don't be silly," he said softly. "It's a fantasy. You know that." He reached out a hand to take Sylvain's. "I really love you. You know that too."

Sylvain reached out with the hand that wasn't clasping Adam's and picked a scruffy little yellow flower. He began to pull off the petals, one by one. *"Un peu..., beaucoup..., énormément..., à la folie,"* he recited, but he stopped pulling the petals off at that point. Adam knew that the incantation went back to zero at that point. *Je ne t'aime pas du tout.*

The next day the fields finally went scarlet, as Sylvain had said they would. Under the hot sun the whole landscape glowed with the colours of fire and blood. Adam was just looking round him, taking in the sight after stepping off the school bus, when a familiar truck came nosing up behind him. Adam peered in before opening the door, just in case it was not Sylvain this time. But it was. "Hop in," he said.

Adam did, dumping his backpack in the foot-well and then dropping his head into Sylvain's lap to go through the village. Sylvain was in shorts today, the first time since Adam had known him, and Adam rubbed his nose along his lightly furred thighs. There was a tang of fresh sweat coming off his sun-warmed skin, which was unusual but not unpleasant. He sat upright after a minute or so to find they were bucking and weaving along the familiar road to Perrogney. He didn't say anything when they whisked past the cart-track to Sylvain's home farm without turning down it, but assumed that he was being taken to the *Licence IV* in Perrogney for a beer. But they were through Perrogney village in a minute and turning left onto the main road at Pierrefontaine. Here they skirted the high point of the plateau, up by the water tower, then looked across the southern slopes where the streams ran downhill all the way to the Med. "Where are we going," Adam asked, suddenly anxious. A road sign pointed to the E-17 *autoroute* junction six.

"To see a friend," said Sylvain evenly. But there was an unfamiliar edge to his voice and his handling of the wheel was far from calm, even by the standards of his usual erratic driving. With an unpractised swerve he swung the truck right, onto the motorway slip-road, then right again at the snake's-tongue fork that offered north or south by two alternative disorienting loops. Adam was too astonished to protest. In a moment they were on the *autoroute* heading south and being hooted by the terrified drivers who had been forced to swerve into the outside lanes by their abrupt manner of joining it.

For a moment Adam became coldly practical. "Have you ever driven on a motorway before?"

"No," admitted Sylvain, "but the principle's the same." They had rapidly zoomed up to the tailgate of a slow-moving lorry. Sylvain braked so sharply that he gave himself a fright, his foot slipped off the pedal and the pick-up lurched forward again, almost into the back of the lorry.

"Look out!" Adam shouted, while Sylvain pulled hard down on the wheel, propelling them unsteadily out into the middle lane like a misfired torpedo. A faster car hurtled past, inches away, its horn screaming. Startled, Sylvain veered back into the slow lane nose to tail with the lorry. Behind them came the blare of another horn. "*Merde*," said Adam. "This is dangerous. You're mad." He was really frightened now.

"Don't worry. I'll soon get the hang of it." Sylvain did not sound entirely convinced by his own answer.

"Before that happens we'll both be dead." Adam remembered the fields of red poppies. "Oh God, oh God, I should have seen this coming."

"It's OK." Sylvain took one hand off the wheel and began to stroke Adam's thigh.

"Don't do that. Concentrate." He wanted to shout: *turn round, go back*, but at this precise moment that was not a real option. Instead, trying to keep his voice steady, he said: "Stay in the slow lane. Come off at the next exit. Then drive us home." As he heard his own voice he realised how near to crying he was. He only just trusted it enough to add, "*je te prie*," I beg you, without it breaking. But Sylvain didn't seem to hear. Without removing his hand from Adam's leg he made another attempt to overtake. This time he refused to be intimidated by the passing traffic but forced it all to jostle into the outside lane with squealing tyres, and ignored its anguished horn-blasts alongside him as he over-steered his way between the high-speed queue he had created to the left of him and the lumbering lorry on his right - each vehicle having its own half-second of distinction as being just then the most perilously close. At last he was able to pull in front of the lorry and with palpable relief accelerated down the empty slow lane ahead of it. Half a minute later they were bearing down fast upon another slow truck.

"Just do what I asked you," Adam said. His voice was fading to a whisper. No answer came from Sylvain, though he did at least seem to be getting over his own fright and his steering was becoming straighter. Adam could see him beginning to look carefully in the rear-view mirror - the ones on the wings were missing - and guessed that he was planning to overtake the new challenge just in front. Adam shut his eyes and was surprised to find himself silently praying: Our Father, who art in heaven...

...But deliver us from evil. Please, please, God, get me out of this. I'll go to church again. I'll never be bad. Never have sex with boys. I'll go on a pilgrimage... Please, God, please... help me.

He felt the tears well up then trickle hotly down his cheeks. Sylvain could hear him catch his breath as he tried not to sob out loud. Adam, his eyes screwed shut, felt a hand alight once more on his thigh. "What's the matter, little one? You're safe with me." As if a dam were bursting, Adam exploded into a paroxysm of tears and howls.

"It's OK. You can wake up now." Sylvain's voice. Adam couldn't believe he had been asleep. He looked around. An unfamiliar landscape was jogging gently past the windows. It was two hours since he had got off the school bus. His parents would be starting to wonder where he was. Not worry yet, but wonder. Adam had kept his eyes shut for some time in sheer terror. He had heard the engine revving painfully fast and guessed that Sylvain was overtaking the second lorry. Then the engine noise had steadied. The ride felt uneventful. Terror had subsided into sulk - and the sulk must have turned to sleep. Where were they? How far had they come? They had left the motorway at some point and were driving through a picturesque region of vine-clad hills. The vines were in fresh full leaf and the sun shone through the undulating rows that draped across the hillsides, turning them into rich necklaces of emerald. He hardly believed himself awake. "Where are we?" was the first thing he said. He was exhausted after his fright, relieved to be alive, too bewildered to be angry just for now.

"I told you: we're going to see friends. We're in the Saône-et-Loire, between Macon and Chalon-sur-Saône."

Adam knew roughly where that was: about a hundred miles south of Langres. "I'm hungry," he said, petulant all of a sudden.

"Nearly there," said Sylvain, though he added disconcertingly, "I think."

"You've been here before, then, right?" Adam checked.

"Three times when I was a boy. I helped with the grape harvest. I had a friend." He sounded proud of all three achievements.

"We're going to see a friend you haven't seen since you were a child? Do they know you're coming?"

"No," said Sylvain.

"Merde."

Two minutes later Sylvain swung the truck off the little country road onto a farm track, just like the one at his home. The farmhouse was already in sight, some distance off: an old, low, stone building. Their pace began to slacken as they approached it, a sign perhaps that Sylvain's confidence in the welcome they were going to get was beginning to weaken. Eventually they drew up to the front of the house and got out of the pick-up. Adam breathed the warm still air. The scent of sun on vine foliage and flower, of distant hay, the aroma of high summer. The scents were wonderful but the silence of that hot fag-end of afternoon felt strange. No sound of barking dogs had greeted them, no sounds of work from barn or hidden yard. No cars were in sight, nor carts or trucks. And all the windows that faced the front were shuttered fast. Sylvain gave Adam a soulful but unpromising look. He seemed unsure what to do. So Adam went up to the front door and knocked upon it. It was painted the same colour, or non-colour, as Sylvain's own. Adam wondered if there was a special range of mud-coloured paints created just for peasant farmers. He knocked again. The sound awoke no echo. Twice more. He turned back towards Sylvain. "Now what," he said. "Plan B?"

"We go round the back and find a way in."

"We can't do that." Adam protested. "It's criminal. Housebreaking. We'd go to prison."

"We're visitors, not burglars. *Viens.*"

"All right." Adam tried to find a wavelength that would work. "But if visitors find the people they've come to see are out, they go away again. They go home. They try another time. They don't force an entry and then wait indefinitely."

"We've come so far," said Sylvain. "They'll understand."

Adam thought this unlikely but could hardly say so. Sylvain knew the people after all, or said he did, and Adam didn't. Miserably he looked around him, especially upwards. If they did get inside... But no telephone wires led to this isolated farmstead. Within his range of vision three or four other lonely houses lay scattered upon the heaving sea of vines, but none was nearer than a mile from here or from its nearest neighbour. His parents would be starting supper. Would they? Would they begin without him, could they manage to eat at all when their only son failed to return home and hadn't made a phone call, had gone missing, was lost? It was an unbearable line of thought. With a great struggle he wrestled it away. Another moment and he'd have been crying again. "OK," he said. "Let's go round the back."

He moved off slowly, reluctantly following Sylvain. What else could he do? He thought for a second of leaping into the pick-up and racing off to raise the alarm, to phone his parents and the police from somewhere, abandoning Sylvain until someone came to collect him... It was a mad

150

idea. On the practical level, he barely knew how to drive and had certainly never tried to do it on a public road. He didn't have a map and couldn't guess the direction or distance of the nearest village. And more importantly, he still loved Sylvain. However mad he might have gone, he could not just run out on his lover, leaving him to the mercies of the police. Until he thought of something better he would have to stay.

At the back of the house was a small yard with long rambling sheds on two sides of it and a little garden with a lawn running away downhill to vegetable plots on the third. At the bottom of the slope a thick line of trees presumably concealed a stream. Everywhere else you looked you saw vines. And heard the same unpeopled silence.

They explored the outbuildings, at first with the very practical aim of discovering a hidden back-door key, but soon curiosity overcame them and they found themselves wandering among the machines and equipment that furnished the needs of a kind of farming unfamiliar to Adam at least. They stepped round a wine-press (hydraulic and hidden by tarpaulins), a grape-picking machine that would bestride the rows of vines like a colossus, found themselves tripping over miles of coiled and hefty plastic pipes. It all looked in good shape as far as one could tell, and was certainly not abandoned here. Equally, given that the *vendange* did not begin before September, it would clearly not be put to use for weeks. Then, remembering what they had come for and giving up on it, they returned keyless to the open air to consider ways of entering the house without one.

Beside the back door they found a shutter that could be unhooked by an exploring finger and, behind it, a small fanlight above a main window which had been shut but not secured. Adam, who was by a small margin the more slender of the two, climbed onto the windowsill with Sylvain's help - help which was quite unnecessary but from Sylvain's point of view impossible to withhold - and stood there for a moment feeling his way inside and down the main window towards the fastening while Sylvain, standing on the ground behind him, massaged his calves. The window sprang open suddenly and Adam almost fell into the dark interior. Sylvain jumped up immediately behind him and followed him through.

Inside the house, which had once been familiar to him, Sylvain's self-confidence appeared to return. He dispelled the darkness by promenading around the ground floor rooms and flinging open windows and the shutters that darkened them, like a character in grand opera. Not that the farmhouse became a temple of light even then. The dark brown and cream paintwork of the interior, old and cracked and foxed with the tar of a generation's *Gitanes*, and the caramel-coloured curtains saw to that. But at least you could see your way around. Adam only peered into the other rooms from the kitchen where he had landed. They were like the rooms on Sylvain's farm, heavy with rough chestnut dressers and armoires. No wonder Sylvain looked at home. The kitchen itself was high-ceilinged and austere. Feeding bowls for dogs, all empty, sat on the floor near the sink. A calendar by the door at least indicated the correct year, which was something.

Sylvain returned to Adam's side. "You're hungry," he said. "Let's see what we can do."

Adam had missed that tenderness in his lover's voice today. Returning, it melted his heart. He would stay here with Sylvain, together against the world, for as long as necessary - whatever the consequences. "I need to pee," he said.

Sylvain unbolted the back door and they both went back out into the yard where Adam unzipped with seconds to spare. He hadn't gone since before leaving school. Sylvain held onto him from behind, lowering his trousers a little way and gently stroking the downy underside of his clenched-up balls until he had finished. He met with no resistance or protest. Then he yanked up the frayed end of his own cut-offs and followed Adam's example.

Back in the kitchen, Sylvain opened the fridge. A light came on, so at least the electricity was working. But the fridge was empty except for some stale milk and a little dried-up cheese. Whoever lived here had clearly not just left that morning. Next to the fridge was a chest-freezer and on opening that they struck gold. More precisely: a collection of unidentifiable cuts of meat, a bag of last year's sweet-corn still on the cob, some blocks of ice-cream and several bags each of wild mushrooms and blackberries. There was a rabbit, curled up in a plastic bag.

"That'll do for us tonight," said Sylvain, dislodging the rabbit from its setting of ice-crystals. He seemed suddenly extraordinarily well in control. He placed the rabbit in the sink, bag and all, and started to run the cold tap over it.

"It'll take ages," said Adam flatly. Sylvain left the rabbit where it was and opened a cupboard. Rummaging around he found a tin of biscuits and held it out, lid off, to Adam. "These'll keep us going for a bit." Adam reached in and drew out a handful. They both ate, then drank glasses of water from the tap. "Come upstairs now." Sylvain guided him, hand on shoulder, towards a door which opened into an enclosed staircase. They creaked their way up and Adam found himself in a short dark corridor from which several brown doors opened off. Sylvain knew where he was. Without hesitation he pushed open the door of one particular room. "This is where we sleep," he said, "if that's OK with you. At any rate this is where they'd put us if they were here."

Adam doubted this. There was only one single bed in the small, barely furnished room. "Is this where you used to sleep before?" he asked, not really needing the confirming nod that was Sylvain's answer. "I don't like it in here," he said. The shuttered house felt stifling and oppressive.

"We only need to come in to sleep. There's a barbecue in the little garden. We cook and eat outside, you see."

"How long's that all going to take?" Adam felt obliged to point up the negative, but he was already beginning to feel better as they descended the stairs.

"About an hour to heat the barbecue, but then the rabbit'll grill in no time."

"How do you know there's any charcoal?"

"I saw a bag in one of the outhouses."

Adam found himself envying Sylvain his shorts this hot evening. And especially if they were going to spend it out of doors. He remembered his school bag in the foot-well of the pick-up and that it contained the gym-shorts he wore for *E.P.S.* This led him to a new question for Sylvain. "Did you bring anything with you? Clothes? Toothbrush?"

"There's a bag of mine behind the driver's seat."

"Mine's there too," said Adam. "My shorts at least. I'll get them both." He went through the kitchen into the front hall and unlocked the front door from inside with a spare key he found hanging there. There wasn't much room behind the seats in the pick-up and Adam could only just see Sylvain's small fishing satchel nestling on the floor. As a fishing bag it did fine but in its new role as luggage or even trousseau it signalled only pathos. He reached through and picked it up, touching something hard and cold that lay underneath it as he did so. He guessed it was a jack or tyre-pump and looked to see. He stopped in mid-movement. He was running his fingers along the double-barrel of a shotgun. Did Sylvain know it was there? Was it always there, unknown to him, unregarded by anyone else? Or had Sylvain brought it specially? He would ask Sylvain about it. But later. He would not mention it to Sylvain at all. He would think about it and decide whether or not to say anything. Later.

He looked around him again. The evening sun was streaming across the billowing vine-slopes, the long shadows highlighting the three-dimensional reality of the landscape. The brilliance of the mid-summer greenness made him catch his breath. How could it be so beautiful here, where he was ... what? A prisoner? A kidnap victim? A conspirator, a

153

willing party to his own abduction? Again he thought about driving off in the pick-up, or setting out on foot for one of the distant, isolated farms. Again he realised that he wouldn't. If only he had forked out for a mobile phone like most of the other people at school. He could have phoned his parents from here, told them he was safe and, roughly, where he was. Then he remembered that the question of how he came to be here and with whom would make it an extremely awkward phone-call. He would need to think about it carefully, plan what he was going to say. Perhaps Sylvain would run him to a phone-box in the car while the barbecue heated up. Even as he thought this he knew it was a non-starter. Whatever Sylvain's plans might be, letting Adam phone his parents tonight was certainly not going to be one of them. His parents would have phoned the police by now, he guessed. He told himself that the police would be very professional and reassuring and that his parents would be less anxious on his behalf as a result. Perhaps it actually wouldn't help anyone if he contacted Hugh and Jennifer or the police this evening. It might simply make things worse for Sylvain when they eventually caught up with him … with them. He decided reluctantly to let the matter go as far as this evening was concerned. Tomorrow he would find a way to persuade Sylvain to drive him home and then all would be well, no harm done.

He went back into the house and through the kitchen, empty apart from the rabbit which still lay under the running cold tap in the sink, and straight out again at the back. At the edge of the lawn the barbecue had been lit and was beginning to smoke and flare. Of Sylvain there was no sign. He stood for a moment in the warm sunshine, then changed into his gym-shorts where he stood, stowing his discarded briefs and trousers in his backpack.

There were garden seats and Adam sprawled in one, feeling suddenly free. He gazed down at his bare legs with approval. Sylvain had been right: his muscles were developing attractively. The light crop of blond fuzz that was burgeoning on his shins and calves caught the sun and sparkled teasingly. Where was Sylvain? Suddenly he felt wretchedly guilty for enjoying the moment so. How silly and selfish he had been, telling himself his parents would feel fine once the police had got involved. Of course they wouldn't. They would be ill with worry, sick with fear. At least *he* knew where he was, that he was safe - for now at least - but they had no such comfort. He tried to imagine what they would be doing right now but could not. He thought about Sylvain's family; they must be worried too. But he had even less success at imagining their state of mind than in the case of his own parents. Yet there was nothing he could do. Not tonight. And it was hardly his fault that he was here...

Sylvain appeared from the kitchen door, lithe and tanned in his denim cut-offs, a snowy T-shirt and nothing else, not even shoes. He was carrying two glasses of red wine.

Adam sat up in his chair. "Where did you...?"

"There's wine in the cellar. Masses of it."

"We shouldn't..." Adam's conscience spoke.

"They make the stuff. It doesn't cost. And we're not going to drink all of it, *P'tit-Loup*. I won't let you go mad." He sounded comfortable with his role as Adam's guardian. Responsibility was new to him and he was enjoying trying it out. His comforting words worked on Adam at any rate; he smiled and reached out for the glass that Sylvain handed to him.

They drank their wine in near silence, admiring the play of sunlight on their own and each other's bodies, awed by the new experience of being alone together in beautiful surroundings that were their own and would remain so for the rest of the oncoming night.

Sylvain went inside to prepare the rabbit for the barbecue, now a mature furnace of embers, glowing dim and hot. He sent Adam on a search of the vegetable garden after thyme or other herbs, plus anything else that took his fancy and would grill in minutes. Adam did find thyme, plenty of it, and shallots as well. He took them into the kitchen and laid them proudly on the table in front of Sylvain. His lover (or captor - Adam's view of Sylvain oscillated from minute to minute) had split the rabbit lengthways with a meat cleaver and was rubbing it with salt and olive oil. He received the thyme with great delight and immediately chopped it up and spread it all over the glistening meat. He gave it to Adam to carry outside on its chopping board, while he followed on behind with two refilled glasses of wine.

The sun was settling into a cleft in the silhouetted hills of the Côte Chalonnaise. Overhead the still sky was as intensely blue as a gas flame. Adam began to imagine that the fantasy he had dismissed as idiotic just a few days ago was somehow coming true: the fantasy in which Sylvain and he lived out their lives in pre-lapsarian contentment in nature's garden, and he charmed the nightingales out from the trees with his cello. It was not so ridiculous, not so unattainable after all. For here he was - living it now.

Bread went on the barbecue. Sylvain had found it in the freezer an hour or so ago and let it thaw in the sun. He turned the rabbit halves over and sprinkled the remains of the chopped thyme over the meat and the hissing shallots and over the embers too. A magical scent arose. With a final blaze of floodlighting the sun slipped between the hills and was gone, leaving the sky to its last blue half-hour of glory. Adam looked at Sylvain, wondering whether he understood him at all, or not. "I love you," he said.

"I love you too." Sylvain gave him a perfunctory kiss. He was getting up to go in search of plates. He returned from the kitchen with a tray on which half the cutlery from the kitchen drawers seemed to be strewn in little heaps, together with salt and pepper and the remains of the bottle of wine. Adam had slipped down from his chair onto the warm grass and Sylvain joined him there. They ate the thyme-tasting rabbit in their fingers, picking it off the bone with their teeth, and mopping up the juices with the grilled bread. It was the first time they had ever shared a meal.

The anger and fear that Adam had felt on being kidnapped had vanished. He recollected them dimly, like the emotions he had felt long ago in childhood's foreign frames of reference. They started to feed each other with titbits of meat and bread, giggling when these went astray and fell down into T-shirts or behind waistbands. By the time the food was finished they were lying together in a tangled embrace. Adam tugged teasingly at Sylvain's shorts.

Sylvain wriggled out of them without protest then removed his T-shirt too, and Adam did the same. They gazed at each other's nakedness, both half-aroused. There was no hurry. "Open another bottle," Adam commanded and Sylvain trotted off obediently towards the kitchen, taking the unused cutlery with him like a well-trained waiter, his bottom - which was slightly less tanned than the rest of him - wagging appealingly like a pale flag in the dusk.

Waiting for him to return, Adam lay back and looked up at the first emerging stars. The grass felt cool now on his back while around him the sounds of evening were starting up. Crickets made ticking sounds like freewheeling bicycles, then the heavier beat of cicadas built up to an all-pervading throb. 'Cicadian rhythm' his father had jokingly called it once on a holiday in Spain... He couldn't think about his father just at present... Nightingales, though. There should be nightingales. But the time of year when you could hear them singing was all but past and, though he strained his ears, there were none to be heard just here. Instead, as if to mock him, a frog began to croak in some unseen nearby pond. It made Adam think of the Emperor's confusion of the two sounds in the fairy story. The barbecue looked rather forlorn, silhouetted against the lighter western sky. But in the east a silver half-moon was rising.

Sylvain reappeared with a freshly opened bottle. "We'll have a proper fire," he said. There was wood stacked against the shed where Sylvain

156

had found the charcoal sack and together they built a fire at the edge of the lawn, where one had been before, both enjoying the novelty of carrying out such an activity stark naked. "Like Robinson Crusoe," Adam said.

They lit it easily, thanks to Sylvain's care in placing the finest twigs, using the dying embers of the barbecue. As the flames began to take hold, their spirits leaped with them and suddenly they found themselves doing an absurd dance together, jigging about, hands together, on the grass. They had to stop for laughing. Then they settled back on the ground again to drink their wine and contemplate each other under yet another change of lighting.

Suddenly Adam said: "What's that?" He pointed to little gleams of light appearing among the grass. Their intensity waxed and waned as he looked at them. They rocked and wobbled slightly. Or was that just the wine?

"Les vers luisants," said Sylvain. Glow-worms. "Come and see." They explored the lawn again, planting their feet gingerly to avoid them landing on the tiny cold white flashes. "Look up and then look down again," said Sylvain. "What do you see?" Looking up he saw the night sky studded with diamond lights, like the dark blue velvet in a jeweller's display, then looking down it was as if he saw a looking-glass image of the same, as if the sky were mirrored in a lake. The movement of his head had made him dizzy and the glow-worms seemed to swim gently before his eyes. "You see," said Sylvain. "The glow-worms make a route-map of the stars."

It no longer seemed absurd to Adam to share with Sylvain the thoughts he had abandoned as childish so few days ago. So he mirrored back to him his lover's dream of living in the woods, embellishing it with the details that had privately occurred to him - like playing the cello for the nightingales. "We'd never wear clothes," he said. "We'd find a country where it was always warm. If we needed money we'd do odd jobs around the local farms. We'd busk in village squares. I could play the cello. You could..." The story of Our Lady's Tumbler went stumbling through his mind. "...You could juggle." He had no idea whether Sylvain could juggle or not. It seemed an unimportant detail. Tonight, when glow-worms lit the roads to heaven, everything must be possible.

Sylvain reached out to him and caught his hands. He walked them back to where their bonfire flared and warmed the air around, then drew him to the ground. He stroked his young lover's shins and thighs, and brushed his neat tight ball-sack with his finger-ends. Adam thought for a second that there were important things that needed to be discussed tonight, things about his parents and about tomorrow. There would have to be decisions and some phone-calls. They couldn't just hide out here for ever. But he didn't want to bring those matters up just yet and so shatter a perfect evening in dragging it down to the mundane. Besides he was no longer sure how he was going to handle the task of persuading Sylvain what was the best thing to do. His mind would be clearer in the morning. Now, with an erection beginning to loom up out of the darkness below his belly, now was not the moment for all that. This was a timeless moment, one of life's best - made to be enjoyed. It did cross his mind fleetingly, darkly, that this night with Sylvain, his first, might be the last one too.

They were in each other's arms. Sylvain had the bottle of olive oil in one hand (at what point had he sneaked it out of the kitchen?) and with the other was anointing Adam's buttock-cleft and thighs. Adam had never felt more relaxed, he was floating on a cushion of wine and summer air, and he offered no resistance when Sylvain rolled him onto his back and lifted up his legs by the calves. Adam felt their weight supported on Sylvain's shoulders and the next thing was Sylvain himself sliding smoothly into him and rendering their separate bodies one. Adam made a small snickering noise. This was so much better than the time before, in the barn loft, when Sylvain had been nervous and rough and his teeth had got chipped. Sylvain seemed in no great hurry but rode him with a rhythmic, sea-swell pulse, but when he came, and Adam felt his excitement inside himself, he gave voice to an explosive whoop of self-congratulation - something that he had not permitted himself on the previous occasion.

When he gently withdrew, Adam was sorry it was over. He hadn't touched himself all this time, though he had wanted to; he had been dreaming other plans. They poured and drank another glass of wine. Sylvain began to be agitated: there was a question on his mind. Sitting up he asked it: "Your blond English *mec*. Did he do that to you - what we just did?"

"No," said Adam truthfully. "But I did it to him."

Sylvain sat thoughtfully for a moment, letting this sink in. "And the other boy?"

"Not with him. He's the one I told you all about at Noidant once. We've always simply done the usual thing."

Sylvain grasped Adam's rigid cock. "Do it now with me." He lay back, spreading his brown legs slightly. Adam felt around for the oil bottle. He wanted to see them glisten in the firelight. "Go, go for it," Sylvain urged.

It was the other way round from the way Sean had presented himself to him. The oil would be the key to everything, he told himself, and applied it plentifully. "That's cold," Sylvain said. But then it was no more difficult than before. Easier, in fact. Slowed down by wine he felt more in control, like when he played the Beethoven with Gary for the second time. The pleasure was intense, and the climax, when it came - not too quickly just for once - felt powerful and steady, like a slowly spreading wave along the shore. They lay still, just as they were, for some minutes afterwards, neither of them willing to move, neither of them quite daring to believe exactly what had just happened. It was as if they could only prove it to themselves by remaining where they were.

In the end Adam didn't exactly withdraw himself at all; diminishing dimensions completed most of that process for him. He rolled sideways and lay back. "Was I OK?"

Sylvain reached out a hand and touched his cheek. "*Et ben oui, mon petit.* It was great. *Tu sais?* Sometimes there's a first time for the older person too." Then he got up to put more wood on the fire.

A third bottle of wine must have appeared at some point. They still had full glasses at their elbows. They began to talk nonsense together while the moon progressed slowly across the sky, its peaceful shadows roaming over the lawn like caressing fingers. At one point an owl hooted loudly from a tree just feet away, and it was a lovely pretext to jump into each other's arms in exaggerated surprise. The last thing Adam would remember of that night was stroking the swirl of hairs between Sylvain's navel and his bobbing cock and saying they reminded him of the fuzzy complex of notes on the final page of the full score of Elgar's cello concerto ... and Sylvain's soft chuckle of a laugh.

When Adam had finally talked himself to sleep and lay flat on his back, purring, on the grass, Sylvain sat looking at him in wonder for some minutes. Then he kissed his boy's face tenderly before lifting him bodily and carrying him, not without the occasional stagger, into the house and upstairs to bed.

FIFTEEN

When Adam awoke he hardly knew who he was, let alone where. Bright sunshine streamed in through shutters that had been weakly shoved half-open. The cavities of his skull seemed to be full of something having the consistency and the weight of mercury, and just as poisonous. When he tried to move an arm, that seemed to be full of mercury too. He was so thirsty that he could scarcely move his tongue, while the inside of his mouth and his throat burnt like the hot sand of a litter-strewn beach. His nose told him that he had been sick over the bed.

A naked and almost pale-faced Sylvain appeared beside him with a glass of something. He leaned over him. "Drink this. It has aspirin in." Adam drank it down in noisy, desperate gulps and was promptly sick again. On the floor this time.

Yesterday came back to him in little ripples of memory, like the first intimations of an incoming tide. They grew to a huge, frightening, swell. He had to phone his parents. Their present state of anxiety, terror maybe, was well beyond the power of his imagination to guess at. He tried to sit up. His stomach convulsed and tried painfully to expel what wasn't there. He leaned over and retched, dryly. Agonisingly. He slumped back under the fouled duvet. He shut his eyes. "I want to die," he whispered. Tears began to ooze from under his closed lids. They ran in separate streams along the sides of his nose and over his temples as if competing to find the quickest way down to the pillow. Despite his closed eyes he still seemed to see Sylvain standing over him, a look of concern pinching up his usually serene face.

"Keep drinking water. I'm coming right back. With mops and cloths."

Adam thought about embarking on a tantrum: telling Sylvain to go to hell and locking the bedroom door against him. But even to think of such energetic activities made his head throb as if it were bursting, and caused a red colour to swim in front of his tight-shut eyes. Instead he smiled feebly and whispered, "Thanks", and to his huge surprise he felt marginally improved.

Adam was ill all the morning and into the afternoon. He heard Sylvain clean up the room around him, but without speaking, stirring or opening his eyes. He would make his real thanks later. Then Sylvain set out cushions for him on a shady area of lawn, found his shorts for him, and took his hand on the walk downstairs. Each new kindness, every tender caress, provoked in Adam a new overflow of silent tears. But he was not so completely self-absorbed as to fail to see and wonder at the change in Sylvain. Over the last few days he had lost that dreamy, half-awake look that had so struck Adam at their first meeting. His eyes seemed bright, not only in the physical sense of being lustrous, as they always had been, but in the meaning of indicating intelligence as well. They shone these days with sense as well as sensibility. Adam wondered whether love alone had brought about that change or if there was also something else. Sylvain was practical too. He was proving a good nurse and kept forcing Adam to drink glasses of water all through the morning. "It was my fault," he said. "Let you drink too much. Gave you no water with it, after a hot day. If it's any consolation, though, I've got a bit of a *gueule de bois* too." He tapped his forehead and grinned sheepishly as he said this. But every time Sylvain left him on his own, and Adam's thoughts strayed towards his parents again, his stomach would gather itself into a knot once more and try unsatisfactorily to expel the thought with the only, excruciating, trick it knew.

By the middle of the afternoon Sylvain felt confident enough of Adam's recovery to leave him while he drove into the nearest town - which he said was called Givry - to do some shopping. He told Adam that it would be better if he went alone: not only would shopping be something of a torture for Adam in his present state of fragility, but there was the probability that they were being searched for by now - they might even have become an item on the national news - and the two of them together might arouse suspicion in a way that Sylvain alone would not. Sylvain laid all this out before Adam in a level-headed kind of way, as if the two of them had run away together, not as if their roles were that of kidnapper and victim respectively. Adam was getting used to seeing the situation from both points of view. One moment he was the imperilled abductee, the next he was the willing party to an elopement, holed up somewhere along the road to Gretna Green. Sometimes he saw both aspects simultaneously. Though when Sylvain said at one point: "We'll keep ahead of them, and if they do catch up with us we'll show them a thing or two, *non?*" he feared for his friend's grasp on reality and only answered with a noncommittal grunt.

When Sylvain had gone, Adam fetched his backpack out into the garden. As it had been packed for school, not for an overnight stay, it did not contain most of the things that might have been really useful, like a toothbrush or a change of underwear. But he did find two handy items when he rummaged through it. There was a tube of sun-protection cream, and there was a book. He rubbed the cream all over himself, even experimentally removing his shorts and applying the cool emulsion to places that had never been so treated before. He felt safe enough then to drag his cushions out from the shade into the leafy sunlight of the middle of the lawn. Then he embarked on the book. It was an old one that Céline had lent him months ago and that he had never got round to reading. Called *Les Carnets du Major William Marmaduke Thompson*, it cast a humorous eye over the differences between the British and the French takes on life. Although many of the incidental details had a dated feel about them, in most respects Adam felt that the book's author, a Monsieur Pierre Daninos, had captured his own experiences and observations to the letter, and before long he was being surprised into audible giggles of appreciative recognition. Céline must have had the book for years. Inside it, on the flyleaf, the unformed handwriting of a much younger Céline had written: *Ce livre appartient à...* followed by her full name and whole address including France and the European Union. At least the book took his mind off the perplexing knots of the predicament in which he found himself, and off the presumed agonies of his parents. He could not imagine, now that nearly twenty-four hours had passed, what he could conceivably say to them if by some magic it were suddenly to become possible to phone them.

From time to time he got up and walked over to irrigate the vegetable plots - the direct if delayed result of all the water Sylvain had forced him to drink during the morning - then he would lie down again and resume his sunbathing and his book, alternating a cheekily face-down position with an even more impertinent full-frontal. Perhaps it was just as well that he was face down when he heard the cricket start up. The insect was startlingly audible, probably because it was the hottest part of the afternoon and all the birds and frogs had fallen silent. But then it got louder, came nearer and stopped. And Adam had to look up then, realising that it was not a cricket but a bicycle.

Adam was looking into the eyes of a boy, perhaps a couple of years younger than himself, who had just pushed his bike round the corner of the farmhouse and who now stood holding it, frozen into total immobility by the sight of the naked sunbather who was lying on the grass just in front of him, and regarding him over the edge of a hardback book with equal astonishment. And thus they remained for a full minute.

He was a nice looking boy, Adam thought, although his appearance was highly unusual for one from the southern half of France. He wasn't wearing very much: just a skimpy pair of white gym-shorts like the ones Adam had recently abandoned, plimsolls with no socks, and a loose, short-sleeved green top. His skin was astonishingly white, although freckled in places, the eyes in his cheerful round face were brown, and

162

his hair was a mass of deep auburn curls like brushes made of copper wire. He had a nicely chunky pair of legs, like a gymnast's. They reminded Adam of Sean's legs, though in miniature, but were quite unlike his own, which were gradually developing the lean muscularity of a sprint runner's.

Adam considered the pros and cons of challenging him. If the boy were simply trespassing he would not know that Adam had no right to be there either. But if he had good reason to be there, then there was a strong chance he knew that Adam shouldn't be. Then it struck him, with a great lightening of the spirit, that neither of them had the right to be there. It was a Tuesday afternoon in term-time and they should both have been at school. So they could deal on an equal footing. The same thoughts must have passed through the other's mind at the same speed and led to the same conclusion, because at the same instant they each gave way to a burst of relieved laughter.

"What's your name?" Adam asked.

"Frédéric," said the boy. "What's yours?"

"I'm Adam."

"You have a funny accent."

Adam sighed. "Because I'm not French. I'm British."

"So is one of my grannies," said the boy. "She's Scottish."

That explained the complexion then. "Interesting," said Adam. "I'm only English myself - which is maybe less interesting."

"I don't see why." The boy seemed to want to be friends. He pushed his bike over the grass - tick, tick, tick - to where Adam lay, rooted by modesty to his cushions, and stood right over him. Adam had to twist his head to squint up at him. And saw with a shock that quite unwittingly the boy was displaying himself with rather less modesty. He found that he had a view, straight up one leg of his shorts, of the boy's stubby cock which peeped out over a neatly sculpted pair of accessories about the size of *mirabelle* plums. He was just sprouting his first soft growth of hair, wispy and pale as thistledown.

Quite unaware of the impression he was making on the English visitor the boy prattled on. "Where do you come from then?"

"In England? ...Oh, you wouldn't have heard of it. In France I live in Langres."

"Londres?"

"No, Langres. Sorry about my funny accent. The Plateau de Langres. Where the water comes from. And the cheese."

This clearly made sense. The boy said: "That's a long way. What are you doing here?"

Be careful, Adam told himself. Don't be put off guard by a pretty view. "Do you have television?" he asked.

"Yes," said the boy. "Why?"

"Anything about Langres on the news today? About people from Langres?"

"Don't know," said the boy innocently. "I don't watch the news."

Disappointment was mingled with Adam's relief at this. He had rather fancied being a TV news item. There were so many things he wanted to ask ... so many opportunities seemed to be presented by the boy's - what was his name? - by Frédéric's arrival. So many opportunities ... and so many dangers. He tried to put his concerns into some kind of order. "Do you have a mobile?" he asked, though there seemed to be little chance that he did have. There was hardly anywhere the scantily dressed kid could put one. Still that distracting view up his shorts. Adam could hardly think straight. Did no-one wear underpants any more?

"A mobile phone? No. Next birthday, maybe." (And when would that be? November. Did Adam need one now? No, not really. Just a passing thought.)

By way of an experiment, as if he had just coaxed a wild creature to feed from his hand and was trying a further step, Adam stretched out a hand and placed it on the boy's leg, just below the knee. Frédéric showed no sign of surprise or readiness for flight. "I suppose you're a friend of the Noirmoutiers," he said affably.

"Yes, of course." (The who?) "Well, actually, they're friends of my friend." (Frédéric looked quickly around the garden) "My friend Sylvain." Might as well give him his real name. The boy hadn't heard about them from the television, and unnecessary lies always led to complications. "He's not here. He's gone into Givry to do some shopping."

"So they've let you stay here while they're away?"

"More or less." Impossible just to leave his hand where it was for ever. He must either remove it or... He ran it quickly, experimentally, up Frédéric's smooth leg and into his shorts.

The experiment was finished as soon as begun. Frédéric stepped briskly back a pace, though only one, and said: *"Touche pas!"* Which was more or less the reaction that Adam might have expected.

"Yes," Adam continued as if nothing had happened. "They said he was to come any time and stay - and to bring me too (which was kind because they've never met me) only ... only they don't seem to be here." Adam made a pantomime of looking all around him as far as his confinement to the horizontal permitted. "I suppose you live round here,

Frédéric?" The boy nodded. "You don't happen to know where they've gone, do you? The ... Nounouliers."

"Noirmoutiers. They're in Lyon. One of their sons is marrying a girl there. A really big do, I heard. We've got all their dogs over at our place while they're away. All except the little one, that is. Pépine goes everywhere with them. I'm surprised your friend didn't know about the wedding."

"Look," said Adam. "Why don't you sit down if we're going to talk?"

"Alright," said Frédéric doubtfully. "But not if you're going to..."

"It's OK, I won't do anything. Not if you don't want me to." He stopped. He had never heard himself talk like this. Yet the words had come automatically as if he had been born to say them. Was this the way adults negotiated their way through these situations with younger people? He had never seen himself in the role of predator before. He had always been able to imagine himself as the stolen child in the Erl-king scenario, even in the role of the bereft father (careful - he mustn't think of that) but never as the Erl-king himself.

"What's the matter?" asked Frédéric. He had plonked himself down close to Adam on the grass, legs wide apart.

Damn it, thought Adam. He must have started crying again and the kid had noticed before he had realised it himself. "It's nothing," he said. "I drank too much wine last night, I think. That's the effect it has the next day, sometimes."

"*C'est vrai?*" said Frédéric in wonder. "I never knew that before."

Neither did Adam, but it was his first experience of a hangover, after all. Did they normally make you so randy and tearful by turns? "To tell you the truth, it was the first time I'd really had too much. Maybe I'm not quite myself." For a second he wanted to blurt out: *Go to the police. I'm stuck here with a madman who keeps a shotgun in his car. We both need help.* But he didn't and the moment passed.

He returned to practicalities. He needed to pee again, quite urgently, and had no idea what to do about it; the proximity of the boy, his recent attempt to grope him and his own nakedness had all conspired to give him a major hard-on which he was pressing firmly down into the cushions. Any move he made would startle Frédéric and embarrass himself. He made himself think about another practicality, one which was scarcely less pressing. "The Noirmoutiers. When are they coming back?"

"Day after tomorrow, in the afternoon. By the way, how did you and your friend get into the house?"

Adam felt suddenly as light as a bird. Here was his salvation. Grownups were coming here in two days. People who knew Sylvain. People who could explain everything to the police and to Adam's own parents and no harm done. Everything was going to be OK. Just wait till he could tell Sylvain... Though on second thoughts, maybe not. Sylvain's ideas were becoming alarmingly unpredictable. He might change his plans and decide they had to drive on somewhere else. Better to sit it out and let the Noirmoutiers' arrival come as a surprise. But anyway, everything was going to be all right. His face was alight with smiles as he remembered that the boy had asked him a question. "How? Oh yes. Sylvain has his own key. He's had it since he used to come here as a child. So he could let himself in any time." It was not only a monstrous lie, it was also highly improbable: nobody gave visiting children keys to their houses that they could then use for a lifetime. But it didn't seem to matter. The boy accepted the explanation with a trustfulness that made Adam's heart ache. "How old are you?" he asked.

"Fourteen," said Frédéric.

Just two years younger than himself. Surely he had never been so innocent, so unworldly as this boy was, and certainly not at fourteen. Then, he hadn't had his physique either, he thought with a futile twinge of jealousy. Had Frédéric stumbled on the skinny fourteen-year-old Adam trespassing in his neighbours' garden instead of the relatively mature sixteen-year-old, he could probably have beaten him up had he felt so inclined. It was a sobering thought.

It couldn't be put off any longer. "Look, you really must... I really have to..." Adam got quickly up onto his knees, twisted round away from where Frédéric was sitting, and emptied his bladder explosively onto the grass. Quick to start but it took an age to finish, and Adam felt himself turning red with embarrassment and wondered if it showed from the rear. At long, long last Adam was able to spin back round and down, rearranging himself in his original discreet position.

Frédéric's eyes looked as if they were on stalks. And not only his eyes ... as Adam observed when he glanced down at his shorts. *"Merde,"* he said in a tone of mixed alarm and envy, *"t'es gros."*

"You're not so small yourself, *P'tit-Loup.*" It was the only possible answer, wasn't it? But he was appalled to hear himself calling the boy by the endearment that Sylvain used with him. What was this kid doing to him? He wanted more than ever to reach out and catch him and then to... And then Sylvain would be coming back. At any moment. And with a shotgun. No, that last bit was a silly thought. Too Hollywood by far. But still... With a supreme effort of will he clutched at a new subject. "Look, won't you burn in this sun, with your complexion, I mean? I've got some stuff here if you want to…"

Frédéric seemed to think this was a good idea. He took the tube of sun-cream when Adam held it out to him and started to rub it into his face, legs and arms. Adam toyed with the idea of offering to do this for him but decided against. He did have time to wonder, though, as he watched the boy anointing himself, what had brought him here in the first place, cycling into his absent neighbours' garden when he should have been at school. He didn't have to wonder long. Frédéric suddenly volunteered the information without being asked. "I wanted to come here because it's quiet. I mean, I thought it would be. Instead of going to school. I do music."

"You play an instrument?"

"Yes, but I mean I write it. Well, not exactly write it. I make it up in my head."

"Sounds good," said Adam. "What sort of music."

"That's the problem. I don't know. It doesn't seem to be rock or anything like it. And it certainly isn't jazz. Maybe it's modern classical. It's really weird, anyway. And if I try and play it, nobody likes it."

"That could well be modern classical then," said Adam thoughtfully. "I know someone in Paris who writes that kind of thing. I'd give you his address if I…" He broke off. Several thoughts had struck him simultaneously.

Frédéric had finished applying the sun-cream. "Do you want me to do you too, re-do you, I mean?" He smiled cheerfully and held out the tube of cream.

"Why not?" said Adam. Oh, what the hell, he thought, and rolled over onto his back.

Frédéric seemed taken aback to see Adam still in the same state of arousal as he had been a few minutes ago. "That's indecent," he protested, gamely trying to make a joke of it, but Adam could see the tent-pole going up in the boy's shorts for a second time as he leant over Adam and started to spread the cool cream on his chest. A moment later Frédéric stopped and went rigid. A tremor ran through him and he drew in his breath, while a blush coloured up his face so deeply that you could hardly see the join between his forehead and his hair. Adam didn't need to peer at his shorts to see what had happened, though he looked there anyway. They had got quite a soaking.

Frédéric scrambled backwards, crab-like, and sat back in his old position, giving Adam a look like that of a spaniel that has been surprised by a harsh word.

"Don't worry," said Adam. "Happens to everyone. You'll dry in no time in this sun." It struck him that this had been a bit of a waste all round: the fun they might have shared, his momentary concern for the boy's innocence, his scruples on account of Sylvain... All in vain. For a moment he thought of salvaging something for himself at least, by simply grabbing hold of Frédéric, pulling his shorts off and taking it from there, but he put the idea out of his mind.

"I think I'd better go," said Frédéric flatly.

"*Ouais*, perhaps."

Frédéric got to his feet.

"Just one thing..." Adam delved into *Major Thompson* and carefully tore out the fly-leaf. Not only Céline's address was written there but also her phone number. "Could you do something for me when you get home? Ring this number. Ask for Céline and tell her I'm OK. You needn't tell her where I am. Best not to, in fact. Just that I'm alive and well and I'll be home in two days. Can you do that?"

"Yes," said Frédéric agreeably enough, taking the paper. Then, with a refreshing open-mindedness in view of what had just happened, "Is she your girlfriend?"

"*En quelque sorte,*" said Adam.

Frédéric turned, picked up his bike and pushed it across the lawn - tick, tick, tick - to the corner of the house. From there he turned back. His mood seemed to have changed for he grinned and gave a childish wave, which Adam returned. "It was nice to meet you," Adam said, as much to himself as to Frédéric. The boy disappeared round the corner of the house.

Adam got to his feet. Sylvain would be back any minute. His friend. His kidnapper. His gaoler. *Son amant, son bien-aimé.* His lover, his beloved. He would pick some flowers for his return. And as he rummaged among the borders for purple honesty and sweet-pea, and at the garden's edge for meadow-sweet and vetch, he imagined himself turning to confront the TV camera of his conscience with a half-snarl and a jabbing index finger and declaring for his own benefit and Sylvain's: "I did *not* have sexual relations with that boy."

Sylvain, on his return, was delighted with the flowers, and with the randy nakedness of the youth who presented them to him, and when Adam fished urgently into his lover's shorts in search of very rapid gratification observed uncritically: "That's hangovers for you. *Ça chauffe*. It's good to see you well again though."

It was not until after some fairly energetic activity on the lawn that Adam inspected the results of Sylvain's shopping trip. Clearly another barbecue was planned. There were Toulouse sausages and lamb cutlets, tomatoes, red and green peppers, an aubergine, three baguettes (neither of them had eaten either breakfast or lunch) garlic and onions. This time it was Adam who took it upon himself to light the barbecue and it was he who, once it was going nicely, made the suggestion, albeit tentatively: "What about opening a bottle of wine?"

"A warm air mass moving northwards from France, bringing hot sunshine but also the risk of thunderstorms later." Sean liked to hear weather forecasts like that in early summer. The promise of heat brought the real summer closer, and the possibility of a storm prevented the outlook from being too tamely predictable. The inclusion of France as the provenance of the benign weather system among the details of the forecast immediately made him think of Adam, something that he did quite often anyway. He remembered with crystalline clarity the details of all the physical intimacies they had so unexpectedly shared less than a month ago. He remembered them with a sort of fascinated incredulity, rather than with recoil or even regret. He remembered with an even greater sense of disbelief that it was he, Sean, who had set them in train, but he could no longer see - if indeed he had ever been able to see - what had led up to it, where all that intensity of feeling and emotion had come from. It was as if he had somehow created a potent magical charm but then lost the formula and also forgotten what it had been intended to achieve in the first place. It had been an extraordinary week altogether, what with Michael getting off with that French boy, Christophe, on the last evening as well. He thought, but was not sure, that the two were keeping in touch, either by letter or email.

Anyway, Adam was not too far from his thoughts this afternoon when the second lesson was interrupted by one of the school secretaries who said that the police wanted to talk to him for a few minutes as part of a routine enquiry. Sean was taken to a small dim-windowed office where difficult interviews were known to take place, interviews with difficult pupils, with difficult parents... Sean had never been in here before; his misdemeanours had always been of a run-of-the-mill nature. He had never been *difficult.*

On the way to the interview Sean had felt curiosity, a little puzzlement, but nothing like alarm. Until, turning into the corridor that led down to the interview room, he saw Michael coming out of it and turning another corner towards his own classroom. Michael hadn't seen Sean at all, and Sean didn't see Michael's face, nor had he time to call out to him. But for some reason a little fist of fear clutched momentarily at his stomach. The principal thing that he and Michael had in common was - Adam.

He was shown in. Two policemen sat behind the desk. They motioned to him to sit down, apologised for interrupting his studies and assured him that they would not detain him long. It was about... Sean waited for the name to come. He knew by now exactly who it would be about. And then the magic formula came back to him. The emotional background to what happened between them in France was restored to his consciousness like the memory of a recovered amnesiac. It was as clear as daylight why he had wanted to go to bed with Adam, why he had wanted to go to France in the first place, why he wanted Adam with him now. And he realised that anything that might conceivably happen to hurt Adam could not fail to hurt him too.

"What's happened to him?" he blurted out in a panic. "Missing? What are they doing to find him?"

"That's where we hoped you might help us," said one of the policemen avuncularly. "You were staying with him recently. Did anything strike you about him that was new, different?"

A whirlwind of memories, of feelings, swept through Sean's consciousness. Everything had been new and different, from the moment he had arrived at the bus station in Chaumont and Adam had sat next to him in the car. Or perhaps before that, when he had decided, at the crazy whim of that powerful emotion, to go to France with Michael to see Adam in the first place. He felt giddy. He looked up at the old-fashioned clock that sat on the wall above the policemen's heads, as if to draw a lesson from its example of poise and balance. He realised, as the policemen's expectant gaze intensified, that his face had reddened.

"He must have made a lot of new friends in France," prompted the policeman when the silence showed no sign of breaking. "Did you meet any of them?"

Sean was at last galvanised into speech by the realisation that he needed to be helpful, to be useful to Adam. Willingly he told the names of all the people, as far as he could remember, that he had met: Thierry, Monique, Céline, Christophe... The second policeman was nodding approvingly; he seemed to be ticking off the names on a list. Sean stopped.

"Was there anyone else?" the first policeman resumed, after a decent interval. "Anyone you heard about but didn't meet? Anyone whose existence you might have guessed at from his behaviour...? For example, a girlfriend he didn't want his parents to know about."

Sean looked dumbstruck. The policeman smiled, then said, more gently: "It's very, very usual, you know."

"Not a girl," Sean heard himself say, hoarsely. "There was a friend he had - a young man on one of the farms. We saw him but we didn't meet him."

"Interesting," said the policeman gravely. "I wonder why your friend Michael didn't tell us that."

"I've no idea," Sean mumbled.

"And how old would this man have been?"

"About twenty-one, twenty-two or so."

The policeman looked at Sean impassively for a moment or two as if he found the youth's face as informative as a well-written report. Then he leaned forward and said: "And what do you suppose the bond between the two of them might have been? I mean, between a young lad who plays the cello almost to professional standard and the relatively uncouth son of a French peasant farmer. What do you suppose?"

The clock on the wall said eleven minutes past three. Plus twenty-eight seconds. Twenty-nine... "It might have been sexual," said Sean, in a voice as thin as a thread.

"Thank you," said the policeman.

Sean left the interview room a few minutes later, weighed down with misery and foreboding. Not the least of his burdens was the fear, a fear made even harder to bear by guilt, that what he had said - had been manoeuvred by the policeman into saying - far from helping Adam in his plight, might land his friend, his lover, in even more dire trouble than whatever situation he now faced.

Adam awoke the next morning in a positive frame of mind. He had shared a bed with Sylvain for the second night running, only this time he had some memory of the experience. He had woken in the dawn and watched the early light play on the sleeping features of his lover, and remembered enjoying the same appreciation of Sean's proximity just a few weeks ago. It was still a new enough experience to contemplate with a certain awe, not something that he took for granted.

They had drunk well the previous night but more circumspectly than before, alternating glasses of water with the product of the vines around them, as they enjoyed a second balmy evening in the garden under the stars, with firelight, and their celestial chart of glow-worms in the grass beside them. Adam felt clear-headed and strong. With the return of the Noirmoutiers tomorrow, which he knew about but Sylvain still didn't, the end of this escapade was in sight. But he had hatched two plans as well, fail-safes, in case of any slips, or of Sylvain's taking it into his head to announce new intentions.

After a cup of coffee and leftover baguette which they dunked in it, Adam asked Sylvain to give him a driving lesson. In other words, allow him to drive up and down the farm track in the pick-up. Sylvain was happy to agree. He sat beside him and entered with pleasure into his new role as teacher of something he was not exactly a master of himself. He told Adam all about gear-changing and the clutch, which Adam already knew because of his occasional sessions with his father, but he was content to be patient and let himself be taught all over again. What he really needed was that practice, up and down the drive that would enable him to do the whole thing in a smooth flow: brakes, mirrors, gear-changes, steering, all at the same time. And after a little while Sylvain let him do exactly that. After another twenty minutes Adam was confidently zooming down the track, just managing to reach fourth gear before it was time to pull up smartly and do a three-point turn in the lane at the end - luckily there was little traffic - before haring back up to the farmhouse. Driving was easy, he discovered, once you had learnt to co-ordinate the footwork. Learning what you needed was the key. It was like school, like the cello, like everything else.

The driving lesson was connected with what Adam thought of as plan B. If, in the last resort, something went wrong - the Noirmoutiers didn't come, there were arguments, or Sylvain decided to re-kidnap him - he now had the final option of unaided flight by road. He felt fairly certain that it would not come to that.

Plan A was altogether simpler. He would telephone his parents that afternoon and tell them, as he had instructed Frédéric to tell Céline, that he was fine and well and coming back the next day. Then he would manage to make it look as if he had got cut off before they had gathered their wits sufficiently to ask him what the hell he had been playing at for two days. He told Sylvain he wanted to come into Givry with him in the afternoon. As Adam had anticipated, Sylvain reiterated the danger of their being seen together in the public street. And, as he had planned to, he put this proposal to Sylvain. Why should Sylvain not drop him on the edge of the town when no-one was looking? Adam could have a walk round Givry on his own (and phone his parents without Sylvain knowing: that was the whole point of the scheme) and then, when he had given Sylvain enough time to go round the supermarket, they could meet for coffee or something as if by chance. That was not the sort of behaviour that suggested either runaways (he told Sylvain) or kidnappers and their victims (he kept this thought to himself). They would then appear to split, but in fact would rendezvous later at another spot on the edge of town.

The spy-story quality of all this appealed to them both, and the more detailed their plans became the more they fell in love with them, and were reluctant to criticise them as being fraught with opportunities for things to go wrong. Sylvain found pieces of paper and a pencil hanging up in the kitchen for shopping lists and drew a rough plan of the centre of Givry. There was a place in the centre called the Lion d'Or, he said. They would meet there, when Sylvain had shopped, for a drink. What about money, Adam asked? He was told not to worry: Sylvain had plenty for the moment. And as there was only the moment to consider - the Noirmoutiers would bring it to an abrupt end tomorrow - Adam was reassured. He would not worry at all.

Lunch was cold aubergine left over from last night's barbecue and more stale baguette. It did not detain them long and they set off immediately after. Adam lay curled up on the floor of the pick-up, his head below the level of the window, in the tradition of all the best spy and gangster films. If by any chance the police stopped them, he would say he had dropped something from his pocket and was looking for it. After what seemed like a very few minutes Sylvain stamped on the brake pedal and brought the truck to one of his trademark halts. "Now," he said. "There's nobody about." And Adam opened the door just as they had arranged, slipped out of it and then crossed the road, giving Sylvain a nonchalant wave as he accelerated away into the town centre.

It took Adam a little longer than he had anticipated to get there on foot - Sylvain had adopted a very cautious definition of the edge of town - but within twenty minutes he had arrived. He spotted the Lion d'Or at once. It was no corner café but the principal hotel in the small town and with its ivy-clad walls and wood-framed conservatory, bright with white paint, it emanated genteel prosperity in a way that Adam realised, with a slight sinking feeling, he very visibly failed to match. He looked down at his crumpled gym-shorts and sockless ankles above dusty trainers. Well, it couldn't be helped. This was the place that Sylvain had said. And besides, in such a place there would be public phones. It would be less traumatic phoning his parents from the comfort of a booth in a hotel lobby than at an open-air installation in the main street under the eyes of *le tout Givry*. He gulped a couple of deep breaths at the foot of the entrance steps, then marched up them, trying not to feel like one of Dickens' waifs and strays, and went inside.

He did not have to look far to find a phone. There were two in the lobby, just in front of him, in coy little cubicles with swing doors that would have shown the heads and feet of the phone users, above and below them, had the booths been occupied. But they weren't. Adam went into one of the booths and dialled his parents' number immediately so as not to give himself time to lose his nerve. He heard the receiver lifted at the other end and then, as a thought suddenly struck him, he slammed down his own receiver as fast as if it had been a dangerous snake. Of course, the police would be monitoring his parents' phone line. A few seconds longer and they could have traced the call. The local gendarmes would be here in minutes and Sylvain would be seized as soon as he walked up the steps. Adam did not want it to end like that. He had his plan worked out. It all hinged on the Noirmoutiers, whom he had built up in his mind as towers of almost super-adult wisdom and dependability. They would sort everything out as soon as they arrived: gendarmes, parents, the lot. And then everybody could go home, stay friends, and live happily ever after. Adam walked out of the booth.

"Can I help you, *monsieur*?" asked the smartly dressed young waiter whom Adam almost walked into in his rapid exit. The *'monsieur'* was uttered in a tone of such deference that the word teetered uncomfortably on the brink of irony, while the waiter looked him up and down rather slowly, taking in the stained T-shirt and shorts, the dusty trainers and the jagged pirate teeth.

Unabashed, because the most difficult thing he had come here to do was behind him, he said that he was meeting a friend and could he wait in the bar and have a drink? For half a second the waiter looked thunderstruck but then his face broke into a smile. Perhaps inside every penguin-suited waiter there might be a youth in a grubby T-shirt trying to get out. "This way, *monsieur*," he said.

Adam was shown into the grand glass conservatory that he had seen from the outside and seated at a table which was laid, like all the others, with a white linen cloth. Around him a few of the other tables were still occupied by people finishing their lunch, mostly with large glasses of white wine at their side. No matter how you were dressed, this did not seem like the sort of place where you ordered a half of shandy. He asked for a glass of the local white wine.

One of the tables was occupied by two very elderly ladies, smartly dressed but so shrunken with age that it seemed as if the slightest draught might blow them away. They had bright little eyes and sharp, hooked noses. Like birds, Adam thought. Miniature birds of prey, perhaps, like hobby falcons or a pair of sparrow hawks. Their toes just reached the floor below the table, their heels did not. They were just finishing a main course that had been served on very large plates. Their waiter asked them something and after a beady look at each other they nodded their heads. He returned a moment later with a salver on which rested the substantial remains of an enormous joint of beef. From this he carved off further slices, one after the other, while the ladies' hook-beaked heads still

174

nodded, until at last the outstretched hand of one of them bade him desist. And then Adam's wine arrived. It came in a goblet that seemed as big and round as the world. The wine was so cool that the moisture in the air had condensed on the outside of the glass and Adam saw the pale clear liquid within like sunshine through a sea-fret. He sipped at it and thought it was like nectar. He had never tasted wine so good. All of a sudden he thought of Oscar Wilde, waiting for the end of his world at the Cadogan Hotel and drinking hock and seltzer. He had one up on poor old Oscar. Hock and seltzer could never have tasted as good as this.

Just then Sylvain arrived. If Adam's appearance had caused a ripple, Sylvain's emergence onto the scene to reinforce the gypsy-like impression he had made created a discernible wave of shock. Adam had not given a thought before to just how brief Sylvain's cut-offs were, or to the fact that his T-shirt didn't really meet them at his waist. Everything that was not concealed by them looked a splendid shade of brown. And his hair, which needed cutting, was turning, thanks to two days without the attentions of a comb, into an impressively wild and wavy black mane. He carried a bulging supermarket carrier bag from which protruded the inescapable baguette. Adam hailed him with a wave. He pointed to his wineglass. "You must try some of this."

Sylvain did. "Of course it's not champagne," he said, tasting it carefully, "or even Chablis. But you have to admit it's pretty good."

Why did people always have to tell you that one thing was not the same thing as something else, Adam wondered? But he was in far too good a humour, and far too much in love with Sylvain at that moment to find fault. At any rate Sylvain seemed to find it sufficiently good to propose that they had a second glass, and while they were waiting for it to arrive Adam was astonished to notice that the two bird-sized ladies at the nearby table had polished off their second lavish portion of beef and were being helped by the waiter to a third.

Another surprising thing happened after that. Three people strolled into the conservatory from outside: two parents and their teenage son. (It was Wednesday, so there was no afternoon school.) The son was not in shorts but in clean cotton slacks, but his flaming head of hair marked him out as different, in all probability, from everybody else in the region. Neither of his parents shared that trait; it really must have been a throwback to his Scottish roots. Adam and Frédéric looked at each other in stunned surprise for a second or two before the stately progress of his parents dragged Frédéric away to a table at the other end of the room where he would be out of Adam's sight unless he were pointedly to look round.

By the time Adam and Sylvain had finished their second enormous glass of Givry, the two small ladies had been served and had eaten a fourth portion of beef and were being asked by the waiter if they might not see their way to managing a fifth. Adam thought that the original joint might have been equivalent to their own combined weight. It was time to go. It had already been decided that Adam would leave first; he had the slower journey to make to their meeting point; Sylvain would pay the bill and leave in a few minutes. As Adam got up and turned to go he got a clear view, momentarily, of Frédéric, sandwiched between his parents, eating an elaborate ice-cream. And Frédéric saw him too. As quickly as he could he made a telephone gesture to Adam and then a thumbs-up sign that his parents missed. Adam returned the thumbs-up with a beaming, grateful smile. Then he and Sylvain enacted what they thought was quite a good pantomime of two people saying good-bye to each other and that they must meet for another drink again soon. As Adam left the conservatory he heard the two old ladies agreeing to ingest just one more plate of beef.

He felt light-headed as walked out into the sunshine and skipped rather than walked the zigzag route through the side alleys of the little town that he and Sylvain had planned together over their map on the back of the shopping list. Twenty minutes later he reached the spot on the outskirts where Sylvain had dropped him a little under two hours ago.

It was not many minutes before he saw the familiar battered pick-up rounding the bend and making its way towards him. He suffered a moment's anxiety as he strained his eyes to make out that the driver really was Sylvain. He was nagged by the thought that his call to his parents had been intercepted even in the short time the connection had been open, and it was a relief when Sylvain's face came into focus through the windscreen and he pulled up to let Adam in.

"*C'est bien passé. Ah oui, c'est bien passé,*" chuckled Sylvain once Adam had jumped into the truck and slammed the door. Adam was inclined to agree. Everything had gone without a hitch. He was particularly pleased that he had engineered the end of the adventure without putting either Sylvain or himself at risk. Céline had been contacted and she would certainly have let his parents know by now that he was safe. Then the Noirmoutiers, arriving tomorrow, would do the rest. Meanwhile there was one last evening to enjoy, frolicking naked with Sylvain out of doors in the firelight with good food (he glanced at the bulging carrier bag nestling at his feet) and good wine.

They had left the town behind them and were in open country, the vineyards around them heavily green in the mid-afternoon sun. Adam

176

guessed they were within three kilometres of their destination. He felt his cock stirring inside his shorts. Everything felt good. "Can I drive?" he asked. "It's an easy road. We're nearly there."

Sylvain looked at him, noticed the promising bulge in his shorts, which quickly triggered a copycat reaction in his own, and said: "I suppose you can." He pulled over, got out and walked round to the other side of the car while Adam slipped across the gear lever into the driver's seat. He felt comfortable and confident. Sylvain dropped into the seat beside him and slammed the door. Adam released the handbrake, let the gears engage without too much of a shock and set a course along the centre of the road towards the place that, now he knew he must leave it tomorrow, he was beginning to think of as home. The feeling of being in control of the movement of the car excited him further and he wasn't surprised to feel Sylvain fumbling at his shorts to open them and then free his pent-up member which popped up like a bottle that has been trapped under water and is suddenly released.

"Oh man, that's terrific!" he exclaimed in English, overwhelmed by the sensation: the bizarre juxtaposition of happening, situation and danger. Sylvain started to masturbate him slowly while, with the other hand, unzipping himself and extracting his own bulging erection. He felt this was the sensible way to go about things: Adam needed to keep both his own hands on the wheel.

By the time they turned up the cart-track that led to the farm Adam was squirming in his seat and taking the bumps and pot-holes in their path without slackening speed, just as he had done when learning to drive the tractor. Sylvain was working away very fast now with both hands. He wanted the climax to come while they were still moving. It did. Adam spurted suddenly over his bare thighs and a second later Sylvain gave a cry and came heavily all over his shorts.

"Oh wow," said Adam, slowing the car down to a more sedate speed. Then he giggled. "What a mess we're both in."

They turned the last bend in the track, which brought them within sight of the front door of the farmhouse. Outside it a large, dark blue car was parked. Adam gulped and braked suddenly in panic. Behind them he heard the sudden emergency brake-slam of the second gendarme vehicle that had driven up the track behind them.

The hair rose on the back of Adam's neck and he felt a strange hot sensation around his groin. He looked down momentarily, and realised to his intense horror that he was wetting himself, just as Sylvain had been in the habit of doing when they first met, three months - and a lifetime - ago.

SIXTEEN

"What happened to all the groceries?" Michael wanted to know. "All the things he'd bought for your supper that night." A typical Michael question, Adam thought. That endless curiosity about even the most trivial details. At school he'd wanted to know how the Irish peasants had cooked their potatoes in the nineteenth century. ("You must know," he'd badgered the teacher. "Boiled? With butter and salt? Baked in their jackets?" Of course the teacher had had no idea.) Now, for the first time ever it struck Adam as one of Michael's attractive qualities.

"I don't know," said Adam, echoing the hapless teacher. He plucked a blade of grass from the lawn. "Perhaps the *flics* took it home and ate it. Maybe it was returned to Sylvain's parents and a receipt signed. Maybe it was left for the Noirmoutiers as a sort of war reparation. You can imagine, it was the last thing on my mind."

The August sun flamed on their bare backs as they sprawled on the grass. Michael had only recently taken to exposing his body to the sun - he had only recently liked his own physique well enough to consider doing so - and he tended to apply the sun-cream a little heavy-handedly, both to himself and to Adam. Adam protested that he didn't need much himself, having built up a healthy colour over the summer - his skin tone almost rivalled Sylvain's as it appeared in his memory - but he protested in vain. Michael's interest in running his hands all over him was not exclusively bound up in his concern about his friend's exposure to ultra-violet light.

One of the peacocks strolled past them, trailing its incandescent plumes over the parched grass. On the top of the house a black redstart repeated his rattling song. Above, the sky was a milky but immaculate blue.

"What shall we do this afternoon?" Michael asked.

Adam shot him a questioning look. "I thought you might want to go and see Christophe, or have him over here."

"Oh, I don't know. Christophe'll keep till tomorrow, won't he? It's you I want to hear about just for the moment."

"Well then, shall we just laze about here? Or I could take you down the *vallon* and show you the springs and the path to the cliff-top in the woods. We didn't go there last time you came."

"You were afraid we'd all run into Sylvain, I think," said Michael.

"Well there's no chance of that now," said Adam, in a tone that seemed to combine flippancy with bitterness.

"You're acting very cool about it," said Michael, sounding almost disappointed. "You don't have to play all stoical with me. I'm for real."

Adam knew that Michael meant that. He didn't say anything, but he submitted uncomplainingly when Michael decided to anoint him with yet another application of sunscreen.

Michael had arrived the previous evening. Hugh had driven with Adam to meet him off the coach in Chaumont and then treated them both to a fine dinner at the Jeanne d'Arc in Langres, for reasons that had less to do with celebration than with the fact that he couldn't face tacking on the cooking of a meal for three to the end of a gruelling working day - one that had already been extended by his having to make a fifty-mile round trip in the car to pick up his son's friend.

Adam had fully expected that Hugh would consign Michael to either Gary's room or the bee room - as the two spare bedrooms had now become designated - and that the idea of his sharing Adam's bedroom would be met with a frown at the very least. Yet when they arrived Hugh cheerfully sent Michael up the stairs to Adam's bedroom. After all that everyone had been through, and despite everything that Hugh had learnt about his son in the last two months, he seemed - unbelievably (wilfully?) - blind to the possibility that his sixteen-year-old son, homosexual by his own admission, and recently involved with such dire consequences with a man of twenty-three, might be sexually involved with another sixteen-year-old, his best friend Michael. Or had he seen the situation clearly, and decided that it and the blind eye he was going to turn to it were the least of possible evils? At all events he gave them their privacy together as soon as goodnights had been said.

By unspoken agreement they had left the telling of Adam's tale until the following day. Michael sensed quite keenly that Adam needed him in other, deeper ways right then than just as someone to unburden himself to. And not just for sex either, though that came into it. First and foremost he needed holding, and Michael was only too happy to oblige as soon as they were alone. They both came twice, though, within a short time of snuggling up in bed together: it was Adam's first sexual contact since his shipwreck; for the first three weeks he hadn't even played with himself - something which, for all his mental anguish, he had found a moment to note dispassionately as an all-time record.

At one point during the night Michael woke up to hear Adam quietly sobbing. He whispered: "It's all right. I'm here." But Adam gave no indication of having heard and Michael concluded that he was crying in his sleep. Although Michael knew about Adam's crisis and his stay in the *maison de repos*, this was the first tangible sign of the hurt he had suffered. Michael had stroked his hair softly until he fell back into sleep himself.

Michael's knowledge of the events of the past two months was patchy. During the evening of that alarming day back in June when the police had interviewed both him and Sean, a female officer had paid a visit to his parents' home - and to Sean's too, obviously - to say that Adam had been found safe and well. What happened to the man in the case (as the policewoman insisted on calling Sylvain) would depend on whether Adam's parents decided to press charges with the French authorities. In any case the British police were no longer concerned in the matter. For further information Michael would have to contact his friend direct. Michael felt unable to do anything that evening, not even to telephone Sean from his parents' house. (Parents could pick up vibes from phone-calls even when they didn't hear the words and were quite capable of asking unnecessary and awkward questions afterwards in a way that they would never dream of doing with a stranger.) So he had to wait in a state of great agitation until school the following morning gave him the opportunity to confer with Sean face to face.

They both balked at the idea of phoning Adam cold and having to deal with his parents at the other end, whether Adam was actually at home by now or not. He had been found, the policewoman had told Sean, in an empty farmhouse in the Burgundy region, well south of Langres. Michael had forgotten to ask her about where Adam had been found. It all sounded awful.

It was Sean who suggested finding out what they could from Christophe. That evening Michael sent a discretely worded email to his parents' house. So cryptic was it that it would have made the most secretive of secret agents proud. Then it was a week before Christophe replied - by letter. Who said that electronic communications would transform the speed of everything? Christophe wrote that everything was very awkward and that it was difficult to find anything out. Adam had not returned to school and there seemed to be a conspiracy between everyone over the age of thirty not to divulge any information to anyone under about twenty-five. Céline had had an extraordinary phone message from a child near Chalon-sur Saône, which she had communicated to Adam's parents while her own father had contacted the police. Everyone at school had been scanning the newspapers and the radio stations, even to the extent of hunting down copies of the local newspapers from the Saône-et-Loire, but there was no mention of the case anywhere. Rumour - there was nothing else to go on - had it that Adam had been kidnapped

180

by a member of one of the more primitive farming families of the plateau region, motive unclear. (*Mais moi, je le sais bien,* wrote Christophe. *Tu m'as parlé une fois de sa petite affaire de coeur. Ça reste, quand-même, notre secret.*) There had been no sign of Adam's parents in the town, and if Christophe's or Céline's or anyone else's parents had been in touch with them, well, they still weren't saying anything. Did Adam know, *à propos*, that Céline's father was a judge? Christophe finished by adding that if Adam's troubles should by any chance bring Michael back to France to see him then he, Christophe, would be delighted and some good would have come out of the affair after all.

Michael and Sean pored over this letter together and wondered what to do next. In the end they each wrote a letter to Adam assuring him of their friendship and support and asking him to give them some news about himself as soon as he was able. They put both letters in the same envelope and entrusted them to the post.

A few days later a letter had come back, but not from Adam. It was an update of the situation from Christophe. Michael (and Sean) would want to know - though it would upset them, of course - that Adam had had some kind of a breakdown and was in a *maison de repos* in the depths of the country near Auberive. The address had been given out to his class at school and Christophe had copied it into this letter for his English friends. He had also heard, thanks to conversations reported back from younger kids on one of the school buses, that a member of the Maury family who lived near Courcelles, a young man called Sylvain, was on *garde à vue* in Chalon-sur-Saône. Michael and Sean could work out roughly what a *maison de repos* might be - it was alarming enough however you tried to render it in English - but they drew a blank with *garde à vue* and had to ask their French teacher. Apparently it meant *in custody on remand.*

Again they wrote a letter to Adam, more or less a repeat of the first one, but addressed care of the *maison de repos.* They had looked up Auberive on the map. It was not far from Langres, just across the plateau from Courcelles-en-Montagne. Again no reply was forthcoming, and a week later the English school term came to an end. Then out of the blue Sean had received a phone-call from Céline.

Adam wanted him and Michael to know, she said, that he was OK. He'd had their letters but didn't feel he knew what to say in reply, in writing at any rate. He'd had some trouble saying anything to anyone for a while, actually, she explained. But that seemed to be getting better. She had been over to see him in his *maison de repos*: she'd been so fed-up with the conspiracy of silence that was being maintained by everybody else. The good news was that he would be coming out in a few days and might be going back to England a week after that. The bad news was that it seemed as if his parents were splitting up.

Sean nearly dropped the phone. "What?" he couldn't help saying. "They choose this moment of all…" Words failed him. He reported all this back to Michael in the course of a private phone-call from his bedroom later.

"Shit," said Michael. "That means he'll be coming back right in the middle of my holiday with my parents. I won't be here."

"Then I promise to look after him for the two of us," Sean had said.

There was no getting out of the family holiday. Michael and his parents were alike conscious that this might be the last time he would want to join them on one, which gave an additional static charge to this year's expedition to Greece. But when the sunburnt Michael came back to England at the end of July he was astonished to learn from Sean that Adam had only stayed in England ten days before returning again to France. "To be with his father," Sean had said. "They're packing up the house there before coming back to England for good. Adam thought he could be useful there." Sean paused for a moment and looked Michael steadily in the eye. "He wanted me to go back with him. I'd have liked to, only … I have to go away with my parents in two days' time." Sean was in the same boat as Michael had been: this would probably be the last family holiday all together before he flew the nest. "So he wants you to go, if you can, instead." Sean could not quite eliminate traces of jealousy and disappointment from his voice as he struggled to deliver this message in a neutral tone.

Michael was silent for a moment as he thought this through. Then: "When?" he asked.

"Next week if it's possible. He said you can ring him."

"Good," said Michael, and produced a brand new mobile phone from his pocket with a flourish.

"Hmm," said Sean, who did not have one yet. "I'm not sure if they all work cross-Channel."

"This one does," said Michael infuriatingly. "Anyway, what about his mother?" he wanted to know.

"Staying here in England. I saw her the other day. You can call on her if you want." Michael said he would think about it. "She's become very different," Sean went on. "Very changed."

"Developed, maybe," Michael said under his breath, and to Sean: "In what way?"

"Well, you know, difficult to say. You'll have to see for yourself." And that became the keynote to all of Sean's answers to Michael's many questions about Adam. Sean's accounts of Adam's present state and

182

what had happened to him were disjointed and difficult for Michael to interpret. Michael found this very frustrating. Sean had met Adam, had spent time with him, during the last two weeks but was able to tell Michael almost nothing, except for something about a mysterious scar on his hand, that he hadn't already gleaned from Christophe's letters. Michael put this reserve, or evasiveness, down to the fact that Sean's relationship with Adam had become complex, not to say weird, during their stay on the plateau and he guessed that Adam's reappearance in Sean's life had made things more complicated rather than less so. Whatever had happened between the two of them during his own absence in Greece he was clearly not going to hear about it from Sean. So he had set about making arrangements to travel to France again, speaking to Adam on the phone and borrowing the money for the coach fare from his parents.

"I came through Folkestone and Boulogne this time," Michael told Adam when they met. "On the Sea-Cat. They have these three tugs in Boulogne harbour, called *Trapu, Costaud* and *Rable.* I translated them as Hunky, Chunky and Butch. You, me and Sean, perhaps?"

"Uh-huh," said Adam. "But then which one of us is which?"

Now that Michael had arrived in Courcelles, he realised that Sean's unsatisfactory account of things was not entirely due to evasiveness on his part. Adam's own recollections of those first few days after the arrest of Sylvain were patchy. Michael began to realise that parts of what he had been through were too painful not only to share with others but even to bring to mind himself.

Adam remembered the drive home from the gendarmerie at Givry in his father's car. He had been given the OK after a cursory inspection by the police doctor who had initially bandaged his hand. He remembered some of his tight-lipped, brittle exchanges with his father, their two pairs of eyes focused firmly on the road ahead, not meeting each other's.

"It's not that I can't accept that you're gay, Adam," Hugh had said. "To tell you the truth, it occasionally crossed my mind that perhaps you were - simply because you didn't have girlfriends or talk about girls in the way that I did at your age, no other reason. I'd always told myself that if that did turn out to be the case I'd give you all the support you needed. But at the same time I wasn't really expecting it. I suppose I just didn't want it to be true. So, forgive me, but it has been a bit of a shock, especially all happening like this. And you're turning out such a handsome, muscular boy. You could have any girl you wanted. I suppose you know that?"

"That isn't the point," said Adam. "You really don't understand. Being able to attract girls or not doesn't come into it. It's not like ... like second best."

"Well, all right," said Hugh. "But what really disappoints me is your lack of judgement, your lack of nous in handling the situation. A farm-worker in his twenties makes an approach to you. You were perfectly capable of saying no at the outset. But his parents tell the police that this has been going on for months under all our noses. You were a fool to get involved. You must have seen no good would come of it." The late dusk of midsummer was falling and Hugh switched on the car's lights.

"He didn't make the approach," said Adam.

His father turned his head for a second to look at him. "Are you saying that you began it?" he asked incredulously.

"Yes," Adam began combatively but then conceded: "I don't know who began it. Who ever knows who begins these things?"

Hugh was silent and thoughtful for a while. Then he said: "I think it would be better if your mother didn't know you were ... how shall I say ... a willing victim in any way. I think she needs to feel..."

"I know," said Adam. "I know what she needs to feel."

Adam could not remember, or could not bring himself to remember, his reunion with his mother. That memory was blotted out by another one. In the church he had gone to in England, when he was small, had hung the usual depictions of the fourteen Stations of the Cross, the Via Dolorosa. In that particular church they consisted of rather realistic wood-carvings, their legends chiselled into a wooden scroll beneath each one. Their usual seat was next to Station Four: the carving was one of the most lifelike and poignant of the set; it had always pained Adam to contemplate it as a child; its caption was: Jesus Meets His Afflicted Mother. This was the memory that had to stand in for any recollection of that evening return home. His last memory of that day was of being in the dark warmth of his bedroom at last, and alone in that darkness that is one of childhood's oldest memories, alike comforting and threatening in its oppressive safety.

It was when he got up the next morning that it became apparent both to him and to his parents that he had lost the capacity to speak. Either he could not, or he didn't want to, say anything. He did not know himself which of the two was the case and in fact the distinction between the two possible explanations for his silence seemed a pointless, academic one since the result was the same. He could remember shutting himself in his room, refusing meals. He remembered the doctor arriving, remembered the trip to the hospital later that day, the lengthy, fruitless, physical examination, the return home.

Next came the visit of a psychiatrist, arranged by the school. This went a little better. Adam found himself willing and able to nod and shake his head in reply to questions. He remembered that the questions seemed rather sensible, practical ones at the time, but what they actually were he had no recollection now, nearly two months later. He did remember lying awake in bed on one of those first nights, hearing his parents talking in the kitchen directly below. They had never stayed talking in the kitchen after he had gone to bed before, they had always used the big living-room, and so neither they nor Adam had discovered how clearly the sound carried up through the kitchen ceiling into the bedroom above. Shreds of their conversations - or recriminations - were wafted up to him. His mother's voice: "If I'd brought him up a strict Catholic as I was supposed to do, instead of going along with you, none of this..." His father's voice, striving to master the situation, telling her to calm down. His mother, recounting a dream she'd had: she'd seen Adam, just his body, very white in the darkness, and then an arm went round his naked shoulder; she'd been comforted to know he had a friend, that he was loved; but then she'd seen how dark the arm appeared against his white skin and she'd looked more closely, looked for the face that went with the arm; she'd seen it and, with a shock, saw that it was the Devil.

All this Adam had heard, thanks to his parents' acoustic miscalculation, and remembered hearing. He remembered how unstoppably, night after night, the tears had coursed down his cheeks.

The school was lucky in its choice of psychiatrist and so, therefore, was Adam. He had had the wit to see that the boy's parents were not only a major part of his speech problem but also the main obstacle to its resolution and Adam's general recovery. It was he who proposed the stay in the *maison de repos*.

Adam was taken off towards Auberive in a car by a volunteer driver. It was a pleasantly anonymous situation, and Adam found it quite nice to be chatted to about the rotation of the crops and EU agricultural policy without being expected to make any sort of reply. He felt that the cure was beginning to take effect already. Perhaps he was right.

Nor was there anything very terrible about the place at which he found himself deposited. It was an old country house in Second Empire style. He had a room to himself; there were communal areas full of air, daylight and newspapers to sit around in with the other, mostly elderly, inmates, and gardens and grounds to explore. The food was surprisingly good and he was even allowed to sunbathe. In no time at all the days had joined together to make a week and then two. His hand was healing well. He found that he was taking a holiday from his emotions; all his feelings were on hold. He didn't feel particularly happy, but neither was he any longer in that wretched state of being that had been his during the few days between the disaster with Sylvain and his coming here. He no longer cried before going to sleep at night, although when, once or twice, he awoke in the middle of the night, he would notice that the pillow was wet. His unconscious, he presumed, was quite busy being miserable for him as if by proxy.

He was intrigued by the nurses and other women who ran the place. Their calm, their placid smiles, their ... what? ... their *fearlessness* in the face of illness, dementia and who knew what else that surrounded them daily. Their quiet preoccupation with cleanliness. The floors, where they were of tile or bare wood, were always in the process of being polished and this was done by one or other of the older women strapping elasticated polishing cloths to the soles of their feet and then slowly skating up and down. It looked a most relaxing pastime and Adam decided that as soon as he was able to formulate the question he would ask to be allowed to try it himself. It was only on about the third day that the penny dropped and he realised that these women who each wore a uniform, knee-length, tartan skirt were actually a community of nuns, members of a nursing order. He felt stupid for not having tumbled to this before. Yet they never asked him about his religion or suggested he might like to visit the chapel on a Sunday. For that he blessed them.

Letters began to come for him. From his parents, short (on the psychiatrist's advice?) but full of love. From his French schoolfriends. There was a card from Gary Blake. 'Get well, pirate captain,' its brief message ran, 'and look life in the eye again as soon as you can.' He liked that. Then there were two each from Michael and Sean. Sean's second letter had ended: 'With Love'. Capital W, capital L. He read the valediction over and over, running his finger along the words as if trying to feel the indentation made by the biro. It was wonderful. He would keep the letter for ever. (And he did.) Michael had signed off his letters with the same words and the same capital letters, but somehow that didn't have the same impact: it was simply what Adam would have expected from him.

Then one day, smelling the cleaning going on around him, he said "polish" to himself, but quite loudly. This elicited nods and smiles of approval all round so he said "tair" and "chable", which did not go down quite so well. But by lunchtime French words had surfaced too, and by the evening he was chatting away to his carers as merrily as a cricket.

His parents arrived the next day. They saw him first together and then separately in his sun-filled room. Jennifer took his two hands into hers and looked into his eyes. "The past is over and finished," she said. "We never need to talk about it or even think about it again. We're turning a new page. Full of promise and opportunity." She had prepared her speech carefully, Adam thought. He noticed she had been careful not to say: *turning over a new leaf.* "Now I'm going to ask you something. When you come home, which won't be long now, will you start coming to mass with me again on Sundays?"

The torments of the last three weeks had aged her visibly, had added new lines to her face and put an altered look in her eye, had even - though perhaps Adam imagined this - accelerated the greying of her hair. For the first time ever he saw in her face the form of the old woman she would one day become. He had caused that change. He alone. No-one else. Coming back from his vanished childhood there flashed into his mind the words from the Good Friday meditation on the Stations of the Cross that was interlayered between the verses of the Stabat Mater: *It is not Pilate but my sins have nailed thee to this tree.* He threw his arms around his mother's neck and wept. Of course he would go to church with her if that was what she wanted.

A little later he was alone with his father. "Now that term is over, your mother's teaching work here has finished. The company needs me for another three weeks or so to finish the project on the dam. She wants to go on ahead to England. To get the old house shipshape again. She'd like you to go with her and help..."

"Dad," interrupted Adam. "You and Mummy aren't..."

Hugh stopped him with that elder statesman look that only Adam could ever see. "We aren't crossing any bridges. If your mother wants you to go with her, then that's what I want too. OK?"

"Yes, but... There'll be a court case, won't there? I'll have to be there, won't I? To give evidence ... or something?" It was not only the first time this had been mentioned, it was the first time Adam had even formulated the thought for himself.

"You're not to think about that," Hugh told him. "It's all being sorted out by Céline's father. You won't have to do anything or go anywhere. You're to forget all about it."

"But Dad..."

"Not today." The elder statesman look again. "We've more important things to think about. Got to get you better." He smiled. "But it's lovely to hear you talk. Even to hear you argue with me." Adam thought he saw his father's eyes glisten.

The following day Céline had come, which delighted Adam. She had driven herself, though in her boyfriend's car. He had gone for a walk in the grounds while she came in to see him. "It's absurd the way they carry on," she said, "as if you're going to be bruised by the smallest piece of real-world information. And all I know is what I've overheard Papa saying on the telephone. Apparently, it's all going to be done in the speediest possible way and with minimum publicity and fuss. That means a *Tribunal Correctionnel*. Sylvain will be dealt with quite lightly; your parents don't want to press charges; it'll all hinge on the question of his mental health. They'll say he's very sick and he'll be sent somewhere for treatment. No further action to be taken, provided he never tries to contact you again. You won't even have to appear."

"But..."

Céline frowned faintly. "Well," she asked him gently, reasonably, "how would you prefer it to turn out? What do *you* want?"

"I don't know what I want," he said. "That's the problem. I only know what *he* wants."

Adam was out of the *maison de repos* a few days later and back in England with Jennifer and his cello a few days after that. They went by train to Paris and then took the Eurostar, under the sea - which was a first for Adam.

He was looking forward to being able to talk to Michael and phoned his parents' house as soon as he arrived. But he got no answer. He then called Sean, who told him Michael's whole family had left for Greece the previous day. "But I am here," he said. That was Sean. Sean who had written: 'With Love' (capital W, capital L). Adam went to his house that very day. He had never been there before. Sean opened the door to him, dressed in a light blue T-shirt and cream shorts. Again that assault on his senses, that belt of pheromones or something, like an electric shock, that always went with a meeting with Sean, and that Adam had half-forgotten. Those blue eyes, like the cornflowers, like the sky. After some hesitation they went up to Sean's bedroom and played a computer game. It seemed to both of them a weird, surreal thing to be doing. Then Adam said: "I love you, Sean," and pushed him playfully backwards on the bed. Sean offered no resistance but he didn't enfold Adam in his arms either, and the serious look on his face made Adam hesitate rather than make that particular move himself.

"And I love you too," Sean said, almost sadly. "But so does this guy, Sylvain, doesn't he? Or maybe he doesn't count any more."

"That's not true," Adam protested loudly, horrified.

Sean ignored this. "And then what about Michael?" he went on. "What's the picture between you and him? So much loving, so much seriousness, so many people. It's not kids' stuff any more when somebody has to end up in prison."

"Don't, Sean. Don't go on."

Sean did take him in his arms at that point and said, "I'm sorry," but Adam understood that the gesture was a comforting one only: it was not intended to be passionate or romantic. Still, Adam had not lost his opportunistic sense. He had a fairly major hard-on in his shorts - his first for quite some time - and he pushed it experimentally into Sean's crotch. He was encouraged by the discovery that Sean was sporting something similar, but then Sean said quietly: "Not now. Not here."

(Not here, Sean? Then where? Christ, man, this is your bedroom! We're lying together, just with shorts on, on your bed!) Adam did not actually say this. He said: "But some time, somewhere, maybe?"

"Maybe," Sean said, his voice now little more than a whisper in Adam's ear. Then: "Sometimes I think you forget I'm just a confused teenager like you. You don't seem to know what you want or who. Well, maybe you need to realise it's just the same for me. But I've never told you anything that wasn't true. Not about love, not about anything. Remember that."

A few days later Sean rang Adam and they met again. Adam had found the experience of living with his newly religious mother rather harder to manage than he had anticipated. Even with the best will in the world, he thought, a couple of weeks entirely alone with her, without the balancing presence of his father, was as much as he could manage at a stretch. It was all very well going to church with her on Sundays but when, a few days after their arrival, she invited the parish priest round for coffee and he, a rotund and florid Irishman, had interrogated Adam for half an hour about his school work and leisure pursuits, he felt that enough was enough. "I'm going back to France," he told Sean. "My mother's said I can. And I want you to come with me."

Sean was surprised to hear of such an abrupt departure but delighted and flattered to be asked along, and he showed his feelings by hugging Adam even though they were taking a walk through the middle of the park at the time. But he said: "Oh shit, Adam," and had to explain about his forthcoming family holiday. Adam had chosen, in retrospect, to put an optimistic gloss on their previous conversation. It had left one potential doorway into the future fractionally open, he had thought, which was better than entirely closed. But Sean's news about his holiday arrangement seemed to imply that fate was trying to tug the portal shut. They walked in the sun and sat and ate ice-creams and talked of other things: the possible break-up of Hugh and Jennifer's marriage, the advisability or otherwise of Adam's giving evidence at Sylvain's

Tribunal Correctionnel, and Adam was surprised to find their discussions more, not less enjoyable, for the omission from them of any mention of love or sex. At one point Adam caught Sean staring at his hand; it wasn't bandaged now. But Sean looked up again when he saw that Adam noticed and said simply: "Have you started up the cello again?"

"Just in the last few days."

"I'm glad," said Sean. He smiled, then pulled Adam's head towards him and kissed his forehead, despite the families all around them at the outdoor tables, eating ice-creams in the park.

It was when they parted that afternoon that Adam asked Sean to deliver his message to Michael when he returned from Greece. Would Michael come to France in Sean's place? And Sean agreed a little sadly to be the messenger, and wondered if the road he had travelled a short way down with Adam had finally reached its end.

SEVENTEEN

Michael was acutely conscious that it was the merest chance - Sean's parents' choice of a holiday date - that had resulted in him being here in France rather than Sean. And he was sensitive enough to realise that Adam was sharing something very personal with him in taking him for that afternoon walk into the *vallon*, the place that - Adam rather carefully explained - had been his and Sylvain's private domain back in the spring and the backdrop to the flowering of their relationship. Not that Adam used those actual words.

Summer was well advanced; most colours were gone except - in the shadier places - for rampant green. Tall seed-heads nodded on either side of them and had to be brushed away where they encroached upon the path. The springs were merely trickles feeding the mossy limestone basins, and the boggy patch across which lay the sleeper path of logs was nearly dry. They followed the path on up, then down a bit, then up again to the grassy clearing on the jutting spur, to the place where the brief length of wooden fence stopped you from missing the U-turn in the path and disappearing over the cliff edge: the spot where he had first made love with Sylvain. Adam didn't tell Michael this; he didn't need to. The opportunity that the spot presented was as clear to him as day.

The two of them stood on the lowest rung of the guard-fence and looked out over the woods beneath. They did what Adam had thought of doing - but had not had time for - on his first visit with Sylvain, and pissed together over the edge, seeing who could spray the furthest and watching their twin arcs rain down upon the treetops below, finishing with little spurts and splashes of diminishing force. Neither of them suggested having sex. In this place, at this time, it would have seemed in bad taste to both of them. Their cocks remained unstiffening, indifferent; they looked briefly without touching, then stowed away and chastely re-zipped.

"The bit you've left out, of course," said Michael, as they strolled back the way they had just come, "is what exactly happened during the arrest. I did ask Sean but he said you hadn't told him either." Michael shot Adam a sidelong look. "Of course I don't know if that was true."

"It was," said Adam. "I think I hid the memory even from myself for quite some time."

"Do you want to tell me now?"

Adam looked around, then led them to an apron-sized patch of grass and sat down, patting the ground beside him. Michael joined him. Adam held up his left hand and pointed to it with the fingers of the other one. Near the outside edge of the palm, below the root of the little finger, there was a sizeable scar.

"I noticed that," said Michael. "So did Sean."

"It all happened very fast. Sylvain threw open the car door almost before we'd stopped. He'd grabbed the shotgun from behind the seat and was out of the car before I'd realised. But I was pretty quick then too. I was out of the car on his side - I don't know how I got there so fast - the gun was halfway to his shoulder, the gendarmes were out of their car now too, and right behind us. It would have been point-blank range. I rugby-tackled him, no time for thinking, then both guns went off together."

"Both guns?"

"The shotgun fired into the ground as we came down and the gendarme's bullet went whistling over our heads. That's when I got bitten. And he wouldn't let go. I didn't know ... I never thought ... perhaps I ought to have guessed that on top of everything else he was epileptic too. I'd heard his mother once talking about his various medicines but never took it in. He recovered just as the *flics* were trying to wrestle him away and that's when he let go my hand. They often don't remember what happens during their attacks - epileptics, I mean, not the *flics* - so he didn't realise what was going on. He just looked at me and said - and this was the thing that hurt me, not the biting - *'Tu m'aimes pas'*. Then they bundled him away."

"Wow." And Michael shook his head, for once unable to come out with a better crafted rejoinder.

"He'd been on all sorts of different medications, I don't know what they were. He'd been on them for years. But for the last three days we were together, and for a few days before that, he hadn't been taking them. I didn't know any of that at the time, only when Céline told me three weeks later. That made a number of things fall into place. It explained why he seemed more together in some ways, driving, cooking, looking after me when I was sick..."

"But more liable to go to pieces when he thought he was under pressure. I see."

"When he saw the police, then everything just seemed to fall apart. Once we were inside the police station - and we were taken in separate vehicles and not allowed to see each other after we got there - they were determined to treat him as the criminal and me as the victim. I must have blanked out a lot that happened but I remember going on and on about

192

that: that it wasn't true the way they saw the situation. That we were in it together…"

"Well, that was hardly true," objected Michael. "You didn't plan to abduct yourself. It sounds as if you both went a little crazy."

"Well, anyway," said Adam, "it didn't do any good, whatever I said. They bandaged up my hand before they let me go home with my father. I can remember looking at the bandage in the car."

"And playing the cello? One has to ask."

"Will not be a problem. Sean asked that, too. I started practising again when I went to England. The wound wasn't in such a vital place, although it seemed to go quite deep. And it's healed very well already. I don't remember it hurting much at the time even. There were too many other things to think about."

"Yes," said Michael. "*You don't love me* is a phrase calculated to induce the extremest state of shock in anyone."

Adam caught his friend round the head with an arm and pretended to wrestle with him. Michael shook himself free. "Did you love him?"

Adam was thoughtful for a second, then he said: "I was in love with him and he was with me."

"Well, at least you've had that experience." Michael sounded a little jealous.

"Yes, but is that love?" Adam asked, suddenly, urgently. "Is being in love the same as love? Do you understand me?"

"I think I do."

"Well then, is it?"

"Why am I the expert all of a sudden?" Michael asked. "It's you that's had all these experiences, not me. You know, with Sylvain, with Sean…"

Adam opened his mouth to say something but Michael stopped him. "I know you've always treasured the things between you and Sean, in a way you never have with me. Don't try to deny it out of politeness. And for some mad reason he feels something of the same for you." Michael pulled a seeding grass head and began detaching the seeds with little spiky movements. "I don't know if falling in love, and being in love, and loving someone are all part of the same thing or something different. I know they're not the same as sex at least. I don't have that confusion."

Adam was unsure if the last remark was a barbed one aimed at him but he let it go unchallenged. He didn't want a re-run of their argument about change and develop. "Well then," he said. "What is love? Adults seem to think it's something that nobody can comprehend or experience until they're about forty. Which would be a bit sad. Make being young a bit of a waste of time. What do you think love is?"

Michael looked awkward for a moment. "Oh I don't know," he said. "But maybe, maybe love should be a kind of journey." He stopped abruptly and looked down at the ground between his legs.

Adam looked at him closely, trying to guess his thoughts, suddenly curious about his old friend in a new way. "Come on," he said. "Let's walk on a bit."

"And what about the tribunal?" Michael asked some time later, as they were walking back through the village to the house. "Where and when's all that?"

"I'm not supposed to know anything about it," Adam told him. "But I do, of course. Céline keeps me up to date with what she knows. It's due to be held in Chalon, or maybe Macon, any day now. The outcome seems to be all fixed too. Sylvain gets sent to a psychiatric institution until he's better..."

"Until he forgets about you, you mean. Sorry to be brutal."

"He's supposed to not contact me, that's all. I don't think forgetting is actually part of the deal. And Céline says it might only be a matter of a few weeks. It's a sort of symbolic gesture. Justice being seen to be done. Though not seen by me. I'm not expected - they don't want me - to be there at the tribunal, so the date's kept under wraps."

"And how do you feel about that?"

"Pretty gutted," Adam said. Then: "Look, enough of that." Even the most self-absorbed of people get tired of talking about themselves eventually and Adam wasn't really one of those. "We'll give Christophe a ring as soon as we get back in. Fix up to meet some time tomorrow." He knew that Michael would wag his tail at this.

But the call to Christophe had to take second priority. A message from Céline waited on the answer-phone. Would Adam ring her back? When he did she told him of a change of plan. The venue for the *Tribunal Correctionnel* had changed. It would be held much nearer home: in Chaumont, half an hour away. The date was two days hence. Céline even knew the time.

"That settles it," said Adam to Michael after putting down the phone. "We're going."

Michael was dubious. "To do what, exactly?"

"I don't know," said Adam. "But it seems like destiny, don't you think? Or God, or fate?"

"Or Adam," Michael said.

***

194

There were five more days before they would all return to England. Most of the family's remaining belongings were boxed up, awaiting the next meandering Pickfords lorry that trundled its way up onto the plateau. On the day of departure Hugh would drive alone to Calais with the car packed to the gunwales with the necessities of existence (this plan had been worked out when Adam was not expected to be here in France at all) while Adam (now that he *was* here) would go back on the bus and ferry with Michael. It was the only practical way to transport his cello.

Having gone back with Adam to England a fortnight ago the cello had returned to France with him ten days later. Since rejoining his father here Adam had taken to playing it out in the garden in the late evening in emulation of Beatrice Harrison. He felt he was entitled now to a certain degree of eccentricity and his father did not try to stop him. He had discovered to his surprise, when he asked his mother to let him come back to his father in France and she had let him, that recent events had given him a new power over his parents. He could stamp his foot, say what he wanted, and get his own way: something which had never been allowed to happen before. This new power did not extend to the nightingales on the other hand; none joined in his al fresco music making; but he found a wonderful and surprising peace out on the lawn under the all-seeing sky in the thickening dusk.

"You're really weird, man," said Michael, when Adam had treated him to two or three of the easier movements among the Bach unaccompanied suites while Michael brushed away moths and flying beetles. "But I think I like you weird. I wouldn't like you any other way."

That night as they lay snuggled together in bed they were both surprised to discover a new tenderness growing up between them, and the sex that they enjoyed together, which up to now had served a predominately functional purpose, seemed to be developing into something else.

Next day they spent with Christophe, who came panting up from the lakeside on his bike. It didn't have to be spelled out to anyone that Adam's house, with his father out all day at work, made the more attractive venue for their reunion. And in fact it was Michael and Christophe who spent most of the day together. Adam surprised himself by his broadminded lack of jealousy, leaving them in peace in the remoter corners of the garden while he practised the cello and put his mind to fine-tuning the details of his plan for the morrow.

It was Hugh's last day on the dam project. There was packing up to do there too plus a final meeting which they called a *bilan*. He was far too preoccupied to question the two boys when they told him they wanted to spend the day in Langres. He even drove them into town. But as soon as they got there they made a beeline for the bus station and took the first bus out to Chaumont where they killed time until the early afternoon.

It wasn't difficult to find the *Palais de Justice*. They took from their pockets the ties they had kept hidden there so as not to unleash astonished questions from Hugh, and put them on while still on the opposite side of the street. Needless to say they had dressed in long trousers rather than their usual summer shorts. Then, taking courage from the memory of his bold entry into the Lion d'Or in Givry two months earlier, when he was much less smartly dressed, Adam took a deep breath and led the way up the steps.

No sooner had they arrived in the entrance hall than they came face to face with someone Adam knew: they had met once or twice at school and teenage parties. It was Céline's father and he recognised Adam too. He stood, broad-shouldered in the foyer, seeming almost to block their way, though that was an impression only; the space around them was open and wide. He wore a dark suit, immaculately pressed, and its knife-edge creases made him look somehow as if he were wearing armour like a medieval knight. "Good afternoon," he said in English. "I wonder what brings you here." He smiled a little reluctantly. "Though I fear that I already know." Still in faultless English he asked to be presented to Adam's friend, and shook Michael's hand with the suggestion of a formal bow.

"Are you one of the judges in Sylvain's case?" Adam blurted out, his carefully thought-out plan blown off-course by surprise.

"No, my friend, I'm not. Though for the best possible reason. Although I don't know the young man myself I do know you. It's never enough in life - at least in my profession - to have clean hands. You have to be ready at any moment to hold them up for inspection too. And that is why - although I'm very pleased to see you, Adam - the pleasure is a little reduced by the fact of its being here. Why did you come?"

"I felt I had to." Adam was still determined to hold his own.

"But to do what, precisely? You're not being treated as a victim. I know you didn't want that, for Sylvain's sake. So that's good, aren't I right? And you're not called as a witness." He lowered his voice. "It's all been looked after very carefully. We, all of us, are on your side. And not against Sylvain, do you understand? But there is a law of the land in France. And all we can do is minimise its severity. With the best will in the world we cannot magic it away. But what we *can* do we can do better without you there. Trust me." He stopped and smiled. "You're not planning to shout obscenities from the public gallery, are you?"

This scenario had actually featured on some of Adam's lists of strategies, especially the ones he'd thought of late the night before. Somehow it didn't seem a very intelligent option now. He smiled a little wanly and said, "No. No, sir."

"I'm driving back to Langres in fifteen minutes," Céline's father said. "Will you do me the honour of accepting a ride?"

There was no argument. Adam had been conclusively if chivalrously toppled from his horse. "If you don't mind the wait, I'll show you a room you can sit in. If I remember rightly there's a coffee machine in there which serves a curiously ghastly brew. At least it's free."

Adam and Michael sat. They were alone. The room was bleak and functional and the coffee was exactly what the judge had said it would be. Then another door opened and someone unseen on the other side of it said: "You can wait in there." And Sylvain, all alone, came into the room.

He stood facing them, motionless, not speaking, for some time. His face was thinner and his hair much shorter than before. He too was wearing a suit and tie, but it was old and too short for him (his father's?) and it had the opposite effect on his appearance from that of Céline's father's suit on him: he looked lost and vulnerable. Adam thought that he had never wanted him so much. Then, *"Mon Dieu,"* Sylvain said, "it's you."

Adam opened his mouth to speak, but it was like a bottleneck of thoughts and words and not one of them would come.

"It's all OK, little one," Sylvain said. "It's going to be OK. It's not for ever. They said I'm never going to see or contact you again. Well, they're already wrong. I have. I will." He took two paces towards Adam and Adam leaped up to go to him but a sudden commotion outside startled them, then both doors opened simultaneously and the little room was full of people, uniformed, gesticulating, angry. Too late for an embrace or even a touch of hand on hand, but something got said, by each of them, that only the other heard. Sylvain was escorted firmly out by two uniformed guards while two other attendants, less threateningly clad but looking just as apoplectic, conducted Adam and Michael through the other door. "Quite the wrong place to send you," they said when Adam protested that Céline's father had told them to wait there. "Extraordinary misunderstanding. *Bon Dieu!*"

Céline's father seemed quite unsurprised to find the boys awaiting him in the main entrance instead of at the place that he'd arranged, and with a beaming but impenetrable smile he escorted them to his car. No mention was made on the journey back of their impromptu meeting with Sylvain; they talked of other things. And when the judge deposited them at the bus station in Langres he said to them: "I'll leave you here, if that's all right. And if by any chance your father, Adam, didn't know you went to Chaumont today, he's not going to discover it from me. *Au revoir, braves gens, et bon courage.*" They were the only words of French they'd heard him say.

Adam and Michael made the most of their remaining days in Courcelles, painfully conscious of the shortness of the time. By day they walked and played and talked in the sunshine, at night they clung ever more tightly to each other, and Michael was heartened by the realisation that Adam had stopped crying in his sleep. On their last evening of all they took a walk along the lane that led west out of Courcelles and up the hill. Adam suddenly said: "I suppose you think I made a terrible fool of myself. Over Sylvain. That I really fucked up. Fucked myself up. Fucked Sylvain up. Fucked my parents up." They were climbing over the gate out of the lane into the field where the log-splitter still stood, a lonely yellow gibbet, on the edge of the wood.

"Nobody fucks their parents up," said Michael. "It's too late for that. Parents are fucked up already. I know mine are."

"Yes, but you know. Mine may be splitting up because of me."

"If they do - though I hope they won't - it'll be nothing to do with you. It'll be an excuse, that's all. A... what's the word? ...A catalyst, something that isn't part of the chemical equation."

"And Sylvain?"

"Yeah, I know that's bad..."

"I seduced him, gave him his first taste of sex..."

"And it sent him off the rails? First, you flatter yourself. Second, he was off the rails already. If anything, he's much more together now than he ever was before. If you weren't bright enough at the beginning to realise what he was like ... well, I suppose I might criticise you for that."

"I suppose I did realise. Everyone called them the funny family. And he was the funniest of the lot. I just didn't want it to make any difference." Dry stubble crackled underfoot.

"But it did. You kidded yourself. That's the only thing you're to blame for. You kidded yourself. Just like your parents kidded themselves they'd brought up a wonder: a goody-goody heterosexual boy with no sign of a libido, the first in the world. Did they stop to think about the improbability of that?"

"I could have handled it if the police hadn't got involved, and if parents hadn't got involved. OK, I made mistakes, so did Sylvain. But we could have sorted them ourselves. We'd have had to part this summer anyway. It'd have been painful but we'd have managed it without

198

gendarmes, and shots being fired, my mother nearly having a breakdown and Sylvain being put in an institution. Why can't they all just let teenagers make their own mistakes and put them right for themselves? Once older people get involved they make it ten times worse."

"Jesus, what's that?" Michael suddenly cried. Two small creatures had leaped out of the stubble at his feet and taken to the air on rattling wings like wind-up toys. *'Ker-ke-ker, ker-ke-ker'* they called to each other.

"A pair of quail," said Adam knowledgeably. "They do that."

"Well I wish they'd give a bit more notice first." They watched the birds abruptly switch to glide mode and plane down in a short curve to disappear again in the stubble a hundred metres off. "Anyway," Michael resumed. "Older people. You seem to be forgetting something: Sylvain is an older person himself. At least, that's how your parents saw it. And that was not exactly a small part of the problem. How do you see your thing with Sylvain, anyway? Was it a kids' thing, like with … with us, years ago?" He made it sound as if those people then were quite different from him and Adam now. "Or was it an adult thing, like Céline and her man, like our parents? Or was it a mixture of the two?"

"Maybe," said Adam slowly, "it's the mixture that's not a good idea. But in our case, Sylvain's and mine, I mean, it wasn't that clear-cut anyway. I treated him as if he was about fourteen and, most of the time, that's how he behaved."

"He seemed quite grown-up when we met him the other day." Michael laid an arm round Adam's shoulder. "You can't keep the adult world at bay, Adam. Céline's father more or less said that. Even Sylvain seemed to have realised that. You have to learn its rules in the end - and then learn to get round them, and make them work for you. That's what Sylvain was saying to you, in his rather elliptic way, and Céline's father too."

They sat down upon the stubble, just where they were, on the edge of the wood, without going into it. On this side of the hill the sun had gone. But where they looked down, across the landscape, it lit the village roofs, clusters of orange round the church spire, and coloured the broad bleached sweep of the eastern plateau all the way to where the cathedral, like a capital letter 'H', indicated the position of the town of Langres. Then a few minutes later it caught the high peaks of the Vosges mountains, impossibly far away and hanging weightless above the horizon, ethereal as clouds. Adam turned his head to look at his friend and saw that Michael had done the same. For a few moments they looked into each other's eyes. Michael had grown rather beautiful, Adam thought.

That night in bed, curled up with Michael, Adam said: "You know? I don't want him ever to forget about me. Is that selfish, arrogant, vain?"

"All of those things," said Michael. "But I understand. You may yet meet again: the world's a funny place. And if you don't, then maybe he'll get lucky with someone else. But if not that, then what he lived with you might just be one beautiful moment for him to look back on, something to treasure, something that was really his. A once in a lifetime experience of tenderness ... or something... Even if it didn't end the way he dreamed. No, whatever happens, he'll never forget you." There was something in Michael's voice as he finished, which took Adam by surprise. He didn't answer him but clasped him a little tighter in his arms and held him a long while, thoughtfully, until they slept.

Hugh didn't take them all the way to Chaumont in the morning. He still had to repack the car and then to make his own long drive to Calais. He drove them just as far as Langres. From there they took the bus to the coach station in Chaumont, each with one backpack and Adam with the cello too. When they arrived they discovered with some annoyance that their coach journey to the Channel port would be a couple of hours longer than advertised due to a diversion 'for operational reasons' via Paris.

"Operational reasons, *mon derrière*," said Michael. "Lack of bookings, more like. They've simply packed two routes into one. *Quel pain in the cul*."

Adam was suddenly struck by an idea, a great wave of optimism, and an unexpected tide of emotion that all arrived tumultuously at once. He put down his cello and took Michael in his arms. If you couldn't experiment with life when you were a teenager, Michael had once said, when could you? And Gary had said to him: though you may fall in love a few more times in your life those times won't be *that* many. Everything seemed so possible now, at just this moment; every door lay open. Sylvain was still alive, they loved each other, they could meet again. Sean loved him too - in his own way, whatever that way was - and he loved Sean: they'd find a way. Then there was Michael... He kissed him on the lips.

"Not here," said Michael, startled. "This is a bus station, not an airport. And we're not even saying good-bye."

"I don't want this to end," Adam said.

"What...?"

"I mean us, together. Not just yet. Maybe not for..."

"Don't be silly. I mean, I don't mean that. I mean ... neither do I. But I didn't know you felt that too."

200

"We don't have to go back to England yet. School holidays go on another month."

"Oh come on, man. Get real."

"I am real. Let our parents sort their own lives out. They don't need us over their shoulders while they do it. Our coach is going to Paris. So are we."

"Are you crazy? We can't spend a month in Paris. Not even a weekend. We haven't any money. We don't know anyone there."

"Yes we do. Gary Blake. He said to get in touch if ever I needed to. Well now I do. Give me your mobile."

Michael fished in his pocket. "You really have gone mad this time." He handed him the phone.

"Yes I have. I want you so much right now and I want so much not to lose you that I'm taking you to Paris. Consider yourself abducted, kidnapped, spirited away. We can phone our parents when we get there this evening."

"This'll all end in disaster," said Michael, affecting a weary tone. "Everything always does with you." Though his body betrayed him and he trembled with excitement.

"But not before it's even started." Then he kissed Michael a second time before reaching in his wallet for Gary's card. With hands that shook, he tapped out Gary's number on Michael's phone.

Also Available From BIGfib Books

50 Reasons to Say "Goodbye"

A Novel
By Nick Alexander

Mark is looking for love in all the wrong places.
He always ignores the warning signs preferring to dream, time and again, that
he has finally met the perfect lover until, one day…

Through fifty different adventures, Nick Alexander takes us on a tour of
modern gay society: bars, night-clubs, blind dates, Internet dating… It's all
here.
Funny and moving by turn, 50 Reasons to Say "Goodbye", is ultimately a
series of candidly vivid snapshots and a poignant exploration of that long
winding road; the universal search for love.

"Modern gay literature at its finest and most original."
- Axm Magazine, December 2004

"A witty, polished collection of vignettes... Get this snappy little number."
- Tim Teeman, The Times

*"Nick Alexander invests Mark's story with such warmth... A wonderful read -
honest, moving, witty and really rather wise."* - Paul Burston, Time Out

*"Perceptive and obstinately optimistic, balances passion and pathos with wit,
whimsy and wisdom."* - Richard Labonte, Book Marks

"Truthful, moving, witty, optimistic... Speaks to everyone."
- Joe Storey-Scott, Gay Times

ISBN: 2-9524-8990-4
BIGfib Books.

For more information please visit:
www.BIGfib.com.